CW01066902

A Reason to Rebel

A Reason to Rebel

Wendy Soliman

A Samhain Publishing, Ltd. publication.

Samhain Publishing, Ltd.
577 Mulberry Street, Suite 1520
Macon, GA 31201
www.samhainpublishing.com

A Reason to Rebel
Copyright © 2010 by Wendy Soliman
Print ISBN: 978-1-60504-540-5
Digital ISBN: 978-1-60504-496-5

Editing by Deborah Nemeth
Cover by Anne Cain

First Samhain Publishing, Ltd. electronic publication: April 2009
First Samhain Publishing, Ltd. print publication: February 2010

Dedication

For Andre, always in my heart

Chapter One

Hertfordshire, England, 1815

"The scullery maid has gone and got herself in trouble." Mrs. Keller pulled her thin lips taut in a grimace of disapproval. "Obviously she's been given her marching orders and now Cook's short-handed, so don't go expecting anything special for luncheon."

Estelle looked up from her embroidery. "Why was I not consulted before the girl was dismissed?"

"It's what the mistress would have done. We don't hold no truck with licentious behaviour in these parts, no matter what those accustomed to Hampshire society might be prepared to overlook."

Estelle refrained from rolling her eyes and reminding Mrs. Keller that *she* was the mistress of this house now. The redoubtable housekeeper ran the household in the same manner as she had during the thirty-year tenure of her predecessor. When Estelle had arrived in Hertfordshire as a nervous bride, Mrs. Keller had blithely ignored her suggestions for changes, her features settling in a curmudgeonly expression as though the word was a contagious disease.

"*Change*, madam?" Estelle recalled her saying caustically. "I hardly see the need for change. *The* Mrs. Travis saw no occasion to criticize our methods. But, of course, if we do not give satisfaction..."

Her words had trailed away yet her beady eyes had remained fastened upon Estelle's features. Her expression of unmitigated dislike dared Estelle to find fault with the domestic arrangements in her new home—tested her. Estelle, inexperienced in the management of recalcitrant servants, knew she ought to stand her ground, that it was a defining moment in which she must exert her authority if she wished to be treated with respect. But she was no match for Mrs. Keller's staunch implacability and eventually gave up on her efforts to reform the household routine.

The death of her husband a year into their union, closely followed by the loss of the baby she was carrying and the subsequent disappearance of her beloved sister, had seen her give way to a prolonged fit of the blue devils. She had long ceased to care what the servants thought of her, leaving the running of the house entirely in their hands.

But now, the notion of a young girl being turned away to fend for herself—when the blame might not lie with her—roused her from her lethargy.

"Who was responsible for the girl's situation? Was it someone under this roof?"

"A footman."

"And he has been sent packing too, presumably."

Mrs. Keller appraised Estelle with an expression of lofty scorn. "We saw no occasion for that. He told Mr. Archer that the girl led him on, so there was no more to be said."

"And Mrs. Travis would have concurred with that decision, I collect."

"She understood how things ought to be done." Mrs. Keller's eyes lingered with evident disapproval on the colourful shawl draped around Estelle's shoulders. "You can't blame young men for trying these things, it's in their natures. It was up to the girl to keep her knees together."

"You would know all about that sort of temptation, would you, Mrs. Keller?"

"Well, really!" She sniffed, her pinched features alight with majestic indignation. "Never did I expect to be spoken to in such a manner beneath this roof."

"I daresay Mrs. Travis, the *first* Mrs. Travis that is, would have treated you with more respect." Estelle could feel the numbness that had cocooned her for the past three months slowly giving way to a burning anger at the injustice of it all, which in turn lent her the courage to face up to her witch of a housekeeper. "What age is the girl?"

"Fourteen, but—"

"And the footman?"

"Three-and-twenty, but that does not signify. Young girls nowadays are very aware."

"Send someone to find the girl and bring her to me. She should not be abandoned in her hour of need."

"It's too late. She will likely be well away by now."

"Do it, if you please, Mrs. Keller," said Estelle in a voice of steely resolve.

"Very well," she said grudgingly.

"Is there anything else?"

"Yes, the fox got into the hen house last night and we lost three of our best layers."

"Oh dear." Estelle did not see what she was expected to do about the situation, other than to recommend the replacement of the unfortunate birds, which seemed rather too obvious to put into words. She wondered why Mrs. Keller had bothered to inform her of the incident. "And what would the previous Mrs. Travis have done about it?" she asked, struggling to keep her lips straight.

"I'm sure I couldn't say, madam," came the frosty reply.

"Really!" Estelle invested a wealth of meaning into the single word. She could have filled a journal with the late Mrs. Travis's miraculous solutions for the tiniest domestic crisis. Apparently she was being burdened with particulars of this latest one only to punish her for daring to issue a direct order. She was obliged to quell a smile at this small triumph. Now that it was almost too late, and the time was fast approaching when she must surrender the supervision of the household to the wife of her husband's heir, she had finally worked out how to best her wretched housekeeper.

The sound of a carriage shuddering to a halt on the driveway saved Estelle from the trouble of formulating a reply to the thorny question of their depleted poultry stock. She dismissed Mrs. Keller with a curt nod. A spontaneous smile graced her lips as she anticipated being reunited with her visitor. Susanna was here at last.

Having declined all other offers of support, especially the half-hearted one received from her own mother, Estelle was now impatient for her friend's company. She was ready to pour out her woes to the one person with whom she could be perfectly frank. She could not wait to inform her of her recent victory over Mrs. Keller. Susanna would have found a way to put the woman in her place long before now, but she would be impressed by Estelle's newfound authority for all that.

The small parlour's frugal fire did little to dispel the chill in the air. Shivering, Estelle pulled herself into a sitting position on the settee and slowly lowered her feet to the floor, moving cautiously to prevent the room from swimming before her eyes. Unaccustomed to ill health, she was finding it increasingly tiresome being incapacitated for so long. Her glance rested upon the shawl which had so incensed Mrs. Keller; a colourful accessory which she always kept by her. Its brightness was indeed inappropriate for a recently bereaved widow but somehow she was unable to dispense with the comfort it afforded her.

Estelle patted stray strands of auburn hair back into place and smoothed the severe lines of her black gown over her knees. Her wan complexion and lustreless eyes bruised with fatigue were attributable to a succession of sleepless nights. She had not spent one comfortable night in the characterless chamber the mistress of this house was expected to occupy; not even before misfortune befell her. But now Susanna had come to her and would make everything all right. All dizziness had left and Estelle sat expectantly, attempting to curb her impatience as she waited for her friend to be shown in.

It took her a while to realize that the voice she could hear booming in the entrance vestibule was not the delicate feminine one of her friend but rather the strident tones of her father. He made no attempt to lower his voice as he addressed Peterson, the footman whom he had sent to this house to spy upon her as soon as her husband had died. Why he thought that necessary when her maid Martha was already diligent in reporting her activities directly to him she could not imagine.

Estelle's heart plummeted. What was he doing here, and today of all days when she was so looking forward to seeing Susanna? Did he deliberately seek to overshadow the one pleasure she had been anticipating since the onset of her misfortunes? Could he really be that vindictive? Her father would be aware that Susanna was expected, of course. Either Peterson or Martha would have been sure to inform him of the fact. He had never approved of Susanna, holding her responsible when Marianne developed an independent streak and dared to question his authority. He had doubtless called to re-establish his dominance over Estelle, aware that having made such a brilliant marriage, Susanna now wielded some influence in the very best circles and would have less reason than ever to keep her opinions to herself.

Estelle dreaded seeing the man whom she had always feared, had little respect for and privately admitted to actively disliking. But she could think of no reason to refuse to see him. Indeed, she would not dare.

"It's all right, Peterson, I do not need announcing. Just have Martha see to Mrs. Travis's packing. In the small parlour, is she?"

Estelle straightened a spine that was already rigidly upright, determined for once not to be intimidated by her father's overbearing presence. Her resolve was immediately tested when she heard him giving instructions for her bags to be packed. Whatever could he be thinking of? Then her heart lifted. He must have intelligence of Marianne; there could be no other explanation. The fact that his visit coincided with Susanna's was pure coincidence, nothing more. Marianne had been found and was asking for her. Naturally she would go to her sister at once, no matter where she was, no matter how long and debilitating the journey. Her own concerns were secondary when compared to the plight of her beloved sibling. At last she would get the opportunity to hold Marianne again and tell her how sorry she was for appearing to take their father's side against her.

"Papa," she said with artificial brightness when the door opened and her father's portly figure filled the aperture. "I did not anticipate the honour of seeing you here today. I trust you are well, sir. Do you bring intelligence of Marianne?"

"Marianne?" Mr. Winthrop's brow creased with confusion. "Why should I be here to discuss Marianne with you?"

Estelle's brief hopes expired and she felt the agony of her sister's disappearance as keenly as though it had happened yesterday. She felt her own guilt at being partly to blame more keenly still. "But I thought, that is to say I assumed, that only something of such moment could bring you so far out of your way."

"Then your assumption was incorrect. I came to see how you fare and was obviously right to be concerned for your welfare." He ran his eyes critically over her gaunt features and scowled. "You are far too thin and clearly not taking care of yourself. What do your servants do all day if not care for their mistress? You clearly allow them far too much latitude and they take shameful advantage of you."

Estelle knew this to be true and could think of nothing to say in her own defence. "It takes time to recover from the loss of a child."

"Stuff and nonsense, girl. Your mother lost three in succession and did not make half the fuss about it that you are doing."

Estelle stifled the retort that sprang to her lips. She possessed more compassion in her little finger than her beautiful yet selfishly remote mother could summon in her entire body. Mama had never recovered from the disappointment of being compelled by financial necessity to marry far beneath herself, and the loss of three children would have been nothing more than a mild inconvenience to her.

"I shall ring for refreshments," said Estelle tightly.

"Don't trouble yourself. I have told Peterson I shall take luncheon with you and will then be on my way."

Estelle tried not to make her relief too obvious. She had supposed her father intended to remain for several days, whilst Susanna was with her at the very least, just to stifle their reunion. The fact that he did not even plan to spend the night under her roof gladdened her heart.

"Such a fleeting visit, sir."

"I am on my way to conduct some business in Leeds," he said, "and came out of my way to call upon you."

"You are too good."

"I shall be returning through these parts in a sennight and came to give you notice that you should be ready to leave with me then."

"Excuse me, sir, I do not understand you."

"You will be returning to Farleigh Chase to live at home again."

"But this is my home now."

"No, Estelle, this is your late husband's home, and his heir will be here before the month is out to take possession."

"Yes, but—"

"You know very well that Travis's son did not approve of his father's marriage to you. His wife bears you no less hostility and will not look kindly upon your presence here."

"But I have every right to reside in this house."

"Which will cut no ice with her. You are a beauty, Estelle, even in your current condition, and such a vindictive woman will not welcome the competition. Good God, girl, you and she are the same age, and she will not wish her husband to daily compare the two of you and be found wanting."

"But that is preposterous!"

"It will happen, just mark my words."

"I do not know what you are implying, Father, or what it is that you think I am, but I can assure you that Mrs. Travis need have no fears in respect of my intentions towards her husband."

"God's teeth, Estelle, I credited you with more sense. There is nothing for you here now. Travis was persuaded to marry you because he needed the money I settled on you. And I sanctioned the match because I wanted you to marry well."

"I did not realize Mr. Travis needed to be persuaded into matrimony."

"Don't get in a taking, girl. Of course he needed to be persuaded, and it cost me a pretty penny to bring him round. He was desperate for funds, so in the end he graciously overlooked your lack of social standing. But your dowry was gambled away even before Travis was foolish enough to break his neck on the hunting field."

Estelle gasped at the crassness of her father's words, but he did not appear to notice how indelicate he was being and carried on in his usual blunt fashion.

"Travis's son called upon me before you were wed trying to persuade me to call it all off. Did you know that?"

"No, I did not, but I do not see how it changes anything. I *did* marry his father on your specific instructions, and even a cold-hearted man such as his son could hardly throw me out when I am still in full mourning."

"Perhaps not, but that does not mean he needs to make you feel comfortable. Now that the money is all gone, he will have no further use for you when he returns to claim what's left of his inheritance. If you had been capable of birthing his step-sibling it might have persuaded me to further generosity when Travis approached me again, which he undoubtedly would have done. But since that did not happen I cannot allow you to remain here to be abused by his wife."

"But I have no desire to return to Hampshire, Father."

"Your wishes are of no consequence. You will do as I tell you."

"I think not, sir." Estelle contained her rising temper with the greatest of difficulty, astonished to find that she was sufficiently riled to stand up to both Mrs. Keller and her brutish father all in the same day. Marianne and Susanna would be applauding if they could but see her. "I will remain here, hand over the running of the house to Mrs. Travis and trust to luck that we may reside together in harmony."

"I do not have time to debate the matter with you, Estelle. You will return to Hampshire with me in a week's time and you will prepare for your marriage to Mr. Cowper when your period of mourning has come to an end."

Estelle gaped in bald astonishment at her father. Even by his standards this was a new low. "Mr. Cowper is engaged to Marianne."

"Marianne is gone."

"But she will be found. I cannot accept that she is irretrievably lost to us—my heart could not bear it. What have your investigators discovered? Presumably they have news."

"They cannot tell me anything since I have discharged them."

"What!" Estelle could not believe what she was hearing. "My sister has been missing these four months—driven away from us by her unhappiness, only to be snatched by brigands or I know not what type of unsavoury character—and you are doing nothing to recover her? What sort of man are you, sir?"

"Enough, be silent!"

"I will not be silent." Resentment lent her the courage to speak her mind. "Marianne has no money and must be living in squalor, too afraid to come home. And you appear content to abandon her to her fate."

"Your sister is as undutiful as your brother. They are both dead to me." Mr. Winthrop dismissed his missing children with an impatient swipe of his hand. "Marianne had every advantage my money could provide, and yet she balked at the prospect of marrying a respectable young man like Cowper."

"For which I do not in the least blame her." Estelle shuddered. "Although to my shame I did not say so and instead tried to persuade her to your point of view. And now I must find a way to live with that guilt," she added, almost to herself. "As to Mr. Cowper, he is a cold, pretentious sort of man, full of his own self-importance, and I never could understand why you so insisted upon their union."

"It is not for you, or for your sister, to understand but merely to obey as dutiful daughters ought. You were Cowper's first choice, which is hardly surprising since you eclipse your sister's beauty and possess a more compliant nature." Mr. Winthrop pinched her chin between his fat fingers as he tilted her head from side to side. He examined her features from every angle as though she was an object being offered for sale in a shop window and he was searching for hidden flaws before agreeing to the purchase. "However, you were already promised to Travis when he asked for you. But no matter; you are free again now and you *will* enter into an agreement with him."

"You have never tired of reminding us all, Father," said Estelle, using the tone of voice Miss Frobisher employed when one of her pupils transgressed the rules, "that you were not born a gentlemen and achieved that status only by marrying Mother. And yet by your actions today I am reminded that

16

gentlemen really are born and not made. You cannot force me into a marriage against my will, sir. Not for a second time. And even if you could, such suggestions should not be voiced, even in private, when I have been a widow for but three months."

"Kindly remember whom you are addressing and refrain from adopting the moral high ground with me, girl. If it were not for your indisposition you would feel the weight of my belt for your insolence, old as you are."

"And so we reach the crux of the matter. I am two-and-twenty, of age to do as I please."

"You are indeed of age, but what can you achieve without money, ah? Answer me that, if you can."

"Money is not everything."

"Hah. If that is your opinion, then it is obvious you have never had to manage without it. Marry Cowper when your period of mourning is over and I will confirm your status as my sole heir."

"Never!"

"Hear me out before you make your decision. In addition to making a generous marriage settlement in respect of your union with Cowper, I will also guarantee you a monthly allowance. It will be yours alone to spend as you wish. All the gowns, jewels and fripperies that your heart desires will be yours. But be warned, if you go against my wishes, I will turn you away penniless and leave all my money to charity." He fixed her with a stern expression. "You know I do not make idle threats, Estelle, and I will have your answer now, if you please."

"And I will not keep you waiting in that respect, sir. My decision is that I must decline your generous offer. Penniless I shall have to be."

"You fool! You have been married and understand the protection that institution affords a lady, the latitude available to her in return for performing less than arduous duties."

Estelle gasped at the crudity of his comment but he did not appear to notice that he was being excessively blunt.

"The alternative is to earn your living through teaching other people's children or being a companion to some dried-up old lady, if you can find one who would hire you, that is. What sort of existence would that be for someone with your looks and abilities?"

"Preferable to being that disgusting man's bedfellow! I will not do it, Father, and nothing you say is likely to persuade me."

"You will do it, Estelle. I know you—you dislike the idea at the moment but unlike your siblings, you still retain a sense of duty. You will return to Hampshire with me in a week's time. We will discuss the matter again when you are in a position to reason it through in a rational manner. When you contemplate all the material benefits that marriage to the impecunious Travis deprived you of, I know you will change your mind."

The door opened and Peterson announced that luncheon was served. From the way he leered at her when her father's attention was diverted, he must have been listening at the door the whole time.

She hated Peterson with a passion, which was probably why her father had foisted him upon her in the first place. But worse, she did not trust him. She felt convinced that he and Martha read her correspondence. And she could tell from his manner that he would not be above taking advantage of her if she forfeited her father's protection.

She shuddered and walked through the door he was holding open, not once glancing in his direction and refusing the support of the arm which her father offered her.

Chapter Two

"Michael, you look quite disgustingly well." Alexander, Viscount Crawley, grinned broadly as he shook his friend's hand. "Married life clearly agrees with you. And Mrs. Cleethorpe, it is a pleasure to see you again." He took Susanna's hand and bowed over it, brushing his lips across the back of her glove. "Welcome to Crawley Hall."

"Lord Crawley." Susanna dropped into a graceful curtsey.

"Married life is excellent, Alex, I thank you," said Michael. "I heartily recommend the institution. You should try it yourself."

"Ah, a splendid suggestion. But one can hardly try such a thing and then change one's mind if it does not suit. Besides, you have plucked the only rose that will not wither when separated from the vine." Alex sighed with such magnitude that Susanna was obliged to stifle a giggle.

"Absolutely!" Michael smiled with smug complacency. "Go and find your own flower, Alex, and stop coveting mine."

"Have we intruded upon a private party?" Susanna's eyes scanned the crowd gathered on the manicured lawns of Crawley Hall.

"My mother is enjoying her first house party since her bereavement."

"Oh, then we are intruding."

"Not at all. She is looking forward to getting to know you," said Alex, his tone reassuring. "It was such a crush at your wedding that she complained afterwards the two of you did not get the opportunity to converse."

"It would appear that I have put ideas into her head." Michael eyed with amusement the bevy of young ladies seated beside their chaperones on the terrace. "Perhaps your mother wishes you to follow my example."

"Is that not how all mothers occupy their time?" asked Susanna.

"I daresay it is." Alex followed the direction of his friend's gaze. "But it would seem that subtlety is a commodity singularly lacking in my particular parent's armoury."

"You do not seem overly concerned." Michael pulled his wife's hand through the crook of his arm as the three of them headed towards the terrace.

"It is her first foray into society since her bereavement." Alex's face clouded with regret at the premature demise of his much-respected father. "I would not spoil it for her by making difficulties."

"And has one of these young ladies attracted your fancy, Lord Crawley?" asked Susanna with an impudent grin.

"They are all so charming, it is quite impossible to choose between them. But now that you are here, Mrs. Cleethorpe, I daresay you will soon be able to regale me with the particulars of their various accomplishments. In fact I would wager that you and my mother between you will have selected exactly the right bride for me before the sun goes down. If you are able to do so, you will save me a vast amount of trouble."

"It would be my pleasure," said Susanna. "But first you must enlighten me as to the particular qualities you seek in a lady. Tell me, should she be tall or slight; dark or fair? What accomplishments do you most admire in the female sex? Should she keep up a stream of light conversation for your entertainment or would you prefer a lady who appreciates the value of silence?"

"Ah, but if I were to reveal all that, I fear it would not only spoil your sport but greatly reduce the field." Alex sighed. "And so I will leave it for you to make that decision for me as well."

"Do not think me unequal to the challenge." She smiled as she cast her eyes over the assembled young ladies in a contemplative manner.

"I have complete faith in your abilities." Alex returned her smile. "But pray tell me, Mrs. Cleethorpe, what did you make of Italy?"

They spoke generally of their travels for the next few minutes. Susanna expressed her delight in all they had seen, her face alight with animation. She admitted that it had been her first journey outside of England and Alex enjoyed her enthusiasm. As he listened to her detailed descriptions of the sights she had seen, he wondered when he had become so jaded, so immune to the simple pleasures of life that he scarcely noticed them any more.

"Mother," he said as they strolled towards the group taking tea on the terrace, "here are Michael and Mrs. Cleethorpe come to join us at last."

"Michael, how delightful! We had almost given up on you."

"Lady Crawley." Michael kissed her outstretched hand with affection.

As school friends, Michael and Alex had spent many a happy holiday romping in the grounds of this vast estate. As a consequence, Lady Crawley was like a second mother to Michael. Alex imagined that, like him, his friend would still be able to find his way blindfolded through the trees in the private woods, so often had they fallen out of them as boys. "I trust I find you well, ma'am?"

"Oh, you know me, Michael, I am always in the rudest of health. That is part of my trouble. And Mrs. Cleethorpe, you are very welcome, my dear."

Susanna curtsied and made the appropriate response. Alex could see Michael watching her closely but he had no cause for

21

concern. She did not put a foot wrong and was clearly comfortable with the company.

Alex had been surprised when his closest friend had declared his intention of marrying a girl so far below him socially, even if she was a beauty of the first order and her father a merchant rich enough to ease the Cleethorpes' acute financial distress. Alex had tried to talk him out of taking such a rash step, convinced he would live to regret it. The friendship between the two of them had cooled for a while as a result, Michael taking offence at Alex's well-intentioned interference.

It was only when Alex met Susanna for the first time that he began to understand his friend's determination. She was not the scheming, social-climbing hussy he had been expecting but a naturally vivacious girl with an enchanting personality and obvious zest for life. She did not appear to take herself or others too seriously and delighted in laughing at the world's foolishness. More importantly, though, Alex could see at a glance that there was genuine affection on both sides, so he worked with Michael then to convince his doubting family to permit the match to go ahead.

"Come and sit beside me, Mrs. Cleethorpe." His mother motioned to a footman to bring a chair. "I wish to hear all about your travels." She dismissed Alex and Michael with a wave of her gnarled hand, much to the chagrin of several young ladies who had been doing their best to attract Alex's attention.

"You did the right thing," conceded Alex as they wandered away to join the gentleman, "and she is a great credit to you."

"I have no regrets on that score. Thank you for helping to make it happen."

"My pleasure. But I am jealous. She has taken you away from me and I miss your society."

"We are home again now."

"Indeed." But it would not be the same. "How long can you stay with us?"

"Just one night, I'm afraid."

Alex raised a brow. "What is the rush?"

"Susanna is concerned about her friend Estelle. She married Bartholomew Travis a little over a year ago. He died just after we left England on our wedding journey."

"The Travises of Hertford?" They turned together at the end of the terrace and set off across the lawn at a leisurely pace.

"Yes, are you acquainted with the family?"

"By reputation only. She must have been a great deal younger than her husband."

"Less than half his age."

"I dare say it was a good match for her. I do not believe the Winthrops frequent the *ton.* I have never encountered them there, or heard of them before."

"Indeed, you are in the right of it."

"But, unlike your own situation, I doubt that it was a love match."

"Hardly."

"Then why does Susanna feel the need to dash off and comfort the girl? She is probably glad to have her freedom restored."

"Perhaps, but there is more. Estelle lost the baby she was carrying due to the shock, and now her sister has disappeared."

"Heavens!" Susanna's friend sounded like a rather careless individual. "And she has poured her troubles on your wife's head and demanded her company as soon as she returned to England. Is that not rather thoughtless of her?"

"Quite the reverse. Susanna knew nothing of any of it until she heard of it by chance from a mutual acquaintance. And now she will not be happy until she has seen Estelle for herself and heard about her troubles firsthand. And no doubt, once she has done so, she will insist upon dragging her back to Fairlands until she has completely recovered."

"They must be very close friends for Susanna to want her intruding so soon after your marriage. Still, with your lot around, I suppose one more makes little difference."

"Quite! And yes, they are close—very. Like us, they met at school and took an immediate liking to one another."

"I see. And did I meet this paragon at your nuptials? I do not recall being introduced."

"No, her husband had arranged something that prevented her from attending." Michael frowned. "Although Susanna would have it that Estelle's father was the one who somehow contrived for her to be absent. He dislikes Susanna and disapproves of her close friendship with his daughter."

"Good God, why?"

"Because he is a tyrant, by all accounts. However, her sister Marianne was there."

"The one who has gone missing?"

"Yes. She is a pretty little thing with blond hair and large blue eyes."

"Ah yes, I think I recall her."

"I daresay you do." Michael chuckled. "If she caught your eye, then I would recommend you not to pass up any opportunity to make her sister's acquaintance."

"I look forward to it." He paused to acknowledge something that was being said to him by another gentleman. "What do you suppose has become of the sister?" he asked when he was able to return to his conversation with Michael.

"Hard to say until Susanna has interrogated Estelle and heard all the particulars. But I do know she was balking at the marriage her father had arranged for her."

"If he was trying to force her to marry someone of Travis's ilk then it is not to be wondered at. She probably took fright and eloped with her childhood sweetheart, or something equally predictable."

"Let us hope that is all it is."

"How did Travis die?"

"On the hunting field. He was trying out a spirited new stallion purchased with Estelle's dowry, and fell at a fence."

"Now that does surprise me. Travis was acknowledged to be a first-rate horseman." Alex shrugged, losing interest in the subject. "Ah well, perhaps he had aged and no longer had the mettle to handle a lively stallion."

"Very likely. But, tell me, how is your mother coping? She looks well enough but I suspect she still feels her loss greatly."

"Indeed." Alex frowned. "She is serene on the surface but I am not fooled by her performance. She is lonely without my father and does not know what to do with herself. It is touching the way she tries not to lean on me. But it is also another reason for her to wish me wed. She would then acquire the daughter she has always wanted."

"I complain about being the oldest of eight, but being an only child must also have its disadvantages."

"It does, believe me. I have business in London which urgently awaits my attention but I am loath to leave her here alone."

"Have you thought about employing a companion to bear her company?"

"Frequently, but she will not hear of it." Alex paused, clasping his hands tightly behind his back as he gave voice to his concerns. "You know how independent she can be. The only way it could be achieved, I think, would be if misfortune were to befall some young lady and the particulars were to reach her ears. She would be bound to want to do something to help her."

"Doing the creature a kindness by taking her in, you mean?"

"Precisely. She is so soft-hearted that she can never help involving herself in other people's misfortunes." Alex shrugged in a gesture of defeat. "But it is of no consequence, since how do I go about locating distressed females of impeccable character? And even if I were to manage that, how would I persuade one of them to descend upon Crawley Hall? I should not know where to begin."

"I daresay it could be managed."

"Perhaps, but I do not see how."

"If you are seriously contemplating such a step, perhaps I could help."

"You." Alex smiled. "Thank you, Michael, but you are no better qualified to bring it about than I am."

"No indeed, but I will discuss it with Susanna, if you like."

"By all means. But what could she hope to do about the matter?"

Michael chuckled. "Trust me, Alex, if anyone can contrive such a scheme convincingly, it is she."

Chapter Three

Estelle was exhausted when her father left but too overwrought to even contemplate resting. She retired to the small parlour instead. It was the only room in the house where she felt safe from the prying eyes of the servants.

To her father's suggestion that she marry Mr. Cowper she barely spared a thought since she did not have the slightest intention of going down that path. Just why Cowper was so important to him that he would try to force first Marianne and then her into marriage with him was not important. What *did* concern her was the fact that he had stopped searching for Marianne. She knew him to possess a cold, unforgiving nature but had not considered him capable of such blithe indifference to the fate of a defenceless young woman—his own daughter.

Well, he might be prepared to abandon her without it troubling his conscience, but her love for her sister ran deep and she knew now what she would do with herself. Somehow she would discover what had become of Marianne. She would find her and rescue her from wherever she had fled to.

And her first port of call would be her brother Matthew. The last time she had heard from him, over a year ago now, he had been in Jamaica, happy in his work as a bookkeeper on his friend's plantation. But she did not know if he was still in Port Antonio or how he could help her if he was. What she did know was that he would not ignore her plea for help.

Just the thought of seeing him again warmed her heart. She had written to him when Marianne went missing but in all likelihood that letter would not have reached him yet. If she wrote again now, that would take months to get there too.

What to do in the meantime? Suddenly she was full of purpose, aware that every day lost whilst she sat idly about feeling sorry for herself could make the difference between life and death to Marianne.

Susanna's carriage must have passed her father's in the driveway, so closely did her arrival follow his departure. The two friends embraced. Estelle was then obliged to endure Susanna's close scrutiny and tuts of disapproval before they settled themselves in front of the fire.

"Bring tea for us, if you please, Archer," Estelle said to the ancient butler who was hovering by the door.

"Now, tell me at once all that has happened," said Susanna in her usual direct fashion. "My poor love, you ought to have let me know. I would have come at once."

Estelle managed a wan smile. "I hardly think that would have endeared me to Mr. Cleethorpe."

With the tea in front of them and the door closed against prying eyes and ears, Estelle, keeping her voice low, told her friend everything in a dull monotone.

"Well, at least you are rid of that dreadful old man."

"Susanna!"

"Don't act so shocked, Estelle. You did not want to marry him, did not love him and he was not kind to you."

"Put like that, I suppose you are right. But it does seem rather shocking to be glad someone is dead. Whatever would Miss Frobisher have said?"

They smiled, easily able to imagine their schoolmistress's outrage at such an unseemly sentiment. Estelle discovered that laughter, something she had heard precious little of in this house even when her husband had been alive, helped ease the tension she had been enduring these three months. Susanna's irreverent company was already aiding her recovery.

"And then you lost your baby. I know how much you were looking forward to his birth. I am sorry for that, Estelle."

"I am reconciled to the loss." Tears stung her eyes.

"Now, tell me everything about Marianne."

"There is little to tell. She came to see me two weeks after your wedding and we argued. After that she disappeared."

"And I suppose you blame yourself."

"Who else is there to blame?" Estelle's hand was unsteady as she poured the tea. "My sister came to me in a defiant mood but instead of sympathizing with her over her troubles, I told her to grow up and remember her duty."

"I doubt that you were so cruel. I know you too well to believe you capable of such heartless behaviour. Tell me exactly what happened."

"Well, she was very distressed about Papa insisting she marry Mr. Cowper. I could not help concurring with her sentiments but knew it would do her no good to balk at the suggestion." Her cup rattled against the saucer as she replaced it with unnecessary force. "I tried to explain that to her. I told her she would have to go through with it and make the best of a bad situation, just as I had been obliged to do in respect of my union with Mr. Travis." Estelle fumbled for her handkerchief and blew her nose. "I told her we had both always known we would have no say in the choice of our husbands. I also pointed out that at least Mr. Cowper was young and suggested she compare him to Mr. Travis before complaining too loudly." She sighed. "But I might just as well have saved my breath. She flew into a rage and said I did not understand, that I always took Papa's side and she did not know why she had expected anything else from me."

"Well, you did always side with your papa," said Susanna gently. "Matthew is a charmer, one who paid lip service to your father's dictates and then did precisely as he pleased. Marianne has independence of spirit, knows what she wants out of life and is not afraid to reach out for it, whereas you—"

"Whereas I am the middle child. The one who is generally considered to be dutiful and sensible. The peacemaker. And that was what I was trying to do with Marianne that day, do you not see?"

Susanna reached across and touched Estelle's hand. "Do not be so hard on yourself, darling."

"I did not mean to overset her, but Marianne has always maintained unrealistic expectations. I knew she would have to do as Father wanted in the end; what choice did she have? And so there was little point antagonizing him and having to endure his brutal punishments if she refused to see reason. I wanted to save her from that," Estelle whispered, a catch in her voice. "But I had no notion that by trying to make her see reason I would only succeed in driving her away."

"Where do you think she is gone to?"

"I cannot say. I have not made enquires because, well because..." She indicated her emancipated body as her words trailed off.

"But your father is looking for her."

"I thought he was." In a low voice, always aware that the servants could be eavesdropping, she told Susanna of her father's visit.

"So that was his carriage I passed at the end of the drive. What a fiend to abandon his daughter so! I had not thought quite so badly of him. No matter," said Susanna briskly. "We must find her without his help, that is all."

Tears of gratitude sprang to Estelle's eyes. "I could not ask you to do that. You are newly married, you have responsibilities."

"Fiddlesticks, this is more important. Michael will understand."

"I did wonder if she had gone to Mr. Porter in Ramsgate."

"The young man articled to your husband's solicitor?"

"Yes, they met here when Marianne came to stay last year, and were much taken with one another. Marianne declared herself to be violently in love."

"Marianne has fancied herself in love on many occasions." Susanna rolled her eyes. "However, it is a possibility, I suppose. Have you asked him if he has seen her?"

"I wrote to him but he sent a formal reply saying he had not had the pleasure of seeing her. Just a few lines, very stiff, which told me nothing at all."

"That is hardly surprising if she does not wish to be found and if..."

"If?"

"Well, if they are living together but are not married. Do not forget that Marianne is not yet of age, so unless they eloped to Scotland there would be no other way for them. We must go to Ramsgate and confront this Mr. Porter in person. I feel sure that he did not tell you the entire truth in his letter."

"I cannot."

"What is to stop you?"

"Well, there is more I did not tell you about my father's visit. He expects me to return to Hampshire with him in a week's time."

"Why?"

"Because he says I cannot stay here when my husband's son takes possession."

"Hmm, he is right about that, I suppose. And surely you would not want to be here with that cold fish and his shrew of a wife."

Estelle smiled at her friend's apt description. "No, indeed, but I do not wish to return to Hampshire either."

"What had you planned to do?"

"To be honest, I had not thought about it. I was more concerned about Marianne. And, of course, I have not been well enough to think beyond one day at a time."

"Oh, Estelle!" Susanna embraced her. "Well, I suppose Hampshire it will have to be, for the time being. At least until you are out of mourning."

"Well, there is a difficulty in that respect too. When I am out of mourning Father says I am to marry Mr. Cowper instead of Marianne."

"Dear God, is there anything that ogre is not capable of inflicting upon his children? No wonder Matthew could not bear it. Oh, come now, Estelle, don't cry, we will think of something."

"Pray, keep you voice down. There are spies all over the house."

"Yea gods, how do you stand it?"

"By pretending it is not happening to me. By living my life inside my head, where no one can reach me unless I permit them to come inside."

"I trust you told your father you have no intention of marrying that popinjay?"

"Yes," said Estelle with a feeble smile. "For the first time ever I stood up to him. You would have been proud of me. But, of course, he does not believe I am in earnest. He is confident that once he has me back in Hampshire he will be able to talk me round."

"Then you shall not return to Hampshire. You will come back to Fairlands with me instead."

"Thank you, Susanna, but that will not do. He will know before we have even reached your home where I am gone and will only come to fetch me."

"Hmm, yes, I daresay he will. But that is of no consequence, we will just have to think of something else."

"Susanna, I thank you for your concern, but do not involve yourself in my battles. Think of what Mr. Cleethorpe will say if you do."

"Michael will understand perfectly."

"Yes, but you know how persistent my father can be. Your husband's parents were reluctant to allow your union." Estelle covered her friend's hand with her own. "If Father descends upon Fairlands like an enraged bull, demanding the return of his daughter and implying I have been kidnapped or worse, it will only give them the opportunity to say they were right about you all along."

"Do not think to dissuade me from helping you, Estelle, because nothing you can say will achieve that ambition. I know very well that if I leave you to your own devices you will eventually be browbeaten into doing as your father wishes. Now, let us stop arguing and reapply our minds to resolving your difficulties instead. What will you do if you do not marry Mr. Cowper, which of course you will not?"

"I do not know, find a position I suppose. A governess or a companion. Miss Frobisher's training has left me well qualified for both occupations."

A slow smile spread across Susanna's face. "I have it! We have just come from Michael's closest friend's estate, Crawley Hall in Sussex. His friend, Viscount Crawley, is in need of a companion for his mother."

"Oh, I do not know—"

"I do, and it is the perfect solution." Susanna's eyes sparkled at the prospect. "Lady Crawley was bereaved a little over a year ago and feels the loss of her husband most keenly. As a consequence her son is loath to leave her alone, which makes things rather inconvenient for him, especially since she refuses to take a companion."

"Well, if she does not crave company—"

"Ah, but she would love you once she meets you. She will soon wonder how she ever managed without you."

"But how can she meet me if she does not wish for a companion?"

"We must invent a history of misfortune for you."

"It hardly requires invention."

"Lady Crawley has the greatest good nature and softest heart imaginable. If she were to think you had been treated unjustly she would adopt you as her pet project in the blink of an eye."

"I would not wish to deceive her."

"We will merely embellish the truth," said Susanna with an airy wave of her hand. "We will say that you have been unwell and your hard-hearted mistress dismissed you from your previous position without a character, just because your poor health prevented you from discharging your duties for a few weeks." Estelle shook her head. "You certainly look unwell, so that part is true. But, of course, if you would prefer to return to your father rather than indulge in a tiny untruth—"

"All right." Estelle, who considered it to be a great deal more than a tiny falsehood, wondered if in all conscience she would be able to go through with the scheme when the time came. "If you think it will work. I will try anything rather than subject myself to my father's tyranny again."

"I am delighted to see you exerting yourself at last."

"He has pushed me too far this time and given me a reason to rebel."

"Good girl! I am persuaded that our scheme will certainly work. It is as though it was meant to be. And Sussex is much closer to Ramsgate than Hertford. It is also much closer to me in Kent."

"That is true." But Estelle was still dubious about the proposal.

"Young ladies," proclaimed Susanna in a perfect imitation of Miss Frobisher's voice, "if you pay heed to the wisdom imparted to you in this establishment you will be equipped to achieve anything that you set your minds to when you quit it."

Estelle giggled. "You have certainly proved her point, Susanna. You have secured a highborn gentleman for a husband, and it is clear to anyone who has seen you together that you are madly in love."

"I am deliriously happy. But we will be at leisure to discuss my domestic felicity once we are safely installed at Fairlands. Before then we have work to do. Come, let us pack you a valise and we will leave first thing in the morning. We should reach Kent before nightfall if you shall not mind making an early start."

"Not in the least, I assure you."

The girls repaired to Estelle's chamber, where Martha appeared so quickly that she could only have been prowling the corridor, on the lookout for them.

"This room gives me the creeps," said Susanna shuddering.

"And I."

"Then why do you not move to another in a different part of the house?"

Estelle lifted her shoulders but had no answer to give.

"Oh, silly me, you could not move whilst your husband was still alive since he would have expected you to occupy the room next to his. And since his death you have not wished to give the servants the trouble of making up a different chamber." Susanna sighed and wagged a finger beneath her nose. "You must learn to be more assertive, Estelle."

"What are you doing?" Martha addressed the question to Susanna, who was pulling garments randomly from the armoire. She made faces at the dull black material of the mourning gowns and threw them aside in favour of brighter coloured attire.

"Mrs. Travis is going on a journey."

"Aye, that she is. She's going to her father's house next week."

"Wrong," said Susanna in a careless tone that Estelle would give much to be able to emulate in her dealings with Martha. Her hateful maid had been appointed by her father. She had a tongue as sharp as a razor, deferred to no one and even Mrs. Keller was wary of crossing her. "Mrs. Travis will be staying with me for a while."

"No one told me about this."

"I did not realize your permission was necessary."

"The master won't like it."

"Oh really." Susanna turned, arms akimbo, and glared down at her. "And who precisely is Mrs. Travis's master?"

"I meant her father," said Martha sullenly.

"Send word to him. I am confident you know how to contact him. You may inform him that he can collect Mrs. Travis from my husband's estate upon his return to Hampshire."

"Very well, but it don't seem right, her gadding about so soon after losing her husband. Still, if your heart's set on it." She turned towards Estelle, who nodded once. "You'd better let me do that then," she grumbled, trying to edge Susanna aside. "And she can't wear those gowns, she's in mourning."

"No thank you, Martha, we do not need your help. Now go." Martha hovered, her face a study in disapproval. "Get out!" The authority in Susanna's tone finally caused the servant to slink from the room.

As soon as the door closed behind her, Estella and Susanna collapsed on the bed in a fit of giggles.

"I wish I could talk to her like that."

"Practice, that's all it takes."

"She's right though, I cannot wear bright gowns." Estelle glanced regretfully at the emerald silk Susanna was in the throes of packing.

"Oh, but you can. You cannot go to Lady Crawley under your real name or your whereabouts will be discovered in no time at all. And you obviously cannot be in mourning either. Trust me, darling, to know what is best for you."

"Well, anyone who can get the better of Martha deserves some respect. Don't forget this." Estelle threw her favourite shawl on the pile to be packed.

"Ah, what memories." Susanna picked up the shawl and held it against her face. "I remember precisely what we were doing as you set each exquisite stitch."

"I was embroidering, just as I was supposed to be, but you seldom were." Susanna pulled a face. "I remember one occasion upon which you spent the entire period sewing the armpits of Lucy Gibbons' favourite gown together in revenge for..." Estelle paused. "What had Lucy done? I do not recall."

Susanna grinned. "She informed Miss Talbot that you had helped me with the household accounting she set me as a punishment, the spiteful witch!"

"Ah yes, that was it." Estelle sighed. "Miss Frobisher's Academy seems a world away now. How innocent and uncomplicated our lives were then. I remember seeing you for the first time. Marianne and I were enchanted. You seemed like an exotic butterfly to us. We were quite in awe of you."

Susanna laughed. "Nonsense!"

"Oh, but we were. You added a new dimension to our limited knowledge of the world. You were so beautiful and self-assured that we felt quite dowdy by comparison. Your lively spirit and irreverent attitude towards authority was like a breath of fresh air. We had never seen anything quite like it in our narrow world."

"That is hardly to be wondered at, given the way your father ruled the roost with a rod of iron and eradicated all traces of spontaneity from your characters."

"What happened to the shawl which you were making when I sewed this one?"

"It is being used as lining in the puppy's basket, which is about all it is fit for. I never could embroider to save my life,

Estelle, you know that. But you," she added, still lovingly fingering Estelle's shawl, "you could make a living out of it."

"I may yet have to."

"Nonsense." Susanna briskly folded a petticoat and placed it on the bed. "We will resolve your problems together. It will be like old times. And who knows, you might come across Matthew as well."

"What do you mean? I have not heard from him for a year. Do you have a letter you forget to mention?" Matthew had directed all his letters to his sisters at Susanna's family home, knowing if he wrote to them in Hampshire the missives would not reach them.

"No, but what about the letter I gave to Marianne a few days before I was married? What news did that impart?"

"What?" Estelle sank heavily onto the side of the bed. "What letter?"

"She did not tell you?"

"No. When she came to see me that last time, she said she had wonderful news. But then we argued about Mr. Cowper and she stormed out." Estelle paused. "Could it have been something Matthew said in his letter? How could she not have told me?"

"Well, something tells me that if we find Marianne, we will also find Matthew. How else could a young girl alone disappear without a trace?"

Estelle could think of several ways but for superstition's sake did not voice her fears. "I hope I do not have to go to Jamaica, Susanna."

"That will not be necessary, darling." She smiled at Estelle's confusion. "Did I not make myself clear? Matthew's letter did not originate in Jamaica. It was posted in Dover."

Chapter Four

"Oh dear, how terrible!"

"Bad news, Mother?" Alex strolled into Lady Crawley's sitting room, dressed for riding in breeches and top boots.

"Yes indeed, from Mrs. Cleethorpe."

"Susanna?" Alex raised a brow. "What ails her, pray? She seemed well enough when she was here the other day."

"Oh, it is not her. She is in good health and writes very prettily to thank me for including her in my house party. What a silly goose! As if we could exclude her and dear Michael from any of our little entertainments. It was such a shame they could not stay longer. Young people are always in such a tearing hurry nowadays."

"Then what does Susanna have to say that so distresses you?" Alex knew the answer was not likely to be straightforward. His mother was perfectly capable of going off on several tangents simultaneously if he did not keep her focused in the right direction. He swished the tails of his coat aside with a practiced flip of his wrist and seated himself as he waited for her to get to the point.

"She mentions a young lady who was until recently employed by a neighbour of hers as governess. Oh dear!" She scanned a little more of Susanna's letter and shook her head. She looked genuinely distressed. "It seems she has been unwell for some weeks. Nothing contagious, apparently, just a debilitating fever that has sapped the poor girl's strength. The dreadful neighbour has lost patience because she has not recovered as quickly as she ought and has turned her away without a character."

"How shocking." Alex forced his lips not to quirk, even as he allowed himself to be impressed. Susanna certainly did not waste time. He hadn't really imagined she would be able to do anything about his mother's stubborn determination not to take a companion. But she appeared to have risen to the challenge, hit upon the answer and lost no time in its instigation. "What does Mrs. Cleethorpe intend to do about the girl?"

"Well, that is just her difficulty, you see. She does not know quite what to do and writes to ask my advice. She would keep her at Fairlands but, of course, Michael's sisters already have a governess. Besides, the girl is still too weak to undertake the education of such lively charges and would just be in the way."

"Perhaps she could stay at Fairlands until she has completely recovered and then seek another position?"

"No, Mrs. Cleethorpe says she has considered that possibility but it will not serve. Fairlands is so full and noisy, the girl would scarce get any rest. Besides, how can she seek another position without a character? People can be so wicked. It quite makes me want to stamp my foot."

"Do not resort to such extreme measures, Mother, I beg of you," said Alex, failing this time to suppress his mirth. "Since she has asked for your guidance you would do much better to apply your mind to finding a solution to Mrs. Cleethorpe's difficulty. It is just the sort of problem you usually excel at."

"Do you think so? Well, perhaps you are right, but in this case I do not quite know what to suggest. It does seem rather hopeless. The poor child obviously needs peace and quiet and I can quite see how that would be difficult to achieve at Fairlands, what with Michael's brothers and sisters being so delightfully boisterous."

Alex arched a brow. Delightful was not how he would describe the behaviour of Michael's high-spirited siblings. But he knew better than to distract his mother by entering into a debate on the issue.

"Besides, where would they sleep the girl?" She frowned, completely taken up with the problem of the unfortunate governess's plight. "She is not exactly a servant but could not be classed as one of the family, either. And then there are the feelings of Miss Gallagher to take into account. She has been the governess at Fairlands for years. She might feel slighted if another member of her profession were to be introduced into the household. Oh dear, it is all so complicated."

"Since Mrs. Cleethorpe had made it clear that she cannot keep the girl, Miss...what is her name, Mother?"

"Miss Tilling."

"Since Mrs. Cleethorpe cannot take Miss Tilling in herself, try and think of someone who would have the goodness to offer her accommodation until she has recovered her strength. I am persuaded that her occupation speaks for her respectability. As likely as not she will be the daughter of some impecunious gentlemen forced by circumstances to make her own way in the world."

"I daresay that she is."

"And if she is well-educated, she is also likely to be well-read."

Alex hoped he had not overplayed his hand by mentioning books, which were his mother's abiding passion, and refrained from making any further comment.

"I should not approve of any young lady who did not take pleasure in reading."

"And you would be in the right of it." Alex paused, adopting a contemplative expression. "Upon reflection, it does seem to be a hopeless case, Mother. I rather fancy that for once you must admit defeat, for I cannot think of a solution. Perhaps you should suggest to Mrs. Cleethorpe that the girl be returned to her family, if she has one to return to, that is," he added, conveniently turning the hapless Miss Tilling into an orphan, a circumstance which he knew his mother would find too distressing for words.

"Oh no, I could not possibly do that. Mrs. Cleethorpe is relying upon me to advise her."

"But if you cannot help and if the girl has no family to take her back..." Alex shrugged. "We must hope that someone else of Mrs. Cleethorpe's acquaintance will be able to think of something. Although Susanna has not been married for five minutes and cannot yet know many people in the locality of her new home. Perhaps that is why she is so anxious for your advice."

"Then Miss Tilling must come here." She nodded her head so vigorously that her chins wobbled. "I knew I would find a solution, even if you had quite given up on me." Alex bowed his head to hide his smile. "I should have thought of it at once if you had not distracted me. It is the perfect answer. If there is one thing we have in abundance here at Crawley Hall it is peace and quiet. And if the young lady feels strong enough, once she has settled in of course, perhaps she will oblige me by reading aloud after supper. My eyesight is not what it once was, and the print in some of the novels I read is quite shockingly small."

"As always, Mother, you have saved the day. I quite underestimated you."

"I dislike being bested, Alex, as you well know."

"Indeed I do." Alex stood, ready to take his ride at last, and brushed his mother's lined forehead with his lips. "Why do you not reply to Mrs. Cleethorpe at once and make your suggestion, Mother? If Miss Tilling has been turned out of her employer's home I daresay it is a matter of some urgency for her to find alternative lodgings, especially if she is feeling unwell."

"Yes, you are right, my dear. I must relieve Mrs. Cleethorpe's anxieties at once; and dear Miss Tilling's too, of course."

"I will arrange for your letter to be sent by express. If Miss Tilling accepts your invitation, perhaps we can look forward to receiving her here at Crawley Hall the day after tomorrow." Alex, conscious of the trouble Susanna must have taken to devise this stratagem so swiftly, was determined to match her for efficiency. He could not but wonder where the obliging Miss Tilling had sprung from at such short notice but was too grateful for her timely appearance to dwell upon the reason for it.

"Yes, yes, that would be entirely convenient. I will have Middleton prepare the spare chamber in the west wing at once. The one that overlooks the small courtyard. Miss Tilling will be assured of absolute quiet in that part of the house. Now, where did I leave my eyeglasses?"

"They are on the end of your nose, Mother."

"Oh, of course they are, how silly of me!" She touched them, just to be sure. "How could I have read Mrs. Cleethorpe's letter without them? Now, I must write at once, there is not a moment to spare. Give me your arm, Alex, and help me to my escritoire."

ᏣᏁᎤ

Two days later the sound of a carriage rattling down the drive in the late afternoon distracted Alex from his business with his steward. Dismissing the man, he reached the drawing room window in time to perceive the Cleethorpe coachman assisting a young lady of above-average height to alight from the conveyance. He was surprised, not really having expected Susanna to act so quickly despite his earlier assurances to his mother. Gratitude washed through him. He could already feel the burden of responsibility for his mother's welfare lifting from his shoulders.

Miss Tilling was attired in a russet-coloured travelling gown. It was trimmed with green braid and complemented with a matching bonnet that struggled to contain an abundance of wayward auburn curls. Several had escaped and trailed across her shoulders in arresting spirals, but if Miss Tilling noticed their rebellious turn she did not attempt to rectify the situation. To Alex's eye her costume appeared rather grand for a governess. He would have expected something more serviceable and less fashionable, but the colour became her so well that he did not dwell upon the incongruity.

The girl was exceptionally thin and walked slowly up the steps to the door, which Phelps was holding open for her. She leaned heavily on the coachman's arm the whole time. Alex raised a brow. Either she really was unwell or she was an exceptional actress. She drew closer to his vantage point and he suspected it was the former, as what little he could see of her face beneath the wide brim of her bonnet was deathly pale.

As though sensing his presence, she lifted her head and turned it in his direction. Alex let out an oath of astonishment. He had not been prepared to encounter such wild beauty. His preconceived notion that all governesses had a duty to be unremarkable was immediately brought into question.

She looked exhausted, ready to drop with fatigue. An air of vulnerability clung to her and her expression hinted at a great sadness. It overwhelmed him with a sudden desire to banish whatever demons afflicted her and persuade her to smile. Her features softened by a genuine smile would, he suspected, be an experience worth the effort required to bring it about. He quickly suppressed the thought. She was to be a temporary guest in his house, a house in which he would spend precious little time over the next few weeks. Provided Miss Tilling proved to be an acceptable companion for his mother, naturally.

Miss Tilling resumed her ascent of the steps and he could no longer see her face, but that was no impediment to his imagination. Her arresting eyes lingered in his mind, tormenting him with their compelling expression. They were quite the most remarkable eyes he had ever encountered.

If this creature really had been dismissed from her position, Alex had no difficulty believing that a jealous wife had seized upon her illness as an excuse to remove temptation from her husband's path. What man worthy of the name would be able to resist the allure of such exquisitely orchestrated features, enhanced by those damned eyes? They were expressive pools, blinking with a combination of curiosity and intelligence as she took in her surroundings.

But what colour were they? For some inexplicable reason it was important he should know. Hazel to complement the hue of her hair, he would be willing to wager. What he did know was that in the brief seconds they had turned in his direction, he could feel the weight of a great sorrow in their reflection. Something more than a slight fever afflicted this child if he was any judge. Once again he felt the overpowering need to act as her protector. For the second time in less than a minute he found himself desirous of witnessing her remarkable features enhanced by a smile.

Miss Tilling entered the house, and his mother would receive her in the sitting room she favoured, which overlooked the terrace and caught the late afternoon sun. He would give them ten minutes to get acquainted and then make himself known to Miss Tilling.

Dismissing the lascivious thoughts the girl's unexpected beauty had engendered, Alex reminded himself that she was here to fulfil a specific purpose. He strode towards the sitting room door, satisfied that he was once again in control of himself. He would not leave the young lady alone with his mother until he had satisfied himself that she had not deceived Mrs. Cleethorpe and inveigled her way into his house through false pretences.

"But, my dear Miss Tilling, I insist that you taste a slice of Cook's delicious sponge cake. I will not take no for an answer. I can see that you are fatigued from your journey but sustenance will immediately revive you. I am persuaded that it is the lightest cake you will ever have tasted—tell me at once if it is not so. Cook made it at my special request because I know how beneficial it can be to those who are not feeling quite the thing.

I am afraid that if you do not take a slice she will be quite offended."

"I fear I have put you to a vast amount of inconvenience, Lady Crawley, and will be happy to try some cake. It is the very least I can do to repay your kindness."

And so it was that Miss Tilling's delightful mouth was full when Alex made his entrance. His mother was fussing over her guest, watching her like a hawk in case she tried to avoid eating the cake, so he was at liberty to examine the young lady for a moment before she became aware of his presence. At close proximity, and without her bonnet, Miss Tilling's appearance was even more arresting. Her posture was rigidly upright, which was no more than one would expect from any governess, and she was every bit as slender as he had at first observed. What he had not appreciated was the curvaceous nature of her body. When his mother succeeded in restoring her to health—a course of action which she appeared to be embarking upon without delay—it could only be enhanced. Already she was pressing Miss Tilling to take a second slice of cake, at the same time demanding to know where she had ever tasted better.

The girl noticed him at that moment and turned her luminous eyes upon him. Yes, they were hazel, quite the most amazing shade of hazel he had ever encountered. Something peculiar happened to him in the few seconds it took for his mother to also notice his appearance. He was taken over by an emotion so alien to him, he was unable to identify it. Until his mother broke the spell by addressing him, he did not think he could have removed his eyes from Miss Tilling's lovely face if his life had depended upon it.

"Ah, Alex, there you are!" said his mother. "Alex?"

She followed the direction of his eyes when he did not immediately respond. They were still fastened upon Miss Tilling's countenance, and he was aware of his mother smiling in apparent comprehension. Comprehension of what exactly he did not care to conjecture. He had merely been appreciating the sight of a beautiful yet transparently vulnerable young lady, as any man in his position would have done. Predictably his mother was drawing inappropriate conclusions from his momentary interest in the chit.

"I beg your pardon, Mother."

"As indeed you ought. No, no, do not get up, my dear. I am sure my son will excuse you. You are not well and must not on any account exert yourself."

"It would be as well to do as my mother dictates." Alex smiled at Miss Tilling and extended his hand. "Take it from one who knows. She will have her way in everything. If she has decreed you unwell, you had best resign yourself to her care since she will not be satisfied until she has restored you to the rudest of health."

"Tosh, pray take no notice, Miss Tilling. My son would have you believe that I intend to invent maladies for you. But anyone with eyes in their head can see that you are quite shockingly thin and your complexion is in urgent want of colour. But, dear me, where are my manners. Miss Tilling, this is my son, Lord Crawley. Alex, this is dear Miss Tilling come to us already, and not a moment too soon by the look of her. The journey has fatigued her dreadfully, the poor dear, she barely has the strength to lift her cup."

"My dear ma'am, pray do not distress yourself on my account."

"She will drink her tea," his mother continued as though Miss Tilling had not interrupted her, "and then I insist she goes straight to her chamber. Middleton lit the fire this morning in anticipation of your arrival. We did not quite know when to expect you, you see. Anyway, she is even now arranging a warming pan for the sheets and you will have your supper on a tray this evening. It is quite evident to me that you are much too ill to come down."

"No, ma'am, I do assure you, I am quite... Oh, pray excuse me." She appeared to notice his hand for the first time and extended her own. "Good afternoon, Lord Crawley. I trust you will forgive my unwarranted intrusion in your house."

"Miss Tilling, you are most welcome. My mother enjoys nothing more than someone to make a fuss over."

"I certainly do not mean to make extra work for you, ma'am."

"Hush, child, we will have none of that." His mother patted Miss Tilling's hand. "When dear Mrs. Cleethorpe wrote and told me of your iniquitous treatment at the hands of your ungrateful employer, she was at her wits end. She is lately married, you understand, and has yet to experience such domestic crises for herself. She did not know what it would be best to do and so very properly wrote and asked for my advice. Naturally, I thought at once that you ought to come here, even though Alex said I would not be able to resolve the matter. But you see, he was quite wrong and here we are now, all comfortable together."

Miss Tilling briefly turned to look at him, and as he met her gaze he again felt that strange lurching sensation somewhere deep inside himself. That she had been living under some sort of strain was evidenced in the haunted expression in her eyes, rather as though she expected misfortune to befall her at any moment and was resigning herself to withstand some new disappointment. She became aware of his prolonged scrutiny and pinkness invaded her cheeks, making her complexion appear even paler in contrast. The transformation was remarkable, only enhancing her loveliness. It caused him momentary apprehension as he wondered just what he had set in motion by inviting the girl into his home.

"Susa—I mean Mrs. Cleethorpe is all goodness."

Alex did not miss the slip of the tongue and was immediately on the alert. Miss Tilling and Susanna Cleethorpe were not strangers to one another, but then was that really any reason for him to be suspicious? His friend's wife had gone out of her way to do him a great service. It was too much to suppose that a neighbour really had turned off her governess just when he needed a companion for his mother. He reminded himself that Susanna's roots did not lay in the privileged classes. She obviously numbered many such Miss Tillings amongst her past acquaintance and had called upon this particular one to do her a service.

He relaxed into a chair and stretched his long legs out in front of him, not surprised to see the sparkle of determination already restored to his mother's eye. He had a feeling that his stratagem would work better than he could have believed possible. Miss Tilling was just what she needed to take her out of herself.

All the same, it would be as well to give her time to settle in before leaving them to their own devices whilst he attended to his business in London. Business which suddenly did not seem nearly so urgent.

Chapter Five

Estelle stretched, wiggled her toes and turned on her side, curling her knees up to her chest. She was conscious of the lifeblood ebbing through her veins as the protective cocoon she had spun round her emotions slipped further and further beyond her reach. She felt warm, cosseted, and soporific as a result of the attention Lady Crawley's servants lavished upon her. They refused to allow her to lift so much as a finger to help herself, shocked that she would even consider doing so.

It was a situation wholly alien to her, even before her marriage. When she had lived in her father's grand establishment, she and Marianne had been expected to wait upon one another to save their father the expense of employing a maid to attend them. Married to Mr. Travis, her situation had been even worse. The opinion of society, led by Mr. Travis's vindictive son, was that she entertained ideas above her station and had no place in a family whose social standing was so far above her own. Since her husband made no effort to dispel that view, Estelle was shunned by the majority of her neighbours as well as her new family and their loyal retainers.

But now, for the first time in her life, she was experiencing the pleasure of being indulged by a kindly matron who could not do enough for her comfort. And it was making her feel guiltier by the minute. She had been at Crawley Hall for two full days, and Lady Crawley's determination to nurse her back to health personally made her more ashamed every time she considered the nature of her deception.

Time and again she considered owning up, only to think better of it, her recently widowed status holding her back. Lady Crawley was of the old school and would find such behaviour bewildering and wholly inexcusable. Estelle would not repay her kindness by distressing her in order to relieve her own conscience.

Oh, if only Susanna was here to advise her, or at the very least to persuade her that she had done the right thing. But Susanna was not here, nor would she be lending her any assistance in the search for Marianne. It had been necessary to stop the carriage twice on the way to Kent because her friend was feeling unwell. She had apologized to Estelle for the unpleasantness, wondering aloud what could be wrong with her. But Estelle suspected she knew and did not scruple to ask Susanna if her monthly courses had stopped.

"Yes, but I did not think." Susanna's hand flew to her face. "Do you suppose? Could I really be..."

"Yes." Estelle embraced her friend. "Indeed you could and very likely are."

By the time they had finished comparing symptoms, Estelle was in no doubt that her friend was carrying her first child. As soon as they reached Fairlands, Estelle, for once exerting herself, ordered Susanna to bed. It took little persuasion for Mr. Cleethorpe to send for the doctor, who confirmed the diagnosis.

"I shall not be able to help you with the search for Marianne now." Susanna pouted. She was already complaining about being confined to bed because of a very slight, almost negligible, swelling in her ankles. "Michael would never agree. He is more efficient than the keenest of gaolers. He would never countenance such action."

"I should think not! Only count your blessings, Susanna. You have a husband who is concerned for your welfare. Mr. Travis took not the slightest interest in my condition and continued to— Well," she said hastily, feeling herself blushing, "never mind what he continued to do."

"That does not in the least surprise me. The man was a monster. Fetch me my travelling writing case, Estelle, if you please. Just because I am forced to idle my time away in bed does not mean that I cannot make myself useful by writing to Lady Crawley to inform her of your misfortunes." Susanna grinned, her grievances temporarily forgotten. "Come along, Estelle, we must invent a convincing history for you in order to invoke Lady Crawley's compassion. Not that that will be too difficult to achieve. Now, darling, what would you most like to have been before illness prevented you from making your way in the world?"

Mr. Cleethorpe was completely taken up with Susanna's condition. He was bursting with pride at the prospect of fatherhood and barely noticed Estelle's presence. Just two days after her arrival at Fairlands she was dispatched in the smaller Cleethorpe carriage. She hugged Susanna and promised to write daily with her news. Mr. Cleethorpe had absently wished her a safe journey as he handed her into the carriage but she doubted if he had even taken in the fact that she was bound for Crawley Hall, much less appreciated the precise nature of her difficulties. He had been too distracted to make more than the mildest of enquiries in that respect and had not appeared to heed her deliberately vague responses.

Estelle sat up in bed. She knew better than to incur Lady Crawley's wrath by rising until breakfast had been delivered to her and her hostess had satisfied herself that her charge was sufficiently recovered to leave her chamber. She looked about the room, so much at odds with her hateful one in Hertfordshire, and smiled with pleasure. It was light and airy, with hangings in soft pastel colours and a fire which had been banked so high, the room still retained its heat this morning. A cheerful maid had already been in to set it ablaze again. She promised Estelle her breakfast would be brought up immediately, now that she was awake. The fresh flowers spilling over the side of a vase, filling the room with a fragrant perfume, were replaced daily. The window afforded an uninterrupted view over a pretty courtyard and beyond towards the orchard, in which the trees were in full blossom.

The opulence of her surroundings and friendly efficiency of the servants, far from setting her at her ease, only added to her misgivings. She could not stay here for long. Indeed, now that she had a purpose once again, she was conscious of the passage of time and impatient to commence the search for her sister. But she did not wish to overset Lady Crawley by disappearing so soon after her arrival. She could pretend she had received the sudden offer of a new position. It was a possibility she and Susanna had discussed in order that she might reasonably quit Crawley Hall when she had recovered her strength without arousing suspicion. But she would need to alert Susanna to send the fake offer and could not, in all conscience, do so for a day or two more.

With a sigh she accepted that she must be patient for just a little longer. Wait another week or two, if she could bear it, until she could be reasonably certain that her father was no longer actively looking for her. She glumly accepted that he was unlikely to give up the search for his one remaining child, upon whose docility and sense of duty he appeared to set so much stock, as easily as he had abandoned Matthew and Marianne. She knew enough of her rapacious parent's character to suspect that he had ambitious plans which required Mr. Cowper's participation. And the price for his assistance was her hand in marriage.

Estelle straightened her spine and discovered that her conscience had no objections to make when she determined she had done her duty by her father. This time she would *not* submit to his will.

Her father would shortly appear at Fairlands, demanding her return. But Susanna would inform him she had already departed for Hampshire and that they must have passed one another on the road. He would not believe her, of course, but

Mr. Cleethorpe did not know where she really was. No one except Susanna did. Her father would doubtless fly into one of his pugnacious rages. Estelle shuddered at the prospect, glad she would not be present to witness the spectacle.

"Ah, there you are, my dear." Lady Crawley bustled into the room as Estelle was finishing her breakfast. "You look a little better today, unless I mistake the matter. There is a touch of colour in your cheeks for the first time, and I see that you have eaten all of your breakfast. Splendid!" She beamed as though Estelle had achieved something remarkable. "How do you feel?"

"Good morning, Lady Crawley. I feel quite myself again, I thank you, due in no small measure to your kind attentions. I am quite well enough to leave my bed."

"Oh, I do not know about that." The countess shook her head, the ribbons that held her cap in place dancing in time to the movement. "It does not do to overexert oneself too soon when one has been so very unwell. You could easily set yourself back."

"But, dear Lady Crawley, it is such a delightful day and I am sure that a little fresh air would be most beneficial. I have spent these two days looking out at your beautiful park and long to take a turn in it."

"Well yes, it is rather lovely at this time of year." Estelle could see she was wavering and smiled winsomely. "Well, I suppose, if you were to dress warmly and lean upon my arm, a half-hour's exercise might aid your recovery."

"Oh, thank you. I shall dress at once." Estelle pushed back the covers but Lady Crawley stopped her, her expression horrified.

"You cannot dress yourself, child. Have patience and I will ring for Middleton."

Having got her way Estelle surrendered herself to the efficient hands of Lady Crawley's dresser. An interminable time later she and her hostess descended the magnificent staircase arm-in-arm. Her heart gave a lurch as she heard Lord Crawley's voice coming from behind a closed door. She was not sure if she was more relieved or disappointed when the gentleman himself did not appear to ask after her health.

Lord Crawley was unlike anyone she had ever met before, and he rather fascinated her. He had an intelligent yet resourceful countenance and features that ought not to complement one another yet somehow managed to exist in harmony. They lent him a raffish air. He had brown curls as wayward as her own and deep-set tawny eyes that sparkled with the same good humour as his mother's. He was taller than most of the gentlemen of her acquaintance. There was about him a suppressed energy and athletically graceful manner of conducting himself which she found strangely alluring.

In spite of his dispassionate-seeming nature and lazy charm, she had already learned that he despised inefficiency and did not readily tolerate excuses, which was another reason not to curtail her sojourn at Crawley Hall. Lady Crawley confided that he greatly mourned the premature passing of his father. The maids answered her questions about the family with pride in their voices, making it evident that Alex Crawley was a firm yet fair-minded master, universally popular and greatly respected.

Estelle and Lady Crawley set out in the direction of the orchard, where a veritable army of gardeners doffed caps and bowed heads as the ladies passed them. Lady Crawley addressed each one of them by name, often pausing to enquire after members of their families and dispensing advice, which was listened to attentively. Estelle soon realized why so many gardeners were necessary. The park and formal gardens were more extensive than she had detected from her chamber window. They were also magnificently maintained.

Estelle's spirits lifted as they strolled along the pristine gravel walks. She revelled in the feel of the soft country air on her face and breathed with appreciation the heady perfume given off by the vast variety of flowers waving lazy heads in the late spring breeze.

Their perambulation came to an end far too soon for Estelle's liking, and they entered the courtyard which she overlooked from her chamber. They sat on a bench to rest.

"My husband laid this out for my enjoyment," said Lady Crawley. "Shortly after I came here as a bride, just because I remarked once that it was a very pretty spot. That was more than thirty years ago now. My, how time flies."

"But the courtyard endures, ma'am. No one can take that away any more than they can steal your memories."

"You are so right, my dear. You are such a perspicacious young lady. That is such a rarity nowadays." She sighed and patted Estelle's hand. "I only hope Alex's wife will appreciate the unique tranquillity of this little oasis as much as I do."

"I was not aware that Lord Crawley was engaged to be married."

"He is not but I daresay he will think about it soon enough. With his father gone he is very aware of the duties that have fallen to him. Between you and me, my dear, I have great hopes of Miss Jenkins. She is the daughter of our closest neighbour, Lord Jacobs, and she and Alex are childhood friends. They have not seen one another for some years, what with one thing and another. But Emma was at my house party last week, the one that dear Mrs. Cleethorpe attended so fleetingly, and they appeared to be quite comfortable with one another. Alex and Emma, that is, not Mrs. Cleethorpe, although Alex is quite comfortable with her too."

Estelle smiled at Lady Crawley's convoluted manner of discourse. It was a characteristic which had confused her at first, but she was fast becoming accustomed to and now found rather diverting. "Do you expect Lord Crawley to make Miss Jenkins an offer, ma'am?"

"Well, I am not altogether sure. It would be so splendid if he lost his heart to her but I would not try to persuade him just because I am partial to dear Emma. To be sure, she is not quite as handsome as some young ladies of our acquaintance, but there are more important considerations when it comes to matrimony than physical appearance, do you not agree? Her family," continued Lady Crawley, not pausing for an answer, "for one thing. It is well established and quite as respectable as our own, which is a factor greatly in her favour. One cannot place too much emphasis on such concerns. And she is well acquainted with Crawley Hall already and confesses to a great love for it."

"I am persuaded that any young lady of sensitivity could not fail to appreciate the unique qualities of Crawley Hall."

"Very likely not." Lady Crawley examined her face closely. "You feel it too, my dear, I can tell just by looking at you. And by how much better you already seem thanks to the tranquillity of the place." She smiled conspiratorially. "Alex thinks I cannot manage alone and that is why he will not leave me. He is such a considerate boy. But that is not it at all." She looked over her shoulder and lowered her voice. "I am sure you will respect my confidence, Miss Tilling, when I confess to knowing how keenly he feels the loss of his father. He tries to hide it from me, of course, but I know him too well to be deceived. And so I exaggerate my need for him in order to give him a sense of purpose."

Estelle allowed her surprise to show. "I would not have thought you capable of such stratagems, ma'am."

Lady Crawley smiled. "When you become a mother for yourself, Miss Tilling, you will understand that it is sometimes necessary to indulge in the tiniest falsehood for the sake of one's children."

C33O

From his library window Alex watched his mother and Miss Tilling walking arm-in-arm at a snail's pace through the orchard. He wondered with amusement who was supposed to be supporting whom. He was relieved to see Miss Tilling out of her chamber at last. It was difficult to tell from this distance, but she appeared to have a spring restored to her step and, if he was not much mistaken, the sound drifting through the open window was that of her muted laughter.

Who was she? Where had she come from? Alex told himself repeatedly that it was of no consequence and attempted to redirect his attention to the papers he was studying. But his steward's recommendation for a series of drainage ditches in the lower acres was as dull as the ditchwater they would be intended to channel and stood little chance of diverting his thoughts from the enigmatic Miss Tilling.

On a whim he quit the room and slipped up the stairs to the chamber she was occupying, unsure what he hoped to achieve by intruding. He searched her belongings, careful to put everything back exactly as he had found it, but found few clues as to her identity. A few gowns of a quality too superior for a mere governess, even if they were no longer the last word in fashion.

The only item of interest was a writing case, the initials *EST* entwined in the leather. Damn, it was locked. It would have been the work of a moment to force the lock. But, even though any letters that might shed light on her background were likely to be inside, he would not invade her privacy to that extent. He left the room, with more questions than answers jostling for position in his brain, determined to discover, at the very least, what the initial *E* stood for.

Returning to his study, he sighed as he directed his attention towards his steward's long-winded report again. He disciplined himself to concentrate but had not got beyond the first page before voices in the hall distracted him. He shuddered when he recognized that of the vicar's wife, who had presumably come to consult his mother about parish affairs. He trusted his mother would not be insensitive enough to expose the convalescing Miss Tilling to the woman's overbearing company. His mother did not disappoint in that respect since, when Phelps approached her a short time later, Alex observed the two of them return towards the house, leaving Miss Tilling in solitude in the courtyard.

He did not pause to examine the reasons for his urgent desire to bear their guest company. Instead he left his study by a side door to avoid any possibility of encountering the formidable Mrs. Gibson, who would be more than capable of delaying him for a considerable time.

"Miss Tilling." He approached her position from the southern path. "I trust I do not intrude?"

She started violently. "Oh, I did not see you there."

"I apologize if I appeared to creep up on you. It was not my intention. May I?" He indicated the seat his mother had just vacated.

"Please."

"May I enquire after your health?"

"Thank you. How could I be anything other than greatly recovered, given the exceptional care Lady Crawley is taking of me?"

"Yes, indeed." He chuckled as he examined her face closely. There was a rosy hue to her delicate features. It had not been present on the only previous occasion he had been in her company, but the haunted expression was still firmly entrenched in her eyes. She bore his scrutiny with apparent equanimity, staring directly ahead, unsmiling. The air of despondency and self-containment he had previously sensed about her lingered still. This girl had learned to keep her aspirations and disappointments to herself, if he was not much mistaken. The realization unsettled him. She ought to be revelling in being young and so uniquely beautiful, not pretending to be someone she was not in order to escape some nameless torment. "I observe that you now have colour in your cheeks and rejoice in seeing you on the road to recovery."

"Thank you." She inclined her head in his direction. "Fresh air and exercise were my only requirements."

"Then I must beg a favour, Miss Tilling."

"What favour, sir?"

"That you do not partake too freely of those remedies." She raised a brow. "I have not seen my mother so happily occupied for many a long month and would not have her newfound purpose taken away from her too soon." He met her gaze and held it. "You comprehend my meaning, I feel assured. Dare I hope you will oblige me?"

"You would have me play the part of the invalid?"

"Do not look so outraged, Miss Tilling. I merely wish you to exaggerate your symptoms for the sake of my mother's well-being."

"I see."

"Is it such a bad thing to concern oneself with the feelings of an aging parent?"

"Not at all."

But she still looked discomposed and Alex wanted to kick himself for handling the situation so ineptly. So convinced was he that Miss Tilling had conspired with Susanna in her efforts to procure a companion for his mother that it had not occurred to him that her story might actually be true. He considered the possibility now. Perhaps she really was a displaced governess recuperating from the fever.

"Forgive me, Miss Tilling, I fear I have offended you."

"No, Lord Crawley, you have done nothing more than demonstrate concern for your mother's well-being, which is laudable." She turned to face him for the first time since the commencement of their conversation. His reaction to the full force of her glowing eyes resting on him was embarrassingly visible and entirely inappropriate. He shifted his position in an attempt to conceal the evidence. "I can assure you, your mother's peace of mind is almost as important to me as it is to you. She has shown me a kindness out of all proportion to my due and there is little I would not do to repay her."

"Then we are agreed." He was aware that his voice sounded strained as he struggled to regain control of himself. "I believe there are worse places in this world to recover from illness than Crawley Hall."

"Indeed, but if I am not to be permitted to roam the grounds then I must find some other activity. I do not care to be idle."

"A consequence of your occupation, no doubt."

"Indeed. But, Lord Crawley, there is something I must ask of you."

"Anything, Miss Tilling."

"Well, the thing is..." Her words trailed off and she looked away from him in evident embarrassment.

"Miss Tilling?" The colour had left her face again and he felt genuine concern for her welfare. "Whatever it is, you may be assured of my discretion."

"No." She shook her head. "It is of no consequence."

In spite of his attempts to persuade her to give voice to whatever it was that concerned her, she refused to be swayed. Being a gentleman, Alex could not insist and politely changed the subject. "Tell me, what does a governess do when she is not supervising her charges?"

She offered him a veiled look. "She has little time for leisure since she shoulders a great deal of responsibility. But when she does find herself with time on her hands she might fill it by embroidering—"

"Did you make this yourself?" He fingered the colourful shawl which was draped over her shoulders on the outside of her pelisse.

"Yes, when I was myself at school."

"I know little about such matters," he said softly, "but even I can see that it is exquisite."

"Thank you."

"But I interrupted you. What other pursuits do you enjoy? If there is something that Crawley Hall is not in a position to furnish, that situation could readily be rectified."

"You are too good." Again she almost smiled and Alex was now determined to entice her to do so, not stopping to consider why it should matter to him so much. "I must own that I also enjoy playing the harp."

"Then nothing could be simpler. My mother will be delighted when she learns of your partiality for that particular instrument, if you have not already confided in her. She herself favoured it when she was younger but has not played now for many years. Her fingers, you understand, do not permit it. But we have an excellent harp in our drawing room and I beg you to feel free to utilize it at your leisure."

"Thank you."

"You are welcome." He smiled at her but she did not reciprocate, rather looking away from him, her attention apparently completely taken up by a vine creeping across the western corner of the courtyard. "Perhaps if you are not too fatigued you will play for us after dinner this evening? I assume you will be coming down this evening."

"If you do not consider that it would be too much for me in my delicate condition." Her response was formal and entirely correct. Even so, Alex thought he caught a glimpse of mischievousness flash through her remarkable eyes and was almost sure she was teasing him.

"I believe it a risk worth taking."

"Very well, but I think it only fair to warn you that I am shockingly out of practice. I have not played these several months."

"Because of your illness?"

"Yes, because of that." She shivered and pulled her shawl more closely about her.

"Come, Miss Tilling, I am afraid you are cold." He stood and assisted her to her feet. "And your timing is impeccable. I believe that is Mrs. Gibson's gig I can hear making its way down the drive. I would recognize the sound of her ancient cob's hooves anywhere." He smiled. "It will be quite safe to return to the house now."

She accepted his hand and placed her arm on his sleeve. They made their way back to the house in silence but Alex was acutely aware of her presence. He was struck by the elegance of her posture, the economically graceful manner in which she moved and the carefully guarded expression he could not begin to interpret. The touch of her fingers on his sleeve was gossamer light at first but as they progressed, she leaned a little more of her weight upon him. He sensed she was tiring and, concerned that she was still so weak, he was ridiculously glad to offer her this small service.

As they slowly traversed the lawn he wondered how she would react if he gave way to the capricious whim that was bubbling away inside him. Whatever would she say if he swept her into his arms and carried her back to the house?

Chapter Six

Estelle went down to dinner that evening, in spite of Lady Crawley's conviction that the exertion would set back her recovery. She wore a cream muslin gown, an old favourite. Her clothing was a little too grand for her supposed situation as a displaced governess but there was no help for that. All her gowns were of the finest quality since they dated back to the days before her union with Mr. Travis. Her father was parsimonious when it came to his domestic arrangements but dressed his daughters in the finest garments his money could procure. He exploited their physical attributes in an effort to establish himself as a man to be reckoned with, looked up to and respected.

Estelle regretted that she had not paid much heed to Susanna's management of her packing. She should have anticipated that Susanna, with her flair for the flamboyant, would not focus on the practicalities of her situation. Upon arrival at Crawley Hall she discovered that only the very finest, brightest coloured of her gowns had been placed in her portmanteau. They were no longer fashionable since no money had been spared for additions to her wardrobe once she had been married, but they were also far from unremarkable.

Fortuitously their inappropriateness did not appear to register with Lady Crawley, who greeted her arrival in the small sitting room with warmth. She exclaimed over and over how delighted she was to see her looking so much better.

"The benefits of fresh country air to the recuperating invalid cannot be over-emphasized," she said, as though she had encouraged her to venture out of doors instead of being seized by dread at the very prospect.

"Indeed, ma'am, I feel a vast deal better."

Lord Crawley stood as she entered the room and examined her lazily from beneath heavily lidded eyes. His scrutiny commenced at the hem of her gown and drifted slowly upwards, lingering here and there, until his gaze came to rest upon her face. From his exacting perusal she suspected the discrepancy in her attire did not escape his notice and that he wished her to be aware of the fact. But he did not put his thoughts into words.

"I rejoice to see you looking recovered, Miss Tilling." He spoke in a laconic drawl as his eyes continued to appraise her person.

She suddenly felt very warm but bore his examination with every appearance of equanimity. Not so much as a flicker of an eyelid betrayed her appreciation for his robust masculinity and the peculiar effect it was having upon her. He was dressed all in black, his broad shoulders emphasising the superb cut of his coat. He escorted her to a chair by the fire. She seated herself and took longer than necessary arranging her skirts, using the time to regain her composure. Only then did she deem it safe to thank him. But she had miscalculated. He was still looming over her like a predatory animal, smoothly formidable, smiling as though he perfectly understood her difficulty. Her eyes collided directly with muscular thighs showcased to perfection by his tight-fitting inexpressibles. She licked at her lips, which seemed inexplicably dry, and averted her gaze.

"Be sure that you do not overtax your strength this evening, Miss Tilling."

"Thank you, sir. I shall endeavour not to do so."

During a very fine dinner Lady Crawley chattered in her usual disjointed manner about people and places unknown to

Estelle. Lord Crawley was adept at keeping his mother's rambling discourse on track without making it apparent that he was doing so. At times Estelle was conscious of such closeness between them she felt she was intruding.

But Lady Crawley demonstrated remarkable sensitivity and drew her into their conversation by frequently requesting her opinion. If ever a lady deserved to have a whole brood of children to fuss over, it was she. She was a natural, so at variance with Estelle's own cold, selfishly inept mother that she had not, until that moment, realized that such warmth and intuitiveness could exist between two generations of the same family. She felt a sadness for all she and her siblings had missed during their austere childhood in that show house in Hampshire that had never been a real home.

Upon learning that Estelle played the harp, Lady Crawley's face turned pink with pleasure at the prospect of hearing her.

"How I wish my hands still permitted me to play." She glanced down at her fingers, swollen and disjointed from the pain of arthritis.

"I should warn you that I have not played for some months, ma'am. I would not wish to excite your expectations only to disappoint."

"Nonsense, child, something tells me you will excel. You are in possession of a great sensibility, and I wager that you intuitively feel the music inside you as your fingers bring it to life. I was once the same. Is that not so, Alex?"

"Most assuredly."

"It is the mark of a true musician, Miss Tilling. To be able to express the passion which the music engenders in one, I mean."

"You are obviously knowledgeable critics. I feel a little fearful about performing in front of you."

"Surely your profession has given you ample opportunity to overcome any such feelings of self-effacement, Miss Tilling?" said Lord Crawley, his tone mildly hectoring. "You must be accustomed to displaying in front of your charges, I should have thought."

"Indeed, but one cannot alter the way one feels inside, my lord."

"That is where you are quite wrong."

"Come, come, my dear, do not allow Alex to bandy words with you, not when I am most anxious to hear you play."

Lord Crawley did not stay at the table when the ladies quit it and offered an arm to each of them as they made their way towards the drawing room. It was Estelle's first foray into the vast chamber and she felt a little intimidated by its splendour. When she espied the magnificent harp situated in the corner she could not prevent an exclamation of pleasure from escaping her lips.

"Another gift from my husband," said Lady Crawley, following the direction of Estelle's gaze.

"It is quite the most extraordinary instrument it has ever been my good fortune to encounter." Estelle ran her hand reverently over the beautifully carved and gilded harp, her nerves driven away by the urgent desire to test it out.

"Please, Miss Tilling." Lord Crawley nodded to the stool at the side of the instrument, as though sensing her impatience.

"Very well, my lord, but pray to not expect anything out of the ordinary."

Estelle seated herself and ran her fingers tentatively over the strings. She trusted that the hours of practice she had put in over the years would compensate for her recent neglect. There was no harp in Mr. Travis's house. Her father had recognized her fledgling talent when she was quite young and spared no expense on instructors. He had made her practice for hours to perfect her performance in order that she might play for his artistic circle of friends and show him up in a good light. No one else played the magnificent harp in the salon in her father's house but he would not hear of her taking it to

Hertfordshire. There had been no one useful to him to hear her play it there.

Estelle settled her skirts comfortably about her and tuned the instrument to her satisfaction. Forgetting about her aristocratic audience, she moistened her lips and anticipated the pleasure she would derive from indulging her passion. She launched into one of Mr. Parry's popular pieces, playing from memory. A smile spread across her face as the haunting melody washed through her. The therapeutic benefits of making such lovely music transported her to a place beyond the cruel realities of her world, a place where no one could reach her with their unreasonable demands.

At the end of the piece she looked up to see tears in Lady Crawley's eyes and an expression of deep appreciation on the face of her son. He applauded her efforts, praising her skill. Having regained control of herself, the viscountess also voiced her appreciation.

"You must forgive a foolish old woman, Miss Tilling." She dabbed at her eyes. "But that particular piece... I was accustomed to play it all the time at my husband's request. How singular that you should have chosen it."

"I am sorry, ma'am, it was not my intention to overset you."

"You did no such thing. My only regret is that I never could execute it as well as you."

"You are too kind." Estelle shook herself. "Now, what else would you like to hear?"

She noticed Lord Crawley's eyes frequently upon her as the evening progressed. Even when she quit her position at the instrument to sit beside his mother and drink her tea, he continued to scrutinize her. Had she done something to incur his displeasure? She hoped that was not the case and met his gaze, an expression of polite enquiry in her eye. But his responding smile lent few clues as to the thoughts occupying his mind.

The next afternoon she sat at the instrument again. Lady Crawley was making calls and Estelle was at leisure to amuse herself. She launched into an ambitious piece she had been trying to master just before her marriage, not having had an opportunity to return to it since. Lost in her own world, it took her a moment to realize that a visitor had called. She heard Phelps show the caller into the adjoining parlour and inform him he would enquire whether Lord Crawley was at home.

Lord Crawley soon joined the mysterious stranger there, asking what business brought him to Crawley Hall. As the visitor responded, his voice full of impatience and displaying scant deference for Lord Crawley's elevated social position, Estelle let out a gasp of sheer despair. Her fingers hit several false notes, froze with indecision and died on the strings. She would recognize that voice anywhere.

The man with Lord Crawley was her father.

છ૪૦

Alex strode towards the morning room. He was annoyed to be disturbed by someone he did not know demanding rather than requesting an audience with the master of Crawley Hall. He would not, as a rule, entertain such a request from a Joseph Winthrop of Hampshire, according to the card he had given to Phelps, since the man was not prepared to state his business. But he had been so insistent, his strident tones reaching Alex's ears even in the depths of his study. Alex would not wish for such a persistent person to call when his mother was here alone, oversetting her with his bullish ways. Better to see what the man wanted and send him on his way.

As Alex entered the room, his visitor was staring at the closed doors to the drawing room. The man was dressed expensively in the very latest fashion, but his well-cut coat did little to disguise his portliness. He had an unremarkable, fleshy and heavily whiskered face. His forehead was creased with a frown and his fingers drummed with impatience against a side table.

"I am Crawley," said Alex. "What is the nature of your business?"

"Joseph Winthrop. I apologize for the intrusion and will not detain you long. I have come to collect my daughter." He extended his hand but Alex ignored it.

Alex was aware of the abrupt cessation of the harp music and was sorry for it. Its lilting melody had been filling the house this past hour. He regretted that this man, whom he instinctively mistrusted, had interrupted Miss Tilling's performance.

"Your daughter." Alex did not need to feign surprise. "I do not understand you. To the best of my knowledge, no daughter of yours resides beneath this roof."

Winthrop's face flushed with anger. "Let us not waste one another's time by bandying words, sir. I believe in plain speaking. Estelle is here, I know it, sent by that interfering minx who calls herself a friend for I know not what purpose—"

"What the devil are you talking about, man?"

"About Estelle. I cannot begin to imagine what she and that interfering Mrs. Cleethorpe hope to achieve by it, other than to vex me. But then that is an occupation Mrs. Cleethorpe excels at. No, I can only assume that Estelle's mind has been affected by her grief, leaving her susceptible to the persuasion of others."

Winthrop's pugnacious attitude only emphasized his shocking want of manners, and the two factors combined to persuade Alex that he was not the gentleman he purported to be.

"I still fail to understand what you are talking about." It usually took a lot to rile Alex. But this man had no trouble invoking his temper. He was not prepared to be addressed with such discourtesy in his own house—or anywhere else for that matter—and strove to take control of the situation. He walked towards the man, conscious that he was a good head taller and at least twenty years younger than his unwelcome visitor. "Why are you disturbing me with such riddles? Since you believe in speaking plainly, kindly do so. Explain yourself before I have you thrown out."

"She is a dutiful, well-brought-up child and knows she should be quietly at home," said Winthrop, acting as though Alex had not just issued him with an ultimatum. "Mourning the loss of her husband. But instead she is gadding about the country and imposing herself upon respectable people."

"Her husband?"

"Yes, her husband, who has not been in the ground these three months. She was to have returned to Hampshire with me three days ago but when I went to collect her she was nowhere to be found. She's caused me a damnable amount of inconvenience, I don't mind telling you, and she'll pay a heavy price for defying me when I get my hands on her."

This extraordinary business was gradually making some sense to Alex. Estelle. *E.S.T.* Estelle Travis, the recently widowed friend of Susanna. The one who had lost her baby and her sister, which no doubt accounted for her ill health. And for her good-quality clothing. Alex was briefly at a loss, but not for long. If Estelle's only option was to return to live under the same roof as this bullying coxcomb, then he would move heaven and earth to ensure it did not happen. He recalled her skittish behaviour since her arrival. Her eyes constantly darted about, as though she could not quite believe she was within the haven that was Crawley Hall and expected at any moment to be snatched away. Now he understood why.

Her sensual expression when she had sat at the harp the previous evening had transfixed him. It was the first occasion upon which he had glimpsed the true nature of the sensitive person lurking beneath the shuttered exterior. His mother had been right about music, it was the key to releasing her inhibitions. She had quickly become totally absorbed by it, forgetting all about her audience as she played from the heart.

71

And the smile he had been patiently waiting to see, a combination of ideology and passion which transformed her beautiful features into something celestial, still drugged his mind.

Alex needed to talk with Miss Tilling—or rather, Mrs. Travis—to find out why she was really here. He needed to understand what she was running away from, although he suspected he was already confronting the answer to that question in this very room. It was now a matter of honour for Alex to be of service to the chit, and only when he had established it was what she truly desired would she be returned to Winthrop's care.

"I regret that you have been misinformed," he said, "and have had a wasted journey. There is no Estelle Travis residing under my roof."

"There must be."

"Are you doubting my word, sir?"

"Not at all. Pray excuse me." Winthrop flapped a placating hand in Alex's direction. "I daresay you do not know who is here every minute of every day, what with it being such an extensive establishment. Perhaps she is passing herself off as a maid of some sort."

"Why ever would she do that?"

"Who can say what a woman might do when she is stricken with grief? No, sir, I must insist that you enquire of your housekeeper if any new girls have been taken on of late."

"I hardly think you are in a position to insist upon anything in my house."

"No, of course not—beg pardon, but I would not have you encumbered with the wretched child. There will be the most damnable scandal if word of her temporary loss of wits were to be spread abroad. I would not subject you to such censure, what with you being a single gentleman, as I understand it. A young gel who ought to be respectably mourning her husband residing without a chaperon beneath your roof would be the very devil to explain away." He eyed Alex with a calculating expression that made him want to plant his fist in the middle of the man's fleshy face. "Best if you send for her right away. I will return her to her mother's care and we'll say no more about it."

"It seems that her mother's care has not been very efficient up until now."

"It is a misunderstanding, that is all, but it will all be resolved soon enough when we have her back." Winthrop gestured with his hand and moderated his bullish tone. "Now, if you would oblige me by making those enquiries, it will resolve the matter and put an end to my intrusion."

"I do not need to make enquiries and I repeat, there is no Estelle Winthrop residing beneath this roof."

"Her name is now Travis and you are mistaken about her not being here. My coachman spoke with the Cleethorpe's driver, who said he deposited the girl here not three days ago. There, sir, what do you say to that?"

"I say that you have been misinformed."

"I think not." Winthrop's expression became calculating. "The man has yet to be born who can sham it successfully with Joseph Winthrop."

"What age is this missing daughter of yours?"

"Two-and-twenty." Winthrop made the admittance with obvious reluctance.

"Then it would seem she is of age and can do as she pleases."

"Disgrace my family, you mean, by gadding about I know not where when she is still in mourning? I think not. What sort of father would I be if I permitted her to make such a show of herself?"

"It seems that you do a good enough job of disgracing your family without your daughter's help." Alex opened the door before his temper got the better of him and called to Phelps. "I can well understand her reluctance to surrender herself to your care. Good day."

"Not so fast, sir! If she is not here, who was that playing the harp when I entered the house just now, tell me that, huh? I know of no one else who can play that particular piece with such feeling."

Before Alex could stop him, Winthrop wrenched open the door to the drawing room, bellowing for Estelle to show herself. But when Alex stepped up to the man, looking over his shoulder with a sense of foreboding, he perceived that the room was empty.

"Get out of my house!" Alex rarely lost his temper but was willing to make an exception in this man's case. "Get out now or I'll throw you out myself."

"I will go if you insist upon it." Winthrop picked up his hat, his face puce with rage. "But I'll not go far. I know she is here and I shall not leave the district until she is restored to me." His eyes lingered on a colourful shawl that was thrown across the back of a chair, the one Alex had so admired the previous day. "I know not what game you are playing, sir, but the law is on my side and I will have my daughter back. Tell her, when she has come to her senses, that I am putting up at the Bull on the Brighton Road. If she sends word to me there, I will call for her and we will say nothing more about her temporary lapse."

He strode from the room without another word but Alex waited until he heard Phelps close the front door behind him before he called to Estelle.

"It is quite safe to come out now, Miss Tilling. He is gone."

But no one appeared. The room was indeed empty.

Chapter Seven

At first Estelle was transfixed with fright. But the sound of her father's voice and the prospect of falling victim to his dictatorial behaviour helped her to overcome her fear. Matthew and Marianne had been right about him all along. She should have paid heed to their warnings but prayed it was not too late to make recompense. If she ever saw either of them again, she would try to make them understand that she had behaved in the way that she had not because she did not love them but through a misguided sense of duty.

She did not know how Lord Crawley would react to her father's appearance. Nor could she could guess how badly he would think of her when he realized she had deceived him and his mother in order to escape her tyrannical parent. The thought of disappointing him weighed heavily on her heart. She would not insult Lord Crawley by considering him in the same disagreeable light as her father, but there was no escaping the fact that they were both men, accustomed to having the ladies under their care deferring to their every wish. If her father could convince him that she ought to be at her family's home in Hampshire, especially as she was still in full mourning, she did not see how he could honourably refuse to hand her over.

Panic gripped her as she glanced round the cavernous room, desperate for a means of escape. There were hiding places aplenty but she could hardly remain concealed in his lordship's splendid drawing room indefinitely when, as soon as he learned the truth about her, he was most likely to want rid of her. There were just two doors, one to the main hallway and the other into the room which Lord Crawley and her father now occupied. The door to the hall was clearly her only option but she hesitated to turn the handle, conscious of her hands shaking so violently that it would have been a difficult feat to achieve at that precise moment. If either of the gentlemen in the adjoining room should quit it unexpectedly, or if they had left the door to the hall open, she would be seen in an instant.

There had to be another way.

Aware that their voices were now raised, presumably combined in their outrage at her want of propriety, Estelle almost gave up the struggle. What was the point? She could not win against them both and was merely delaying the inevitable. But her every sinew balked at the prospect of giving up her hard-won freedom so easily. Now that she finally understood how right Matthew and Marianne had been to stand up to their father, she was determined to match their stance. Besides, the very thought of marriage to the obnoxious Mr. Cowper was sufficient to reinforce her rebellious streak.

Reapplying her mind to concealment, Estelle considered the possibility of taking refuge behind the heavy drapes. But that would not serve. The huge window which they adorned overlooked the drive. The wide seat behind them would comfortably accommodate her but she dismissed the possibility without even trying it out. She would immediately be observed by her father when he descended the front steps towards his waiting carriage if he chanced to look back over his shoulder.

There had to be another means of escape, and it did not take long for her to find it. Hidden in the panelling immediately behind the harp was a door she had not noticed the previous evening. She did not scruple to turn the handle.

She found herself in a dim passageway, as cold and musty as a tomb. Its purpose was not immediately apparent and she did not pause to consider what it might be. She shuddered, pushing her fear of the dark to the recesses of her mind. It had to go somewhere and as long as it took her away from her father, she was desperate enough to follow wherever it lead.

Estelle screwed up her eyes and plunged recklessly ahead, hands stretched in front of her to feel for obstacles in her path. It reminded her of the extensive network of passages at Farleigh Chase which she, Matthew and Marianne had explored during their childhood. They had been their only escape from their all-seeing father, who was unaware of their existence. Those passages had held no unpleasant surprises, and she could only trust to luck that those in Crawley Hall were equally innocuous.

After what seemed like an eternity, but in actuality could not have been above two minutes of moving with extreme caution, she was confronted by another door. She hesitated. What if it took her directly into the adjoining room, straight into her father's path? But that would make no sense. She had not travelled far but she was fairly certain that she had moved in a different direction from the morning room. She listened intently, ear pressed against the heavy door, trying to make out any sounds beyond it, but she could hear nothing.

Something alive scurried over her slippered feet and she almost shrieked. Galvanized into action at the prospect of disturbing the rats which lived in this dark hideaway, she marshalled what little remaining courage she possessed and turned the handle.

With a sigh of relief she stepped into an unoccupied study. The walls were lined with shelves of books, and comfortable-looking furniture suggested the room's owner had stamped his personality upon a space where he spent much of his time. Papers lay in disarray on a large desk, left there as though someone had been interrupted whilst reading them. A substantial fire danced in the grate. She could sense Alex Crawley's presence as surely as if he was still occupying the huge chair behind the desk, his eyes resting upon her with a disarming expression of intelligent curiosity. She must have stumbled into his private domain, which was another reason for him to resent her intrusion into his house.

Instead of making good her escape before he came back and could add the invasion of his privacy to his list of her transgressions, Estelle looked about her with interest. She thrust to the back of her mind the depressing fact that her father had managed to run her down after only three days.

Her gaze swept the room, pausing on the portrait over the fireplace. It showed a gentleman and lady, the lady unquestionably Lady Crawley in her youth. Estelle stared at her image for several minutes she could ill-afford to waste. She admired the beautiful lines of her classical features and the lively spirit shining from eyes that had been skilfully captured by the artist, a spirit that was still visible in their faded depths even today. The gentleman must be Lord Crawley's father. Indeed the resemblance betwixt father and son was unmistakable. Instead of looking at the artist, his eyes were fixed on his wife's smiling face with a look of such slavish adoration that it stole Estelle's breath away.

To be so comprehensively loved simply for oneself was a gift that she was never likely to experience firsthand. To live the feeling vicariously through her brief contemplation of this painting was a temptation too great to resist. She understood at that moment why Alex kept it here rather than on display with the other, more formal family portraits in the main gallery upstairs. It must catch his eye every time he glanced up, giving him pleasure and acting as a reminder that the future of the Crawley dynasty now rested in his hands.

Hearing the sound of the front door opening jolted Estelle from her reverie. Her father must be leaving and Lord Crawley would return to this room as soon as he was gone. Without hesitation she opened the door to the hall and peered cautiously round it. Finding the vestibule temporarily deserted she slipped up the stairs without being seen.

Gaining her own chamber, Estelle flopped onto the sofa in the window embrasure and contemplated her situation. She battled to regain both her breath and composure. Even the slightest exertion still fatigued her. She was safe from Lord

Crawley and his very natural questions if she remained in here, where he could hardly beard her.

But once she ventured downstairs again, he was bound to seek her out and demand answers. That being the case, she would use her illness as an excuse not to show herself. That would be considered natural enough after all her recent unaccustomed activity and Lady Crawley would immediately take her side.

Estelle suppressed the guilt she felt at playing upon that lady's sensibilities, pushing it to the back of her mind as she tried to decide what best to do. Never had she felt the need for Susanna's advice more. And Marianne's too. She would listen to it this time and take it to heart. But Susanna and Marianne were not here and could not help her when she needed them most. No one could. She was on her own.

And so, what to do? *Think, Estelle, think.*

She gathered some of her things together and threw them haphazardly towards her portmanteau, a plan forming in her mind. She would plead fatigue as her excuse for not appearing at dinner and then, when the household had settled down for the night, she would slip out. And away.

She paused in her efforts to pack. She would have to leave most of her possessions behind. Getting out of the locked house undetected would be difficult enough. Attempting to do it whilst toting a heavy bag and then walking as far as the village to catch the mail coach first thing in the morning would be impossible. She would just have to take the bare essentials in her small valise and make do as best she could.

But where would she catch the coach to? Where did it go to from here? She had a vague idea about getting to Ramsgate and quizzing Marianne's suitor about her whereabouts. She checked her reticule. She had barely enough money to pay for the journey and a night or two's lodgings. If she did not find Marianne or Matthew immediately then how would she live? Questions without answers flooded her mind. Were it not for the fact that she had already taken shocking advantage of Lady Crawley's good nature and been caught out in deception by her son, she would be tempted to bide her time here in this lovely house that so soothed her jaded spirit for just a little longer.

A light tap sounded at her door.

"Come in." She straightened up, expecting the maid to be bringing her afternoon tea. "Oh!" A hand flew to her mouth when she saw Lord Crawley on the threshold. "What do you want?" Her nervousness made her forget her manners. "You cannot come in here."

His only answer was to step into the room and close the door behind him. He looked at the contents of her wardrobe scattered across the bed and raised a brow.

"Going somewhere?"

"I, er, I...that is to say—"

"Miss Tilling, or should I say Mrs. Travis?"

"I do not know what you mean."

"I sent him away," he said softly. "He will not get past the gates again. I have given instructions to that effect, so you have nothing more to fear."

She turned away from him lest he read the overwhelming gratitude in eyes that were swimming with tears. He had not asked for her side of the story but could not doubt that she had sought to deceive him. Her continued presence in his house would only visit troubles upon him but he had still taken her part. No one had ever displayed such faith in her before, other than Susanna, and finding an unlikely defender in this handsome stranger made her feel weak with gratitude.

"Tell me about it?" He leaned against the closed door and folded his arms.

Estelle's head was spinning, a fact attributable as much to his presence as to her difficulties. She was acutely aware of his commanding presence and was in danger of being overwhelmed by his kindly expression. His desire to be of service to her only increased her giddiness. This room, which had once seemed so commodious, now felt crowded as he prowled around it, covering the distance between them with lithesome grace. He stopped a foot or two short of her position by the window.

She wanted to fling herself at his feet and beg him to protect her from her brute of a father. She longed to make him understand why she could no longer do her duty by an authoritative parent who was blind to her finer feelings.

But she knew she would not behave thus. This was her battle and she must somehow find the strength to fight it alone.

"I do not understand your meaning, sir," she said, unable to meet his eye. "But I do know that it is not at all seemly for us to be alone in this bedchamber."

"You found the passage to my study, presumably?" She nodded. "I was hoping you would. The other branch leads to the cellar and through a trapdoor directly to the stables. Very useful it is too."

"Why was it constructed?" She had no real interest in knowing but needed to divert his attention away from her own situation.

"Some dissolute ancestor, wishing to enter and leave the house unobserved, I have always surmised." He smiled. "In any event, most of these old houses have something of that nature. Very useful for secret trysts, plotting against the monarchy, that sort of thing."

"I suppose so." Estelle's gaze was focused on the orchards below as her mind continued to whirl. He was being so kind to her, doing so much to put her at her ease. She felt ashamed of the trouble she was causing him and could not bring herself to look in his direction.

"Come, Estelle." He whispered her name in a voice loaded with such gentle compassion it was as though she was hearing it for the first time. His somnolent smile was full of persuasive charm. His eyes locked upon hers and caused her resolve not to confide in him to falter. "Tell me what I can do to be of service to you."

"There is nothing. I—"

"You have no reason to be afraid of me." He brushed her shoulder with a gossamer touch that set her senses reeling. "You will find that I am a very sympathetic listener, one who is not easily shocked. Besides, unless I mistake the matter, you are of age and can do precisely as you please."

"It is not that." She swirled away from the window, frowning as she placed distance between them. Her mind had a tendency to become addled when he stood too close to her, preventing her from thinking straight. But she knew better than to give way to temptation and lean upon him just because he was being gallant. "It is something I have to work out for myself."

"You may depend upon my discretion. You and I understand the ways of the world, I think. After all, you can hardly lay claim to being a skittish miss, not if half the things that posturing brute claimed are to be believed."

Estelle let out a gasp of betrayal. She had almost given in to his gallantry and shared her troubles with him. How could she have been such a simpleton? She should have known better than to imagine that he was really on her side. He now knew she had been married and intended to take shameful advantage of her.

He was no different than Mr. Travis's awful son, and others too, who had seen her married to a man so much older than herself and thought she would welcome their advances. By refusing her stepson's overtures with contemptuous disregard for his pride, she had made an enemy of him, which was partly responsible for her current difficulties.

And now history appeared to be repeating itself. She would not offer herself to Lord Crawley and would very soon find herself homeless again as a consequence.

"Please leave," she said.

"I only wish to be of service to you."

Estelle could easily imagine the service he had in mind. "I do not require anyone's assistance."

"Oh, but I think you do." A flicker of understanding passed across his face and his expression hardened. "I cannot imagine what you think I have in mind but I suspect you have misinterpreted my intentions." He threw her shawl on the bed and turned towards the door. "Winthrop was most interested to observe this garment in the drawing room," he said, closing the door softly behind him.

Estelle wanted to weep with frustration, even as she wondered why she was so disappointed to discover that Lord Crawley was no different than all the rest of his gender. Despite his pretence at an innocent reason for wishing to assist her, she knew better than to believe him. She had seen the look in his eye when he called her by her name, had seen the same hunger in the eyes of too many other men since the time of her marriage to mistake its meaning. She knew what he would expect in return for aiding her and, in spite of the fact that she had no one else to turn to, she was not prepared to oblige him. She had finally had enough of being exploited.

Lady Crawley would most likely seek her out upon her return. The notion helped Estelle to banish her introspective thoughts. She hid her efforts at packing and reclined upon her bed, which is how that lady discovered her not half an hour later.

"My dear, you look worn out. I am afraid you have overexerted yourself."

Estelle was overwhelmed, once again, by Lady Crawley's concern for her welfare. It was clear that her son had not yet revealed her true identity—presumably because he was unaware of her return. Estelle could not but wonder how much distress she would be responsible for causing when it did become known. She stifled a sigh and would have given much to make it otherwise.

"Yes." Estelle sat up and managed a weak smile for her hostess's benefit. "I fear your wonderful harp proved to be too much of a temptation and I played for longer than I ought. I completely lost track of time."

"Yes, my dear, Alex mentioned to me when I came in just now that your beautiful music has been filling the house for most of the afternoon."

"Oh, did Lord Crawley say that?"

Estelle was now very confused. So he had spoken to his mother but had not chosen to mention Estelle's deception. Why? Presumably to protect his mother's finer feelings. Or did he hope that by remaining silent she would feel obliged to warm his bed through a sense of gratitude?

"I have asked for tea to be sent up here," said Lady Crawley. "We can be quite comfortable and you need not exert yourself. And then, my dear, I do think it would be advisable if you remained in your chamber this evening and recovered your strength." She patted Estelle's hand. "You are looking altogether too pale and I blame myself for that. I should have known that harp would be your undoing. I would not have been able to resist it either, had I been in your position."

Estelle smiled and thanked Lady Crawley. She felt more dispirited by the minute for deceiving her but did not scruple to obey. She had known the dictate would be issued the moment the viscountess saw she had taken to her bed.

"Lady Jacobs is to hold a house party in two days' time," said Lady Crawley, once tea and a delicate selection of cakes had been delivered and the maid had left them alone. "She reminded me about it this afternoon. Dear Miss Jenkins will be there too, of course. Alex and I are expected and although I said we would attend, I do not now see how I can go. I cannot possibly leave you when you are so unwell, although I daresay Alex will still wish to form part of the party."

"Oh no, Lady Crawley, you must go. I insist!" How much more guilt would this charming lady unwittingly heap upon her already overburdened shoulders? Estelle did not think she could bear it. "I would not for the world have you miss the entertainment because of me. Besides, I daresay you would not wish to miss an opportunity to further Lord Crawley's intimacy with Miss Jenkins. House parties are ideal situations for matchmaking, are they not?"

"Oh dear me, yes, there is that. Lady Jacobs and I referred to the matter just this afternoon. We both have such high hopes in that regard and Miss Jenkins herself is, I believe, not averse to the notion. It does seem like too good an opportunity to pass up. Dear Miss Jenkins was looking quite pretty today. I wish Alex could have seen her in her pink dimity. Oh dear, I really do not know what it would be best to do."

"My dear Lady Crawley, do not spare me a thought, I beg of you. I shall be quite comfortable here. Of course you must go."

Lady Crawley left Estelle alone after they finished their tea but came to check on her after she had taken her dinner alone with her son. She sat with her for over half an hour, chattering away, fuelling Estelle's guilt. When, yawning discreetly behind her hand, her ladyship declared that she too would retire early, Estelle was at last satisfied there would be no further interruptions and set her plan in motion. She placed the most serviceable gown she possessed in her valise and packed the other few items she could not manage without, including, naturally, her favourite shawl.

She stared out of the window, impatiently tapping her fingers on the sill. She was not surprised to notice that even nature had conspired against her, providing only a miniscule amount of moonlight by which she would have to navigate her way towards the long driveway and thence to the village. She shuddered, aware that her fear of the dark was about to be tested for the second time in one day.

All was in readiness and she must wait now until she was sure the household had settled for the night. Her only remaining task, and a crucial one, was to pen a few lines to Lady Crawley to account for her sudden departure. Easier said than done. Half an hour later she had still had not written a single word. Compounding a falsehood by committing it to paper was so much more difficult than merely living a lie. But eventually it was done. A sudden summons to a new post received late the previous day was a wretched excuse and one which would not stand up to the mildest scrutiny. But she could think of nothing better to account for her sudden disappearance. She added that she had left the house at first light, walking the short distance to the village in order to catch the early mail coach, since she had no wish to give further trouble by requesting transportation. She ended by offering warm thanks to her hostess for so diligently restoring her to health but avoided any mention of where she was headed.

Estelle could imagine Lady Crawley's distress when she read this most inadequate of letters. Picturing her kindly face wrinkling with confusion and concern, she had never liked herself less. She sighed and propped the missive on the mantelpiece in her chamber where it was sure to be seen and handed to Lady Crawley by the maid.

Dressed in her warmest travelling attire, Estelle slipped from her room, valise in hand, and crept down the stairs in the direction of Lord Crawley's study. It had been very obliging of him to mention that the secret passage had two wings. She had not noticed that it split off in different directions and was grateful that she happened to have chosen the correct route earlier. It also meant that her escape from the house would now be expediently achieved.

As expected, his lordship's study was devoid of human presence, only the embers of the dying fire lending it any light. But that was sufficient for Estelle to make her way to the concealed doorway and slip behind it. Only then did she appreciate that she should have thought to bring a candle with her. She told herself it was no gloomier now than it had been this afternoon. The darkness of the night could not penetrate these hidden passages. But the thought did little to reassure her and she hesitated, suddenly unsure of which direction to take.

Only the sight of a pair of inquisitive eyes staring beadily up at her compelled her to gather up her skirts with a shriek and move her feet. She shuddered, her skin crawling with repulsion. Where there was one rat very likely more were lurking. She was so appalled by the thought that for a moment she considered giving up her bid for freedom. But only for a moment. She had come too far to turn back now and told herself not to be so pathetic, aware that she must now move quickly if she was not to lose her nerve altogether.

She sped along the dank passageway as fast as she dared, touching the walls on either side with her valise and reticule respectively. She spoke aloud in the hope that the commotion she was making would scare off the more inquisitive members of the rodent population. Only when she sensed a change in the draughty atmosphere did she slow her pace. Aware that she must have reached the point at which the paths divided, she stared straight into the eyes of the one rat which had refused to be deterred by her noisy intrusion into his territory.

"Which way do I go now, then?" she asked him, strangely comforted rather than alarmed by his determination to accompany her.

The rat regarded her with an air of complacent superiority and a twitch of his whiskery nose but offered no opinion.

"You are no help at all," she admonished, shaking a finger at him.

She forced herself to take several deep breaths as she waited for the confusion that was clouding her mind to dissipate. As it gradually did so her powers of reasoning were restored to her. She decided that if she had approached from straight ahead this afternoon, and she was sure that she had because she did not recall turning any corners, then her path on this occasion must lay to the right. Blindly stretching out her hands she turned in that direction, cursing as she struck her head on an overhang which knocked her bonnet askew. She ducked beneath the offending rock and followed the path as it turned sharply to the left, fervently hoping that her subterranean journey was coming to an end. Instead she was almost blinded by the light glowing from a wall scone.

"Ah, there you are at last!" The owner of the rumbling male voice levered himself from the wall against which he had been sprawled. "I was beginning to think you must have taken a wrong path."

Estelle gasped, her heart pounding against her rib cage. This was simply too much for her fragile grasp on reality to cope with. She had defied her father; overcome her fear of the dark and her repulsion for rodents, only to be challenged by some nameless male figure of authority before she had even escaped the confines of Crawley Hall. Her head was swimming and she staggered backwards a few paces, dizziness rendering her actions ungainly, as she struggled to come to terms with her spectacular failure.

Her last memory before her world went completely black was of a strong pair of arms catching her, preventing her from crumpling to the floor in a dead faint.

Chapter Eight

Alex cradled the unconscious Estelle against his chest and carried her back through the passageway into his study. All the while he cursed his stupidity. He should have kept his temper in check and devised a less dramatic means by which to challenge her contention that she was a stranger to Winthrop. He should also have realized that these passageways would be a daunting enough test for any lady's sensibilities, and that one weakened by illness was bound to be especially susceptible to their terrors. His confronting her in such a crass manner could have resulted in her injuring herself.

She weighed nothing at all. Carrying her and her bags, Alex was not even out of breath when he regained his study and laid her gently on the settee in front of the fire. Rekindling the flames, he was soon rewarded by the sight of them chasing one another up the chimney. He removed her bonnet and loosened her pelisse, gently tracing the line of her deathly pale face with his palm. Opening her valise he found what he was searching for almost immediately and placed her beautifully embroidered shawl across her knee. Perhaps the sight of it would soothe her when she opened her eyes. He sat on the edge of the settee and removed her fine kid gloves, taking her hands and rubbing them together to infuse some warmth into her.

Alex felt great admiration for her courage. She was heartrendingly beautiful yet virtually defenceless against her brute of a father who treated her more as a possession than a person. The man terrified her to such a degree that she was prepared to venture alone into an uncertain future rather than live beneath his roof. Her vulnerability brought out his protective instincts in spades.

But there was more to her dilemma than a domineering parent, he would wager his fortune on that, and would not be satisfied until he knew precisely what she sought to evade. If he was to make recompense for his boorish behaviour by being of service to her, he must first persuade her to place her trust in him and reveal the precise nature of her difficulties.

Alex cursed himself for being the cause of her current anguish and would have given much to be able to relive the evening. How differently he would have managed matters then. He had been angry with Estelle and had wanted to teach her a lesson for doubting his integrity. But he could now appreciate the situation from her perspective. The growing attraction he entertained towards her had made his offer of assistance sound clumsy, open to misinterpretation. In retrospect he could scarce blame her for all but accusing him of dishonourable intentions. It was an insult of the first order for a gentleman of his ilk—one which rankled, causing him to temporarily lose his grip on reason and making him desirous for a modicum of revenge. He had deliberately mentioned the other passageway, knowing by her haphazard attempts to pack her belongings that she was intent upon escape and that she would swallow the bait.

"It was you!"

The sound of her voice jolted Alex out of his introspection. He looked down into eyes which were clouded with confusion, her lashes sweeping repeatedly across her translucent cheeks as she struggled to reclaim her senses.

"I apologize for startling you. How do you feel?"

She ignored his restraining hand and sat up, carefully twisting her head from side to side. "I have a mild headache, which is hardly to be wondered at. Still, having survived your juvenile prank, I ought to be thankful that I am still in possession of a head at all, I suppose. Whatever did you imagine you were about?"

"Here." He handed her a glass of water.

"Thank you." She took several sips. "Where did this come from?" She fingered her shawl and cast a suspicious glance at him.

"I thought you might find it comforting."

"That was thoughtful but would not have been necessary if you had not scared me half out of my wits. And you still have not explained why you acted in such a manner."

"I apologize once again." He bowed his apology, to which she made a derisive sound at the back of her throat. "Shall we start again, Mrs. Travis?"

"Please do not call me that."

"I doubt, having witnessed your father's unconscionable behaviour, you would find Winthrop any more acceptable."

She inclined her head, a ghost of a smile playing about her lips. He could not tear his eyes away from them and stared, mesmerized, wondering how they would taste if he were to kiss them. "True."

"Then I shall simply address you as Estelle," he said, relieved to see that her temper was subsiding and she had ceased pressing him for explanations. She clearly was not one to bear grudges, a discovery which heartened him.

"As you wish."

Distant haughtiness had returned to her tone, reminding him that he would likely have to undertake a vast amount more grovelling before she would even consider trusting him. And since being of service to this indescribably endearing creature was currently of vital importance to him, grovelling it would have to be.

"I think it is time you told me what is going on, Estelle, so that I might make recompense for my behaviour by helping you out of your difficulties." He held up his hand when she made to interrupt him. "And the truth this time, all of it, if you please."

She was quiet for a long time, staring into the fire as though seeking inspiration in its embers. Alex did not speak again, knowing this time that whatever she chose to tell him would indeed be the truth. The only question was, how much of the truth would she be prepared to reveal?

"Susanna Cleethorpe and I are not strangers to one another. In face we have been friends for years," she said at last.

"You met at school?"

"You knew that?"

"I surmised it. You gave yourself away when you first arrived by almost referring to Mrs. Cleethorpe as Susanna."

"I did not think that anyone noticed the slip."

"I did."

"And then my father arrived and confirmed the fact."

"Your father made a great many assertions, none of which I was prepared to take at face value."

"I daresay that he did, and I thank you for not being taken in by his bluster." She paused. "I should have admitted to the truth when we spoke of his visit earlier. I can see that now, but I thought, well, you know..." Her words trailed to an embarrassed halt. Then she turned her remarkable eyes upon him, all artifice gone from their expression. The naked vulnerability they now displayed fired his passionate desire to act as her protector. More significantly, they fired his passions as a man. Never before had a woman affected him so comprehensively. He hid the discomfort of his reaction by shifting his position and inclining his head, an invitation for her to continue speaking. "I apologize for dissembling but I was not sure, that is to say..."

"Do not distress yourself, my dear. We have neither of us behaved as we ought but it is not too late to right that situation, if you could just bring yourself to trust me."

"I do trust you, sir—now." She smiled briefly, a gesture which lit up her whole face and enhanced her aesthetic beauty. "But I have learned, through necessity, to be cautious about whom I place my trust in."

"I knew of your late husband by reputation," he said when her words appeared to have stalled again, "but I collect he did not make your happy."

"He had to be persuaded to marry me, apparently. My father will tell anyone who asks that it cost him a fortune to marry me well. Mr. Travis only reluctantly took me even then, not because he was desirous of another wife but because he so badly needed the blunt."

"Good God!" said Alex, surprise taking precedence over good manners.

"I did not actually know that until my father was kind enough to inform me when he called on me a week ago. But it should have been obvious by the way my husband treated me. I was never made to feel a part of his world, and it was clear that he resented my presence in his house. He did little to ease my path into society and nothing at all to abuse his acquaintances of their belief that he had married beneath his station. I have never been more lonely in my entire life."

Her quiet dignity made him want to dispel the hurt in her eyes by pulling her into his arms and kissing her witless. "Iniquitous behaviour!" Travis clearly had not resented her sufficiently to exclude her from his bed, any more than it had prevented him from impregnating her. Alex clenched his fists. He would like to bring the bounder back to life. Then he could enjoy the satisfaction of inflicting excessive physical damage upon him before dispatching him back to his grave.

"Indeed, and my father filled the house with his spies. My maid has always reported my every activity to him—"

"You should have dismissed her."

"It would not have served. He would have found another way to keep abreast of my activities. That much became apparent as soon as Mr. Travis died and he sent others to keep watch over me."

"But why?"

"That is what I did not understand at first but since my father's visit last week it has all become so much clearer. He did not trust me, you see, to keep faith with Mr. Travis or to resist...well, to resist..."

"I perfectly understand, Estelle. Please continue."

"My sister Marianne also knew she would not be permitted to follow her heart when it came to matrimony. When my father told her she was to be engaged to a business acquaintance of his, a Mr. Cowper, she agreed at first but then took fright and ran away."

"And you fear for her safety as a consequence."

"Yes, you see my brother also escaped from Papa's tyranny. My father comes originally from the north of England, from Leeds. His father was a bricklayer who set himself up in business by winning contracts to construct cheap cottages for mill workers. My father inherited that business but cast his net wider, making a vast amount of money through his construction projects. But he was always ambitious and never intended to remain a member of the lower classes." Estelle paused to take a sip of water. "His most obvious means of bettering himself was to use his money to marry well. My mother is the youngest child of the Earl of Dorchester and he thought that by marrying her, society's doors would be opened to him as a matter of course."

"But they were not?"

"No. My father is not without intelligence but he has a northerner's blunt manner of expressing himself deeply ingrained. He sees nothing wrong with the fact that he has achieved his wealth through hard work and his own ingenuity, and discusses the particulars with anyone who will lend him an ear. That sort of language, as you can imagine, does not go down well in the best salons."

"To have made his money through trade is one thing but to even hint at it, much less flaunt the fact, is simply not done."

"Precisely. My mother hides her disappointments at the direction her life has taken by being totally self-absorbed. She only sees that which she wishes to see and accepts my father's complete dominance without question." Estelle sighed. "I do not know how things were between them when they were first married, but I have not known her to strive for any sort of independence."

"I see." And Alex rather suspected that he did. He had been wondering why Estelle's mother had not come to her daughters' aid. Now he understood. The mother was clearly as cold and disinterested in her family as the father was determined to exploit its members for his own ends. "Pray continue."

"Well, when society proved to be less than enamoured with my father he chose another path. By using his wealth he developed a reputation as a patron of the arts. He holds regular soirees in Hampshire, encouraging all up-and-coming artists, writers and musicians to attend his salons, and offers patronage to those whom he considers to have the most potential. He has an uncanny knack of knowing what the latest trend will be before it has become fashionable and exploits the appropriate protégées in order to be seen as a forward-thinking philanthropist."

"Which is why he encouraged your musical ability, presumably."

"Yes. I was made to play at all of his gatherings, simply to show him in a good light and make it appear as though he knew what he was about."

"And your brother's role in this?"

"Well, papa's ultimate aim was, of course, to enhance his reputation by exploiting Matthew's artistic knowledge. He did not entirely trust anyone else to advise him."

"And your brother fell in with that scheme?"

"Yes, he was miserable but had no choice, other than to be cut off without a penny. But no sooner had he graduated than Papa told him he was arranging for him to marry a Lady Isobel Bruton—"

"Lord Bruton's daughter?"

"Yes."

"Ahh, I see!"

"You know her?"

"Indeed." Alex shuddered at the memory of the outspoken woman whom he had met on several occasions. She made little effort to make the best of herself, or conform to the dictates of society. "And I suspect that was when Matthew decided he had been pushed too far."

"Yes, it was. Lady Isobel had nothing whatsoever to recommend her. She had no personality, no accomplishments, not even a passing beauty or a pleasing figure. But of course it was her title that interested my father. Because her family were not only in such straightened circumstances but also despairing of ever getting Isobel off their hands, he knew they would eventually accept an offer from Matthew."

"The offer was made?"

"Negotiations had commenced and I had never seen Matthew so distraught. He came to me one night, the last occasion upon which I spoke to him," she said, her voice filled with a combination of guilt and regret, "telling me he simply could not do it and would run away rather than endure marriage to such a girl. He had such romantic notions, you see, but to my eternal regret I told him not to be so melodramatic. I knew he had little choice in the matter and suggested that Father would let up on him if he did what he wanted. I assured him it would all work out for the best in the end." She sighed. "The next time I heard from him was a letter sent from Jamaica. He had a close friend at school whose family has a plantation out there and he accepted a position as a bookkeeper."

"And he is still there?"

"I thought so, but apparently he wrote just before my husband died and the letter was sent from Dover."

"Do you think your missing sister might be with him now?"

"If it were so, it would be the answer to my most fervent prayer."

"Have you any idea where they might be?"

"No, Susanna and I were to search for them together. But that is no longer possible because of her condition."

"Her condition?"

Estelle smiled. "She has only just found out."

"Ah, I see." Alex too was now smiling. "Michael has not wasted any time."

"Indeed, but Susanna is disgusted that he will not now let her out of his sight."

"I daresay." Alex doubted his friend would have taken too kindly to his new wife traipsing all over the country in a well-meaning search for displaced siblings. It was just as well that she was now confined to Fairlands. "But tell me, who is this Cowper whom your sister took such violent exception to?"

"Well, that is the strangest thing. Lady Isobel and Mr. Travis were both of the upper classes. I did not approve of either of them but understood why my father was so desirous to ally our family to theirs. But Mr. Cowper is just an agent of my father's, employed to oversee his business dealings in Leeds."

"He still handles construction work in that county?"

"Yes, it is still the bedrock of his business empire."

"Then I do not understand why he wished for your sister to marry such a man."

"No more do I. But then I had always been the dutiful sibling who never questioned his decisions. I told Marianne that at least Mr. Cowper was young and that she ought to count her blessings." She dropped her voice to a hoarse whisper. "That is the last time I saw her and I fear more and more for her safety as each day passes."

"But you do not feel able to return to your father's establishment and persuade him to instigate a search for your missing siblings?"

"No."

"Why not?"

"Well, since I am being so frank, there is more you should be made aware of." She paused for so long that he was on the verge of prompting her when she spoke again. As her tale slowly unfolded he was obliged to conceal his abhorrence at her father's callous attempt to manipulate her. She blushed as she related the problems inherent to living beneath the same roof as Travis Junior. That blush told him a great deal, not least why she had misinterpreted his earlier offer of assistance. A fresh surge of anger ricocheted through him as he contemplated the number of inappropriate proposals she must have received since her unlikely union with Travis.

"But that is not all. My father also told me he has given up his search for Marianne." Tears sprang to her eyes. "All that had kept me going these past months was the belief that he would be throwing his resources behind the search for my sister. To think she is out there somewhere, with no one to protect her and no one to turn to for advice, makes me sick with apprehension."

"Calm yourself, m'dear, we will work something out." Alex took her hand and stroked the palm with his long fingers, soothing her as though she was a skittish filly. "Now, if you feel able, please tell me the rest. I believe there is still more."

"Indeed there is. My father also told me that when I was out of mourning I was to marry Mr. Cowper in my sister's stead..."

"Good God!"

"I feel God has little part to play in the scheme," she said with a wistful smile.

"No wonder you felt compelled to escape. You are what, no more than three months a widow?" Estelle nodded. "And already he is marrying you off again to further his own ends."

Alex ran his hand through his rebellious curls, his eyes narrowing as a succession of unsavoury thoughts tumbled through his brain. "I would give a lot to know what is so special about Cowper that your father is determined to tie one of his daughters to him."

"I wondered about that too. He said I had been Mr. Cowper's first choice but I was already promised to Mr. Travis when the question of him marrying one of us came up."

"Travis's demise came at a convenient time then, just after your sister disappeared and Cowper might have looked elsewhere for a bride."

"Yes, I suppose it did. I had not considered the matter in that light before. My father said that if I married Mr. Cowper he would make me his sole heir, thinking that would persuade me."

"Then he cannot know you as well as he supposes." Alex stroked the hand he was still holding in his. "Not if he thinks you will be persuaded by material considerations."

"He probably believes that if he can entice me back to Hampshire he will soon be able to talk me round. That is why he is so anxious for my return. It has nothing to do with my happiness and everything to do with his ambition."

"And so when he found you gone he would have been greatly vexed."

"Yes, and blaming Susanna, no doubt. But she would not hear of me returning home. She told me of your mother's need for a companion and, well…" She raised her eyes to his face, making no attempt to reclaim her hand from his grasp. "I regret deceiving your mother, Lord Crawley. She has been prodigiously kind to me. But you must understand that I was desperate and did not stop to consider the consequences of my actions any more than I appreciated how agreeable I would find Lady Crawley's company. I also did not anticipate that my father would find me so quickly and cause you so much trouble."

"Think nothing of that."

"I should have anticipated that he would gain information from the servants and track me down by that means."

"Do not distress yourself. I knew you were no governess the moment I laid eyes upon you but did not object. Indeed, I was grateful when I saw how readily my mother took to you and how your being here so lifted her spirits. Anyway, I asked Susanna to find someone to bear her company so can hardly complain at a little subterfuge."

"You are very understanding."

"So tell me, where did you hope to escape to?"

"Why, to find Marianne, of course."

"Alone? Do you have sufficient funds and somewhere to stay?"

"Well no, not exactly, but..."

"Where do you imagine she might be?"

Estelle explained about the solicitor's clerk in Ramsgate. "His reply to my letter did not ring true at all. The more I think about it, the more sure I am that he must know where she is. He informed me that he had not had the pleasure of seeing her but did not ask any questions about my reasons for enquiring. Nor did he ask if there was any way he could be of service in locating her, which would surely be the natural thing to do."

"Indeed, and so it seems we must go to Ramsgate without delay."

"We?"

"You cannot possibly travel there alone," said Alex, his mind alive with the possible consequences of such action.

"Oh, but I must."

"And my mother?"

"I left her a note explaining my sudden departure," she said, averting her gaze.

"This?" He reached across to his desk and held up the letter she had left in her chamber. The seal was broken. She watched in stupefaction as he committed it to the flames.

"What are you doing? Where did you get that?" When he raised a brow but said nothing she became agitated. "You were watching me?" She placed her hands on her hips and glowered at him. "You saw me leave my chamber and knew I would head for the passageway, which is why you told me about it."

"I needed you to trust me." He chuckled at her stony expression. "It was a good notion to suggest you had received a sudden offer. But to disappear like a thief in the night. That was not kind, Estelle."

"It was necessary. My father will find a way to get to me if I remain here."

"You do not appear to set much stock by my abilities to protect you."

"You should not have to. I am not your responsibility."

"But what if I wish you to be?"

"Why would you wish it?"

"Because it pleases me to be of service to you. Now," he said, waving away the further objections he could sense her formulating, "if you can bear to wait until the morrow, we shall arrange for your offer of employment to arrive by more conventional means. I shall then invent business that takes me away immediately, thereby offering you a seat in my carriage for part of your journey."

"But you are not desirous of leaving your mother alone."

"Ah, but Lady Jacobs has obligingly arranged a house party that commences tomorrow. My mother will attend and will be quite taken up by all the activity there for several days. She will not miss us and we will be at leisure to pursue our enquiries."

"Oh, you are too kind, but that will not serve. You are expected at the house party as well. Your mother was only telling me yesterday how much she was depending on it, and it would not do for you to disappoint her as well."

Alex offered her a wry smile. "I fear she would be more disappointed if I did attend. Emma Jenkins is a dear friend but she is not the one for me."

"So you know of your mother's aspirations in that respect?"

"She is not quite as subtle as she imagines."

"Yes, but—"

"No buts, Estelle. I am determined to help you find out what has become of your sister and there is nothing you can say that will dissuade me."

Chapter Nine

Alex went in search of the ladies the following morning and found them occupied with their work in his mother's sitting room. He had scarce bid them good morning before Phelps entered the room on feet that appeared to glide soundlessly across the floor and stopped before Estelle.

"An express has just come for you, miss," he said, offering her a missive balanced on a silver salver.

"For me?" Estelle's feigned expression of surprise impressed Alex, especially since he was aware how much she disliked the idea of deceiving his mother. "I cannot imagine who could be writing to me here. No one of my acquaintance knows of my whereabouts."

Lady Crawley looked up from her embroidery and frowned. "It must be important if it came by express. I do so hope it does not signify bad news, my dear. It is my experience that unexpected letters often bear distressing tidings."

"Let us hope that is not the case in this instance." Estelle broke the seal. "Oh, there is no cause for concern, Lady Crawley, it is from Mrs. Cleethorpe."

"How thoughtful of her. What does she have to say and why, I wonder, did she feel the need to send her letter by express?"

"Well now, let us see." Estelle scanned the closely covered page and adopted a commendably convincing expression of surprise. "Goodness me, I can scarce believe my good fortune!"

His mother laid her work aside, giving up all attempts to conceal her curiosity. "Is there some difficulty, my dear?"

"No, indeed not. Quite the opposite, in fact." Estelle smiled in apparent delight but Alex noticed she could not bring herself to look directly at his mother. "Mrs. Cleethorpe writes to say she knows of a lady in London who is in urgent need of a new governess. Her own has had to leave without giving notice to care for her ailing mother and Mrs. Cleethorpe has kindly recommended me for the post."

"Oh." Lady Crawley's face fell. "What a wonderful opportunity for you. It is such a shame that you are not well enough to take up the post."

"But I am so much better, ma'am. Besides, I cannot let Mrs. Cleethorpe down when she has gone to so much trouble on my behalf."

"Well yes, it is true that you look better, but that is only due to the country air here at Crawley Hall. If you were to be subjected to the dirt and pollution of London I am sure it would only set you right back." His mother nodded decisively. "No, no, it is prodigiously kind of Mrs. Cleethorpe to go out of her way to find you another position but I am persuaded she cannot appreciate quite how unwell you have been. If she did she would not even have suggested it."

Estelle smiled and, observing her, Alex conceded that she did indeed look a great deal better. The dullness in her eye had given way to a sparkling vitality, her skin was flushed with a delicate hue, and her defeated demeanour had been replaced with one of resolute determination.

Alex suspected that having at last found the courage to defy her father was a liberating experience, at least as much responsible for the transformation in her as the country air his mother set so much stock by. She had been used as a bargaining tool and, he suspected, subjected to a barrage of improper propositions during the course of her short marriage. Seeing her emerge from the shadow of her oppressive father's influence, ready to do whatever was necessary to locate her missing siblings, was all the reward Alex required. Her lips curved upwards in a specious smile of sweet sensuality. She lifted her eyes and held his gaze, colour heightening her complexion. Alex was totally bewitched and forgot all about his mother's presence, not noticing the marked interest she took in his preoccupation.

"Alex, what is your opinion? We urgently need your advice." His mother's words only penetrated his sensuous thoughts when Estelle collected herself and dropped her eyes to the letter in her lap. "Dear Miss Tilling has received a letter from Mrs. Cleethorpe suggesting an acquaintance who is in need of a governess."

"But surely that is good news, Mother?"

"Well yes, of course, in the normal way it would be. But I do not think Miss Tilling is sufficiently recovered to travel all the way to London for an interview at this juncture."

"Oh, but my dear ma'am, indeed I must go. Mrs. Cleethorpe has advised her friend, Mrs. Fanshaw, to expect me there tomorrow."

"There, you see," said Lady Crawley in a satisfied tone. "I told you it was impossible. I emphatically do not understand how poor Miss Tilling could possibly travel to London, by mail coach of all things, in her debilitated condition. No, no, it is impossible. I will not hear of it. You had much better stay quietly here with me, Miss Tilling, until you have recovered your strength. There will be other positions available when you are well enough to consider them."

"I do not think so, ma'am. You must remember that I do not have a character, or anyone to recommend me. It will not be so easy for me to procure a respectable position without such credentials and so I cannot afford to waste opportunities such as this one."

"If Miss Tilling is of a mind to go I can be of service to her in that respect," said Alex. "Through great good fortune I have business that calls me to London tomorrow and I would be happy to take her up in my carriage. There, Mother, would that ease your mind?"

"No, indeed. I mean, yes." She looked up at them both, her expression greatly troubled. "I do not know what I mean. It is all so sudden that I do not know what to make of it at all. Nor do I understand the need for all this gadding about, for such haste."

"But, ma'am, Mrs. Cleethorpe is at pains to explain that Mrs. Fanshaw needs a new governess at once. It is a wonderful opportunity for me and if I do not attend the interview then I am afraid she will engage someone else. My circumstances are such that I cannot afford to take that risk."

"Oh yes, well I do see that, I suppose. I daresay you are very concerned about your future." Estelle inclined her head and averted her gaze but Alex could still detect guilt in her expression. He suspected that only the thought of her sister and the danger she might be facing prevented her from giving up the scheme and agreeing to stay at Crawley Hall. "But, Alex, I am sure you did not mention before that you were for town tomorrow."

"Urgent business that cannot wait, I am afraid, Mother."

"But you cannot go now. It is Lady Jacobs's house party tomorrow, which I am so anticipating, and you are expected."

"I have just now sent a note to Lady Jacobs with my regrets."

"Oh, oh I see. Oh dear, poor Emma."

"Emma, ma'am, what is she to do with it all?"

"Oh well, nothing exactly, but she was so looking forward to seeing us both. I am sure I do not know what she will make of the sudden business that keeps you away. But then, if you were to postpone it, dear Miss Tilling would have no means of getting to town. We could send her in the carriage, I suppose, but I do not care to think of her travelling unescorted."

"Then my suggestion must best serve."

"Well yes, but Miss Tilling, you must promise to return to us here immediately after you have conducted your business with Mrs. Fanshaw. If you are offered the position, and I am sure I do not see how you could fail to suit, Mrs. Fanshaw must be made to understand that you are convalescing from a grave illness and will not be ready to take up your new duties for at least another month."

"But, ma'am—"

"No buts, my dear, I really must insist. I shall expect Alex to have returned you to me by the time Lady Jacobs's party comes to an end in five days time."

"Very well, Mother." Alex exchanged a speaking glance with Estelle. Neither of them had expected his mother to be so firm about Estelle's return to Crawley Hall. But it was obvious she intended to extract a promise from him in that respect and he could hardly demur at such a reasonable request, even though so short a space of time would restrict their ability to conduct their investigations.

"Now, Alex, you must install Miss Tilling in the town house and ensure that Mrs. Parsons takes prodigious good care of her. Oh dear, should I send a note to make sure she airs the sheets and warms the bed? After all..."

"Calm yourself, Mother, Mrs. Parsons knows her business better than either of us. As our guest Miss Tilling will naturally receive every courtesy."

CRBO

Early the following morning Alex assisted Estelle into his luxurious coach and four. His mother looked very small and full of concern as she stood on the front steps and waved them off to town. He experienced a pang of guilt at being the cause of her anxiety. Aware of Estelle regarding him with a quizzical expression, he waited for his two liveried tigers to scramble up behind and gave his coachman the order to drive on.

"I feel most ungrateful," Estelle said, "deceiving Lady Crawley in such a monstrous fashion."

"And your way would have better served your conscience?" He raised his arm to his mother for a last time before putting up the window.

"No, of course not, and I would not have you think I do not appreciate your intervention. It is just that I cannot help regretting the necessity to play her false."

"Then let us hope that our business might be speedily concluded."

"Indeed, but if we are so fortunate as to recover my sister I do not see how I can return to Crawley Hall. I shall have Marianne's welfare to consider as well as my own and can hardly foist another deserving cause upon Lady Crawley."

"So what do you intend to do?"

"I cannot say with certainty. In fact I own I have not thought that far ahead. Devising a means of discovering Marianne's whereabouts and taking her to safety has occupied all my thoughts since learning that my father is no longer looking for her." She paused, nibbling at the end of her gloved index finger, a contemplative expression filtering across her lovely countenance. "Perhaps we are both destined to become governesses after all. We are amply qualified to fulfil such a role thanks to our tenure at Miss Frobisher's Academy for Young Ladies."

"I daresay." Alex chuckled at the vision this conjured up. He glanced out of the window as they approached the outskirts of the village. "I say, look out!" He clasped her shoulder and in one fluid movement pulled her head towards his lap.

"What is it?" The alarm in her voice was apparent even though it was muffled by the close proximity of her lips to his thigh.

"We are passing through the village, past the inn where your father has put up. I can see him talking to his coachman at the archway to the mews. No, no, keep down, he is looking this way."

"Has he recognized you?"

"He can hardly have failed to do so. But do not be alarmed. He will only have observed me sitting alone inside my carriage."

Winthrop broke off his conversation with his man and turned to glare at the passing carriage. His features were cold and full of suspicion. He lifted his head to ask a question of the inn's ostler. Presumably he wanted to know whose carriage it was bowling past them at such a cracking pace. Alex assumed a bored expression and looked straight through the man.

"He will suspect something nonetheless."

"It will get him nowhere."

"No, I suppose it will not." Estelle sounded far from certain as she twisted her head sideways on his thigh, presumably because she found it uncomfortable speaking to the fabric of his breeches. Alex stifled a groan. He was finding it uncomfortable too, but for a very different reason. "But he will now know that you are not at home and will very likely try to gain access to Crawley Hall and to your mother."

"Pray do not concern yourself. He will not get past the gatehouse. And by now my mother will be in the curricle, on her way to Lady Jacobs's party, where she will remain until I have returned and can collect her myself."

"But he will not give up, even then." Alex could hear renewed anxiety in her voice and had to suppress the almost overwhelming urge to comfort her in the manner which spontaneously sprang to mind. By some extreme effort of will he resisted taking such an improper course, making do with stroking her slender back, soothing her as though she were a fractious child. "He will undoubtedly set about quizzing your staff, or more likely get his man to do so."

"And what will he discover?" Alex lifted his shoulders. "That I have removed to London, that is all, and there is nothing remarkable about that. I visit the capital on a regular basis."

"But he might also learn that you were accompanied on your journey by a lady who has been a guest in your house."

"Perhaps, but only if there is someone in my employ who values his position so little that he is prepared to reveal that information. I have given specific orders that your visit should not be mentioned to anyone and I seriously doubt that those orders will be disobeyed. But even if he does somehow gain that intelligence, what then?"

"Well, he might look for me in your London home."

"Where he will have no better luck than he did here." He transferred his attention from her back to the trembling shoulder resting on his knee. "Have courage, Estelle. I know you are fearful of him and I comprehend your anxiety. But take comfort from the fact that he cannot get near you or force you to do anything against your will when you are in my company."

"And when you are not with me?"

"I shall not leave you unprotected until this matter is resolved."

"That is not what I meant." She popped her head up, only for him to push it sharply back down again. The only sounds inside the carriage as they passed through the outskirts of the village were the wheels gliding over the rutted road and Estelle's anxious breathing.

"It is all right," he said after a moment or two more during which no words passed between them. "We are beyond the village now and it is safe for you to get up."

"Thank goodness!" Bonnet askew and face drained of all colour, she lifted her head, her insecurities on plain view as she gazed at him through trusting eyes.

Alex cursed beneath his breath. It was beyond his ability, would likely have been beyond any man's power, to resist her as she appeared at that moment. Her eyes were wide with anxiety, and he was mesmerized by the sweep of her extravagant lashes as they fluttered to rest against her pale cheeks. The rise and fall of her breast as she struggled to contain her fear only added to his dilemma. To Alex she had never appeared lovelier or more vulnerable. His arm was still resting on her shoulder and he pulled her head against his chest, intent upon reassurance. Her eyes opened wide with surprise and he thought she was about to object. But she made no attempt to evade him. Encouraged, Alex's free hand moved to set her bonnet straight and then pushed a springy curl behind her ear.

"You worry too much," he whispered. "It is not at all flattering that you set such little stock by my abilities to protect you."

"It is not that, it is just that I—"

"Shush, no more talking."

She was looking directly up at him, her lips plump and so achingly tempting that Alex gave up all efforts at restraint. Slowly, giving her ample opportunity to object, he dropped his head, angling it to avoid colliding with the now straight peak of her bonnet. With infinite gentleness he covered those lips with his own. Savouring the sweet taste of her mouth, he gradually increased the pressure. His body pulsated with desire when he discovered that she did not have the slightest idea how to return his kiss. The knowledge both heartened and infuriated him. Her brute of a husband had clearly not taken the time to allay her very natural fears about her marital responsibilities with soothing preliminaries before forcing himself on her.

All to the good, Alex decided, putting his heart into pleasing her. He teased her lips apart with his tongue and lazily explored the contours of her mouth. As he drew her closer and deepened the kiss she let out a tiny sigh, whether of outrage or pleasure he was not entirely sure at first. But when her arms wound their way round his neck, a feeling of triumph ripped through him. That she was following her instincts and actively seeking to prolong the moment became apparent when she pressed her body more closely against his side. It was a headily sensual gesture underlined with a sinuous grace that left him breathless and aching for more.

Her action, and the sensations that threatened as a direct result, brought Alex to his senses. Disciplining himself to ignore his growing need, he reluctantly lifted his head and released her. Another cry, and this time it was definitely one of protest, passed her lips.

"Better?" He raised a questioning brow as he removed his arm from around her shoulders and settled her back in her seat.

"Is that how you resolve all the problems with the females under your care?"

Alex's lips quirked. It was too late for her to pretend disinterest. Her cheeks were scarlet. She put up her chin in a belated attempt to appear dignified, looking everywhere except at him. Her response to his kiss had told him far more then she could possibly imagine. He would wager his fortune that she had never before acted so impulsively and was doubtless overwhelmed with guilt for enjoying the experience. She did not yet appreciate that she possessed a passionate nature and was clearly embarrassed by what had passed between them.

And so she was attempting to place the blame at his door, which was indeed where it belonged. It had been most ungentlemanly to impose himself upon her when she was so totally dependent upon his patronage. He should not have given way to his impulses and vowed that he would not do so again.

With considerable difficulty Alex wrenched his mind away from the alluring prospect of awakening her passions and the peculiar effect the prospect was having upon him. He had bedded more women than he could remember. What was so special about this one? He did not know and disciplined himself not to dwell upon the issue. There would be time enough for introspection when they had found her wretched sister.

But then what? It was a question which had cost him much sleep the previous night and one which he had yet to find an answer to.

"We are bound for Ramsgate but that is all I yet know. Tell me more about this callow youth whom your sister developed a *tendre* for and why you anticipate finding them together."

"Mr. Porter is articled to Nesbit and Jones, the solicitors who took care of Mr. Travis's business affairs."

"Yes, so I apprehend."

"Marianne was staying with me in Hertfordshire, a month or two before Mr. Travis had his accident. Whilst she was there, Mr. Porter called about some business on behalf of his employers. It detained him in Hertfordshire for several nights, which threw him into frequent company with Marianne, since he dined with us each evening. He is an intelligent and engaging young man and it did not harm his cause with Marianne that he is also frightfully good looking."

"I daresay it did not, but I feel persuaded that your father would not have approved of a mere clerk paying court to your sister."

"Indeed he would not have. However, he was not there and I did not think there was any harm in it. Marianne almost swooned when she first espied Mr. Porter. I could tell immediately that her partiality for the young man was returned by the way they looked at one another and the excuses they made to be together. I caught the two of them in close conversation several times, conversation that ceased when they noticed my presence. I also found them alone in the summerhouse shortly before he left."

Alex chuckled at her expression, which failed in its effort to be censorial.

"Very remiss of me, I know. I am unaware how long they had contrived to be alone. I am not much of a chaperone, you see." She turned dancing hazel eyes in his direction. "And once he had left, Marianne could not stop speaking about him. She whirled around the house saying it was love at first sight—"

"She was that smitten?"

"My sister has a flair for the dramatic. But even so, I thought as you do, at first anyway. I had seen her in love before but her partiality for Mr. Porter did not wane when he left, so I was gradually persuaded that this time it was different. There was an indefinable air about her; about them both when they were together, which was impossible to misinterpret."

"But you did not encourage her partiality?"

"No, for I knew it was useless. She was determined to wait until Mr. Porter was out of articles and could make a life for them both."

"They had talked of such matters? It had progressed that far?"

"I believe so, from some of the remarks she subsequently made. I reminded her that she had agreed to marry Mr. Cowper. But she just waved the notion away and said she would find a way to avoid that fate."

"Which is why Porter's one-line response to your enquiry after Marianne makes you so sure she must be with him?"

"Quite. As I said before, I could see how taken he was by her. Indeed what man could resist such a jewel? But even if he was not, surely politeness alone would require him to ask why I was seeking her and if there was any way he could be of assistance? I cannot understand it at all," she said, frowning. "Mr. Porter's manners are punctilious and his attraction towards Marianne was absolutely genuine, I would stake my life on that. And that is why I cannot accept he would be so unconcerned about her welfare."

"Which," said Alex, covering both of her hands with one of his own, "is precisely why we are heading directly to Ramsgate now. Try not to worry. We shall soon have all the answers."

"Thank you, my lord."

She spoke quietly, with heartfelt dignity. Strange things happened to him as he felt the full force of her gratitude shining from the luminescent eyes that rested upon him with transparent faith in his abilities. He knew then that he would move heaven and earth, do whatever was necessary, to ensure that her trust in him was not misplaced.

"But presumably, when your sister first went missing, you acquainted your father of your suspicions in respect of her attraction towards Porter?"

"Well, no, actually I did not."

"Really!" Alex did not have to feign his surprise.

"I suppose I should have done so but, even in my anxiety for her, I did not wish my father to know that I had allowed her partiality for the young man to develop beneath my roof. I decided to write to Mr. Porter myself, thinking that if Marianne was with him he would not be so cruel as to prolong my suffering and would confess to it. And, of course, the situation was delicate. Had she been so, well…"

"Had she been living with Porter they would have had to marry and your involvement need not have been disclosed." He inclined his head. "I understand completely, you have no need to berate yourself. Anyone in your position, with such a parent to answer to, would have acted in a similar fashion."

"Thank you."

"But you still did not alert your father to Porter's possible involvement when you received his reply to your letter?"

"No, I did not. But you must appreciate that I had just lost my husband, my baby and my senses and was not thinking coherently."

"The fact that your father is ignorant of their attraction towards one another is to our benefit. He will not think to look for your sister in Ramsgate—or for you either, since what possible reason could you have to visit the town?"

"Indeed, that is a comforting thought, my lord."

Alex shifted away from her, profoundly moved by her apparent faith in his ability to keep her safe. "Since we are now partners in this investigation, perhaps it would be more expedient for you to address me as Alex."

She inclined her head. "Thank you. When we are not in company I shall, but I would not presume to do so in front of others."

"As you wish." He leaned his shoulder against the corner of the carriage, wriggled into a more comfortable position and closed his eyes.

"We have some distance to travel yet," he said. "It would be as well to try to rest."

Chapter Ten

Alex fell asleep immediately, evidently untroubled by the guilty conscience that prevented Estelle from following his example. She had been relieved beyond words when he insisted upon sharing the burden of responsibility for her sister's welfare. Watching him set about doing so in a competent manner that suggested he was unused to failure encouraged her to hope.

But that did not mean she intended Lord Crawley to take complete control of matters. She wondered whether she should wake him in order to emphasize her determination in that respect. She was on the point of doing so but the sight of his craggy features relaxed in repose, of the unruly curls falling across his brow making him appear years younger than he was, gave her pause. There would be time enough later to make her feelings known.

Estelle turned her thoughts to that kiss, her face flooding with colour as she recalled its searingly passionate nature. She should not have permitted it, of course, and certainly should not have allowed him to see quite how much she enjoyed it. But having reached the conclusion that he entertained no such aspirations she had relaxed her guard and his advance had taken her completely by surprise. Her reaction had been entirely spontaneous and for once she simply went with her feelings instead of trying to decide how she ought to behave.

And thus the elegant sophisticate sprawled on the seat beside her had, with one impulsive gesture, engendered in her an explosion of sweet sensations the like of which she had long ago despaired of ever experiencing. But the memory would have to last a lifetime. She would be more vigilant whilst in his presence in future and it would not happen again.

Satisfied that she had her emotions under control, Estelle closed her eyes and attempted to sleep, convinced she would never manage it. Which was why, when she felt the carriage slowing and opened her eyes, she was so surprised to discover that they were pulling to a halt in front of Fairlands, Susanna's home. It was a good two hours away from Crawley Hall, which meant she must have slept soundly the whole way.

"What are we doing here?" She sat up and blinked the sleep from her eyes.

"We need to travel on in something a little less conspicuous. I do not think it likely that your father will send his spies in pursuit of me but, just in case, it is better to be cautious."

"Yes, that is true, I suppose." The distinctive Crawley family crest was emblazoned on the doors of their current conveyance. Estelle was grateful for Alex's caution yet miffed because he had not bothered to share his thoughts with her before turning in the direction of Fairlands.

"I was rather hoping that Michael might loan us a phaeton. I will then send my coach back to Crawley Hall and we can travel on anonymously."

"Do you not have a phaeton of your own? Is it really necessary to throw ourselves upon Susanna and Mr. Cleethorpe at a time when Susanna is not feeling quite the thing?"

"Of course I possess a phaeton but I could not have concealed you in it so easily. If your father was abroad, as proved to be the case, he would have seen us driving away together."

"Oh, I see." The stinging retort she had been formulating died on her lips.

"Oh look, here are Michael and Susanna."

"Estelle, is that you?" Susanna broke away from her husband and tripped lightly down the steps. She embraced Estelle as soon as Alex assisted her from the carriage. "What a delightful surprise. But what brings you here, darling?"

"It is a long story." Estelle blushed self-consciously, aware of Mr. Cleethorpe looking from her to Alex and back again, a flicker of amusement in his eye.

"Then come inside and relate it." Susanna linked her arm through her friend's. "And you are just in time to join us for luncheon."

"Thank you," Alex said. "We are famished."

The meal was a rowdy affair, attended by all of Michael's sisters. They greeted Alex with casual affection and proceeded to bombard him with a litany of impertinent questions, which he countered with an air of tolerant forbearance. When they had eaten their fill, Alex and Michael retired to his library for a few words in private, the girls returned to their lessons, and Susanna and Estelle were finally in a position to exchange their news.

"Now tell me at once what brings you here, alone with the dashing Lord Crawley."

"Well, he discovered who I really am, found out about Marianne and now insists upon helping me to locate her."

"Does he indeed!" Estelle was not surprised when Susanna's grin broadened, doubtless already drawing inappropriate conclusions. "I wonder what could have moved him to such feats of chivalry."

"My father, most likely." Estelle explained about his unexpected appearance at Crawley Hall.

"Fustian! Does the man never give up?"

"I have never known him to be swayed from his purpose before but perhaps he has met his match in Lord Crawley."

"Very likely."

"Which is why we wish to borrow a phaeton from your husband, just in case he has somehow contrived to have Lord Crawley watched."

"Humph, I would not put it past him." Susanna ground her teeth. "How I wish I could accompany you to Ramsgate, what fun we should have! But, of course, Michael will not hear of it."

"I should think not, in your condition."

"I am perfectly well but I shall go out of my mind if I must spend the time until my confinement being mollycoddled. Michael does not allow me to be alone for more than two seconds at a time. If he is not able to bear me company himself at least one of his sisters is always by my side. It is as though he does not trust me to behave myself."

Estelle chuckled. "He clearly begins to understand your character."

"I suppose he does." Susanna pouted. "And I would not have you think that I resent his sisters' company. They are enchanting, all four of them, but I miss my freedom and your society. But I daresay you have scarce spared me a thought, what with Lord Crawley being so keen to be of service to you." Susanna's mutinous expression gave way to one of devilment. "And pray, what is the precise nature of the service he wishes to offer you?"

"You are reading too much into his chivalry." Estelle wagged a finger beneath her friend's nose, furious that her cheeks flooded with colour when she recalled the nature of the kiss they had enjoyed. "But I suppose that ought not to surprise me."

Susanna watched the blush creep up her cheeks and grinned triumphantly. "I thought as much!"

"He merely wishes to assist me in locating Marianne."

"Of course he does! Which would explain why his eyes scarce left your face during the course of luncheon."

"Nonsense!" Estelle blushed deeper still. "He hardly looked in my direction. Besides, his mother expects him to make a splendid match and he is all but engaged to his neighbour's daughter."

"Then why is he gallivanting around the countryside with you?"

Good question! "That is different, I think that—"

Susanna chuckled. "Estelle, my darling, I think you underestimate your charms."

The door opened to admit Lord Crawley and Mr. Cleethorpe, for which Estelle was exceedingly grateful. She had no wish to be the subject of Susanna's wild conjectures. It *was* rather singular, the manner in which Lord Crawley was putting himself out for her. But Susanna's partiality for her was clouding her judgment. Lord Crawley's future lay with the likes of Miss Jenkins. Lady Crawley had made that abundantly clear. And even if Miss Jenkins did not suit, Estelle was realistic enough to appreciate that the middle-class daughter of a bombastic bully would never be considered a viable alternative.

"Everything is in readiness for our departure, if you feel sufficiently rested," said Alex.

Estelle rose gracefully to her feet. "I am more than ready."

And five minutes later they were bowling down the Fairlands drive, waved off by Susanna and Michael. All four of the latter's sisters were there too. They had seized upon the excuse to abandon their French verbs and wish their guests a rowdy adieu.

"Thank you for thinking to stop here," said Estelle, her annoyance at his arbitrary actions forgotten as they passed through the village and Alex set the matching pair of bays to a steady trot on the Ramsgate road. "It was pleasant to see Susanna. I had been concerned about her but she appears much better."

"I would never be forgiven if I passed this way without stopping to see Michael."

"His sisters are a lively bunch."

Alex smiled with obvious affection. "They are wild hoydens, every one of them, but I have known them since their infancies and have become accustomed to their impertinent ways." He rolled his eyes. "Charlotte has her come-out next season but the prospect does not appear to have tamed her behaviour in any discernable fashion."

"She has years ahead of her to be sensible. Let her enjoy her freedom whilst she can."

"True." He was silent for a moment. "Are you quite warm enough?"

"Yes, I thank you."

Estelle enjoyed being driven by such a competent whip and watched the passing countryside with interest, not feeling any need to fill the silence between them with mindless chatter. Far sooner than she would have imagined possible they reached the outskirts of Broadstairs.

"We will put up here for the night." He reined in his team and turned into the mews attached to the Albion Hotel without waiting for her to voice her agreement. Two lads came running to take the horses' heads as he assisted her to alight. He tossed a coin and one of them caught it in mid air, doffed his cap and still kept one hand on the bridle of the near-side horse.

Estelle released his hand as soon as her feet touched the ground, her mellow mood replaced with one of annoyance. Once again he was taking control without troubling to consult her first. "But we are not yet in Ramsgate. There is plenty of daylight left and the horses are not tired. I think we should continue."

Alex grasped her elbow and steered her towards the hotel doors. "And I think we should stay here tonight." He glanced down at the mutinous set to her features and chuckled. "Trust me, I have my reasons."

"I daresay you do." She tossed her head in a disgruntled manner. "But how can I know what they are if you do not choose to share them with me?"

The landlord bustled up to them, summing up the status of the new arrivals with one practiced sweep of his eyes. Satisfied that they were in possession of fat pockets, his face broke into an anticipatory smile. Alex's request for his best rooms for himself and his wife was met with a stifled gasp from Estelle and a regretful shake of the head from their would-be host.

"I am sorry, sir, we are full to bursting just now, what with the fair being in town. I have only one chamber remaining, although it is the best in the establishment."

Estelle barely heard this exchange since she was hot with embarrassment and could not decide whether to voice her objections in the landlord's hearing or wait until they were alone before tearing him off a strip. This time Alex had gone too far. Why had he pretended they were man and wife but then requested separate rooms? Presumably because he understood she would balk at sharing the same chamber with him. So why not simply say that they were brother and sister, which would better account for their requirement for separate rooms? The implication that they were married seemed completely unnecessary, unless he had a sound reason for it, in which case he ought to have been courteous enough to explain it to her in advance.

The incident served as a reminder that she had unconsciously relaxed her guard in Lord Crawley's presence, which was a most unwise thing to do. He was chivalrous to a fault but that did not mean he lacked the baser instincts inherent to the majority of his sex, and she was not convinced he would resist taking advantage of her vulnerable state.

"Then we had better look at the room." Alex's languorous voice intruded upon her thoughts. "Come, my dear." He took her arm and followed the landlord up the stairs. "My wife is greatly fatigued and cannot travel further today."

"I am sure you will be very comfortable sir, and the lady, too. I have never had any complaints about this room."

"Your wife?" Estelle hissed in Alex's ear.

"Shush." He patted her hand. "I will explain later."

She narrowed her eyes at him. "Indeed you will."

CR&D

The room was vast, with a bow window overlooking the esplanade and an uninterrupted view of the sea. It looked clean and comfortable and Alex had to hide his amusement as he watched Estelle's remarkable eyes darting around it, seeking reasons to object and looking everywhere except at the vast bed which dominated the space.

"I daresay we will be comfortable enough," he drawled, clasping his hands behind his back. He retreated to the window embrasure and stared at the people strolling along the parade below him, giving Estelle the opportunity to recover her composure and curb the wild temper he had seen flashes of during the course of the day. When she made no immediate response he nodded to the hovering landlord. "Have our bags sent up, if you please, and some hot water."

"At once, sir."

"Is there a private parlour in which we can dine?"

The landlord shook his head. "They are all taken, sir."

"Then we shall dine in here." He nodded towards the small table in the alcove where he was standing. "In an hour's time."

The moment the door closed behind the landlord, Estelle, hands on hips, swirled to face him. "Explain!"

"What would you like me to explain first?"

"Everything. Why Broadstairs, why you are calling yourself Mr. Jenson, why you are so anxious to dine in private and, well...and why you think it necessary to pretend we are married."

"Ah that," he said, cool amusement in his tone. "I should have anticipated it might anger or, at the very least, embarrass you."

"No, sir, what you should have done was to consult me on the matter first."

"And what would your answer have been?"

"Why, I would have declined to be part of such a deception, of course, especially since I can see no necessity for it."

"Precisely! And that is why—"

A knock at the door heralded the arrival of their bags and shortly thereafter a maid with ewers of hot water. Both intrusions failed to deflect Estelle's requirement for an explanation. She tapped her foot impatiently and as soon as they were alone again she faced him, her eyes raised in anticipation.

"Since you insist, I shall endeavour to answer your questions in the order that you asked them."

"Very obliging of you."

"I chose Broadstairs because I am known in the best hotels in Ramsgate."

"Why should that matter?"

"Because your father would be able to find me very easily if he chose to look for us in that location. He will devise a means to discover if you are still at Crawley Hall and although I have attempted to anticipate his every stratagem, I cannot be sure to have outthought him on every suit. Anyway, I am not convinced that he will give up looking for you as easily as he abandoned your sister, since you appear to play an important part of his ambitious plans. Also, if we were to put up in Ramsgate, people I am acquainted with would discover me travelling with a lady— alone."

"Ah, I see." She paused, determined not to permit the meticulous nature of his planning to impress her. "That explains why you are not using your correct name here, I suppose, and Broadstairs is very convenient for Ramsgate." She stopped speaking and nibbled her index finger, a habit he found strangely compelling. He felt his expression soften as she attempted to find ways to refute his logic. "But why pretend that we are married and why is it so important we dine alone?"

"If we were to mix with the other clientele we would not be able to help conversing with them. As anything other than my wife you would be subjected to unwarranted attentions and I would not have you thus exposed. And since you still wear your wedding ring, I thought it the best way to resolve the matter. Unfortunately I did not anticipate that there would be insufficient rooms available and for that I apologize."

Alex sensed when the tension left her. He was aware that she was fair-minded and whilst he might have given her cause to take offence, he suspected she would be equally quick to see reason.

"I can see that you were motivated by the best of intentions," she conceded, and set about removing her gloves, bonnet and pelisse in a series of economical movements that prevented him from reading her expression. She turned her attention to her skirts next and took an inordinate amount of time to shake the creases from them. "But before we go any further, my lord, I think we ought to get one or two matters straight. Grateful as I am for your assistance, I do not at all care for your taking matters into your own hands. You must agree to tell me what you are thinking in future and consult me before making arbitrary decisions. Are we agreed on that point?"

"Perfectly agreed." Alex bowed his acquiescence. "Tomorrow we will beard your Mr. Porter in his own lair and doubtless discover more about your sister's whereabouts. But in the meantime—" he indicated the steaming jugs of water, "—our dinner will soon be delivered and you may wish to wash the dust of the journey away first."

"Indeed, my lord, but later...we need to establish—"

Alex adored the way she blushed whenever she was embarrassed. "I shall sleep on the truckle bed over yonder," he said with a wolfish grin. "I daresay it was intended for a maid but I shall not mind the discomfort in the least."

"It is no more than you deserve." She turned away from him with a swish of petticoats and a sanctimonious expression on her face.

The dinner was surprisingly good, as was the claret. Alex made light conversation during the course of the meal, doing his best to set Estelle at her ease, and by the time they finished their repast he was a fair way to succeeding. She laughed at some of his anecdotes and the transformation in her countenance was profound. It made her delicate features appear as though they were lit from within.

He had never met another woman who could claim to be her equal for beauty and courage. His fierce determination to protect her—one of the reasons for their sojourn in this room as man and wife—intensified. The thought of seeing other men attempting to ingratiate themselves with her, as they assuredly would, had to be avoided at all costs. She would not realize what they were about and would be quite unequal to the task of fending them off.

But damn it, when she looked at him as she was at that moment, her laughing eyes full of confidence in his abilities, he cursed the presence of the fair which had caused the shortage of available chambers. He was compelled to grind his teeth and transfer his thoughts to his steward's drainage report, a surefire way to control his carnal desires and prevent him from disgracing himself. To be on the safe side, he rose to his feet before temptation could get the better of common sense and told her he would spend the next half hour in the tap room.

"I feel sure you would welcome a little privacy," he said. "But do not open the door to anyone whilst I am gone."

"I am not entirely without wits, you know."

When Alex returned to their room a little under an hour later, she had retired for the night. She had drawn the hangings across the bed but had left a gap, and he paused to look through it. He wondered if she really was as sound asleep as she appeared or whether, like him, she was tense at the prospect of their spending the night together in the same chamber, albeit innocently.

Reluctantly turning away from her, he stripped off his outer garments. He sat on the edge of the truckle bed, upon which she had thoughtfully placed a blanket and pillow, in order to remove his boots. It lurched beneath his weight. Before he could recover his balance, the bed tilted. He let forth with a string of smothered oaths as he was rolled unceremoniously onto the floor.

The sight that greeted him as he sat up and rubbed his head set him swearing again for a very different reason. Estelle, her glorious hair escaping from a long braid and framing her face with a cloud of curls, was peeping round the curtained bed, her eyes brimming with helpless laughter.

"I am gratified that you find the situation so diverting."

"That bed obviously was intended to take the weight of a slight maid." She gasped, clutching her breast as though in physical pain.

"So I apprehend." He stood, mindless of his state of undress, and bestowed an angry frown upon the bed in question. What the devil he was supposed to do now? With a resigned shrug he dragged the straw mattress in front of the fire.

"There is room for you here." Estelle indicated the other side of the large bed.

"Thank you, but I hardly think—"

"I was angry with you because I thought you intended to...well, never mind that. But I can see now that I got it quite wrong and cannot expect you to sleep on the floor when you are only here in the first place because of me." She placed a stout bolster down the centre of the bed, busying herself by positioning it to her satisfaction. She did not once look in his direction. "There, I daresay we shall be quite comfortable."

Alex raised his brows but bit back the retort that sprang to his lips. She might be comfortable sleeping in such close proximity to him, but he'd wager Crawley Hall on the fact that the same would not be true in his case. He had shared a bed with any number of attractive women in the past, but never chastely—and never with one who fascinated him as comprehensively as the siren who was so casually inviting him into hers.

"I think it would be for the best if I stuck to the floor."

"Nonsense! Pretend I am your sister, if my presence embarrasses you."

Alex was experiencing many difficulties at that precise moment, but embarrassment was definitely not one of them. What was he doing, standing in the middle of the room, half-dressed, probably looking faintly ridiculous, trying to talk his way *out* of a lady's bed? Why was he even hesitating?

"Lord Crawley." Estelle's impatient voice recalled his attention. "I am greatly fatigued and in need of sleep, even if you are not. Make up your mind, if you please?" With that, she made a big play of turning as far away as possible from the side of the bed she had allocated to him. She pulled the covers up to her ears, thumped her pillows into a comfortable nest and wished him a curt goodnight.

Alex sat beside the dwindling fire and finally managed to remove his boots. Swearing quietly, he made for the bed, stretched out beneath the covers and let out a long sigh. He was convinced he would not be able to sleep a wink.

Chapter Eleven

Estelle turned on her side, pretending to be sound asleep. She was acutely aware of the mattress sagging beneath Alex's weight, of the warmth of his body, the sound of his breathing as he stretched out full length beneath the coverlet. Whatever had she set in motion by so recklessly inviting him to share her bed?

Afraid to move a muscle for fear of rolling closer to him, she remained rigidly on her side and tried to ignore his presence. Fatigue must eventually have won the day and she fell into a restless sleep. A loud clap of thunder directly above the hotel woke her in the early hours. Disoriented, she sat bolt upright and instinctively cried out.

Alex sat up too. "Are you all right?"

"Yes. No." She was trembling and there was little she could do to disguise her fear. "The noise startled me, and I could not remember where I was for a moment."

It was a feeble explanation which did not appear to deceive Alex. He pulled her into his arms and stroked her back with his soothing, capable hands. "Shush now, you are perfectly safe. I will not allow anything to happen to you." He tangled his fingers in her hair and held her a little tighter. "Why are you so afraid of the storm?"

"It is hard to put into actual words." She tried to formulate a rational explanation, grateful that he could not see the shame in her expression as she grappled with long-suppressed memories. "When we were children Marianne and I enjoyed thunder. The excitement broke the monotony of our routine."

"But not any more, it seems. Why is that?"

She sighed. "One night there was torrential rain, just like now. I recall opening our chamber window and leaning out, inviting Marianne to join me. I enjoyed the feel of the rain lashing against my face and the wind blowing away the cobwebs in my head. The forces of nature were in full rage, lighting up the sky in a pyrotechnic display of bad temper which was quite spectacular." She paused, unable to suppress a shudder. "But then the lightning struck in the nearest field, bringing down a tree and trapping new-born lambs beneath its branches. I have never been able to get their terrified cries out of my head. I will never forget the mournful bleating of the ewes calling to the doomed babies either." She lifted her shoulders and made a huge effort to compose herself. "I dare say you think me foolish and are vexed with me for waking you. I apologize. I am quite myself again now. You can go back to sleep."

She tried to move out of his arms but her efforts made no impression upon the bands of steel that circled her body. Lightning danced across the curtained window, briefly lighting up the room so that she could see his face. She was astonished to observe that he was looking at her not with annoyance but with deep compassion in his eyes.

"Mother Nature is having a bit of a tantrum," he whispered, "and so we will simply wait for her to recall her manners. But have no fear, she will not harm us." Another flash of lightning illuminated the sky. "Count with me, Estelle. Let us see how long it takes for the thunder to come."

"One, two, three," they counted together, conscious of the sound of the rain pouring down in torrents before the next loud crack rattled the windows.

"The storm is already three miles away," he told her.

"How do you know?"

"For every second that elapses between lightning and thunder you can assume one mile. Did you not play that game as children?"

"No, I have never heard of it before." Estelle shook her head against his chest to emphasize her response. She was still trembling, although not nearly so violently as before. There was something indescribably comforting about being held in a pair of strong arms and she simply surrendered herself to his protective care. Their peculiar situation made it ridiculous to worry about the propriety of her actions.

"Hush, don't worry, it will soon be past." He brushed the hair from her forehead with such gentleness, such infinite care, that she felt herself responding to his gossamer touch somewhere deep within her core.

It did not take long after that for her to forget all about the storm. Gently his lips claimed hers. His kiss effectively banished everything else from her mind until all she could think about was the exquisite pleasure that rippled through her. His tongue invaded her mouth, and his hands stroked the length of her body with profound sensuality. She trembled more violently than when the thunder had been directly overhead. Each dizzying sensation was more intense than its predecessor.

When he eventually broke the kiss they were both breathing heavily. Her head came to rest on his chest again and she could hear his heart beating fast. Empowered by the knowledge that she was responsible for his excitement, she tentatively reached out a hand and touched his hair. She realized now that she had wanted to touch him, to explore his remarkable physique, since the first time she had set eyes on him. She had never harboured such salacious thoughts about any gentleman before. Far from being shocked by her wantonness, she felt liberated, especially when he let out a groan that implied anything other than pain.

"That's right, sweetheart, touch me. Let your fingers explore. Do whatever comes naturally." She sensed the smile in his voice. "Touch me in the way that I touched you just now."

He guided her hand and let out another soft groan as her fingers tangled with the hairs on his chest.

Estelle had never touched a gentleman in an intimate manner before. Mr. Travis had not expected anything from her other than that she lay beneath his fleshy weight, night after night, in silent capitulation as he did whatever he wished with her. Oh, how she had hated it! He was harsh and appeared to enjoy hurting her, emphasizing his total domination over her. He seemed to relish punishing her for his myriad disappointments, simply because he could.

She had not realized until that moment that it was all right to take pleasure from such activities. The discovery ought to have shocked but her passions were stirred to the point that she no longer cared about anything, just so long as Alex's hands did not stop their sublime journey across her body. He tantalized and teased her with his long fingers, heightening her perceptions until she was pulsating with such an inexorable need that it transcended every other thought in her head.

Alex, his eyes aflame with desire, met her gaze and held it. "You are incredible," he said, his voice gravelly with passion.

"There is nothing remarkable about me."

He chuckled, a deep throaty sound, intimate and self-assured. "Allow me to be the judge of that." He untied the lace at the throat of her nightgown and exposed breasts now covered only by the thin fabric of her shift. This too he removed. It was shocking, she ought to protest, but no sound escaped her lips. Slowly, so slowly she thought the sight of her naked torso displeased him, he bent his head and applied his lips to her breasts. The pleasure he sent cascading through her was primal, and when he lifted his head again, a small cry of protest escaped her lips. "Perhaps we should not do this."

"It is a little late for an attack of conscience now," she said, daringly reaching up to place a kiss on his lips. She spoke with assurance but her heart plummeted. Her earlier thought had been correct. He did not desire her. How could she ever seriously have supposed that he might?

"I do not wish to take advantage of your vulnerable state."

"Have you considered the possibility that I might wish to be taken advantage of?" In the intense, rarefied atmosphere of his embrace she found the courage to admit to her feelings. She was beyond worrying about the consequences of her actions, no longer even hearing the sound of the rain pounding against the windows and the distant rumble of thunder as the storm slowly moved away.

"Very well." His hands sought her breasts once again and she half rose to meet them, too impatient to be submissive. "Tell me how this makes you feel."

"Is it all right to talk about it?"

Her voice must have reflected her doubts because he laughed aloud at her prim response. "Oh yes! And not only that, but it's all right to enjoy it, too. You have no reason to feel guilty."

"Hum, well perhaps guilt will come later but for now I feel pleasure spangling through my entire body. I have never known anything like it. It pools somewhere deep inside of me. Somewhere that I didn't know existed."

"Here perhaps." His hand came to rest at the top of her thigh.

"Yes, that is exactly the place." Her breath was coming in shorter and shorter gasps. She heard herself moaning aloud as he did something pleasurable with the hand that was still caressing her thigh.

The caresses stopped abruptly and she moaned again, this time in protest. She was aware of the mattress shifting beneath his weight as he stood up. Reluctant to leave the place to which he had transported her, she was slow to open her eyes. Disjointed thoughts tumbled through her head. Why had he left her? Was he shocked by her wanton response to his attentions? Estelle had been married but this situation was entirely alien to her. She gathered her courage and glanced in his direction. He was shedding his clothes, with no apparent concern for their welfare. His pristine white shirt was pulled over his head and tossed onto the floor in a crumpled ball.

Next came his breeches. Estelle did not think she ought to look but could not tear her eyes away. Completely naked, he met her gaze and held it. The extent of his tumescence both shocked and thrilled her. He was magnificent! Pure predatory, devastatingly robust male. Anticipation tingled down her spine. Tentatively she reached out to touch him. He groaned and fell back beside her on the bed, pulling her beneath him and kissing her as though his life depended upon it.

"Are you sure?" he asked her when he finally broke the kiss.

"Yes, Alex, please!"

He chuckled and kissed the end of her nose. "As you wish."

She could just make out the contours of his face as he entered her, could detect his tortured expression as he ignored his own needs in order to fuel hers. She shivered, lifting herself to meet him. Something inside her broke and an intense, rushing sensation that she would never have imagined possible exploded through her entire body.

Alex kissed Estelle's brow, cradled her in his arms and told her to go to sleep. She curled up beside him, made herself comfortable, and did just that. Her feline smile nudged his recently sated body back to life with almost indecent haste. For him sleep would be a long time coming. He had not planned to seduce her, even when circumstances had compelled him to share her bed. It would have been too ungentlemanly for words when he knew her to be both vulnerable and reliant upon his continued assistance. And even when she had been so distressed by the ferocity of the storm, his initial intention had been merely to calm her. The feel of her feminine curves pressed against him ought to have alerted him to the danger he was in. But her expression of transparent faith in his ability to keep her safe, the warmth of her body beneath the thin silk of her nightgown, only added to his eventual undoing.

Alex roundly cursed the storm for placing such temptation in his path. He was becoming obsessed with Estelle Travis. And experiencing the full extent of her remarkable passion and the enthusiastic manner in which she surrendered herself to pleasures previously alien to her only served to fuel that obsession. He reached down and placed a protective hand on her hip, smiling at her somnolent form, and waited for sleep to claim him.

CঙEৎ

"Good morning."

Alex was woken by the soft timbre of Estelle's voice and judged it to be well past the hour when he was accustomed to rise.

"Good morning." He leaned up on one elbow to better examine her face for signs of regret, encouraged to discover that none were immediately apparent. "I hardly need to enquire if you slept well. Your features are all aglow."

"I feel very well rested." She gazed up at him with a smouldering expression that was wholly uncontrived.

"I am glad to hear you say so." He tore his glance away from her to peer through a gap in the curtains. "There is no need for you to stir just yet. It is still raining and the roads will be difficult."

"I see." She raised her arms above her head and stretched. A tangle of copper curls cascaded over her shoulders and onto her naked breasts. She followed the direction of his gaze and made no attempt to cover herself.

"I shall see about breakfast." He pushed back the covers, intent upon escaping whilst he still had the strength of will to do so.

"I am not in the least hungry."

A Reason to Rebel

"But I am famished."

Her hand came to rest on the small of his back and he flinched as though he had been scalded.

"Then perhaps it is my turn to ease your discomfort?"

Her sweetly innocent smile banished his half-hearted determination to behave himself and all thoughts of food left his head. And since it was not in his nature to let her get away with such impudence, he was obliged to punish her with a searing kiss. She responded with the enthusiasm he was starting to expect from her and he was lost. His body was already on fire, pulsating with need. He ignored it, drawing upon every last vestige of his self-control as he tried to decide how best to satisfy her.

Which was why they did not set out for Ramsgate until after luncheon. As he drove, Alex cast frequent sideways glances at his companion and would have given much to know what occupied her thoughts. Did she regret what had passed between them? Did she now hold him to blame for seducing her? It was important that he should know. But how to phrase the question?

She turned her face towards the wind, allowing the fresh, invigorating air to cool her flaming cheeks. Not once since leaving the inn had she looked directly at him.

"Are you feeling yourself, Estelle?" He took one hand off the ribbons and covered both of hers with it, seeking to reassure.

"Yes, thank you. I am perfectly all right. Why ever would I not be?"

"No reason. It is just that you seem preoccupied."

"What shall we do when we reach Ramsgate?" she asked, clearly anxious to change the subject.

"I shall leave the phaeton at one of the inns. After we have refreshed ourselves we shall then go in search of Porter's place of employment."

"And talk to him there, in front of his employers?"

"No, I think not." Alex paused as he guided his team round a large pothole filled with muddy rainwater. "If he was reluctant to reveal any information to you in a letter, he is hardly likely to do so in person. And if anything he said showed him in a bad light, it would leave his employers with no alternative but to dismiss him."

"Yes, possibly." Estelle fell into deep contemplation. "Perhaps he was being cautious because he felt that anything he said in a letter could fall into my father's hands. If he sees that you and I are alone, then surely he will confide in me?"

"It is possible, but I suggest we wait for Porter to leave his place of business and then follow him to his home. If we tackle him there, we will have a better chance of convincing him that we are not acting as your father's agents. And by not embarrassing him in front of his employers, he will be more likely to trust us."

"Yes, I can see the sense in what you say, but I am frustrated by the need to delay by as much as one hour."

"Have patience, sweetheart. It will not be long now." He turned his team into the mews adjoining one of the better hotels. Trusting to luck that no one of his acquaintance would be within at such an hour, he surrendered the conveyance to the care of the ostler. "Come, we shall take some refreshment before we seek directions to Nesbit and Jones's establishment."

Alex watched the arresting young lady seated across from him in the best parlour of the inn, her back ramrod straight as she sipped her tea, and tried to fathom her thoughts. His attraction towards her prevented him from making much of a fist of it and in the end he gave up trying. They were alone in the parlour and, without dwelling upon the wisdom of his actions, he asked her the question to which an honest answer was becoming essential for his peace of mind.

"Estelle, about last night..."

"Yes." She looked up but avoided meeting his eye. "What about it?"

"Do you consider that I took advantage of your fear of the storm to...well, to...?" Alex's words trailed off and he raked his hand through his hair as he tried to think how better to phrase his question. His first attempt sounded completely wrong. Never in his life before had he felt so tongue-tied. "What I mean is—"

"What you mean to say," she responded with a smile that melted his heart, "is that I ought not to make anything of it."

"No, no, I—"

"Think no more about it." She waved a hand dismissively. "I was equally to blame. You gave me ample opportunity to demur. I realize now it was a mistake but that is of no consequence since it will not happen again. We were merely forced together by circumstances and did what came naturally at the time, finding comfort in one another." She sat straighter still, something he would have considered impossible, and bestowed an arch smile upon him, even though she still did not meet his gaze.

"No, no, you completely misunderstand me. Damn!" he said under his breath when a brisk knock heralded the return of the landlord with the information he had requested.

"Excellent!" said Estelle when the man gave them directions to Nesbit and Jones's premises. She stood and looked expectantly at Alex. "Come, we have dallied for quite long enough. Besides, I believe we understand one another quite well and there is nothing more to be said in respect of our previous conversation."

Alex, who ought to have been relieved that Estelle was adopting such a reasonable approach, was perversely annoyed by her attitude. He considered there was a great deal more to be said, but the presence of the landlord prevented him from voicing that opinion. He settled their account, donned his hat and gloves and escorted Estelle from the establishment.

Following the landlord's directions, they easily located the premises which housed the solicitors' office. From a convenient position across the road they were able to watch the door without being observed. Within fifteen-minutes a respectable couple emerged, being bowed away by an older man with extreme obsequiousness.

"That is most likely Porter's employer and those must be his last clients of the day," said Alex. "And pretty important ones too, judging by his demeanour."

The man they took to be the solicitor soon re-emerged from the premises, fitted his hat onto his head and directed his steps towards the tavern on the corner. Two more people came out a little later, neither of whom was Porter. It was another five minutes before that person eventually showed himself.

"There he is!" Estelle cried.

"All right. We shall fall in behind him and see where he leads us." Alex took Estelle's arm in case impatience got the better of her and she spontaneously approached Porter. "Let us hope that he is not bound for the tavern too."

Fortunately he was not, and ten minutes later he approached a neat house in a respectable road and produced a key from his pocket. But before he could insert it in the lock, the door was flung open. A young lady threw herself at Porter in a flurry of petticoats, squealing with joy as she welcomed him home. He caught her in his arms and kissed her mouth. Then, looking quickly up and down the road, he persuaded her to return indoors.

Estelle took a sharp intake of breath and a beatific smile invaded her face.

"That is Marianne!" she said, and burst into tears of relief.

Chapter Twelve

"Come." Estelle dried her eyes. Endless possibilities regarding her sister's situation tumbled through her brain. Anxious for answers, she gathered up her skirts and moved away from the stoop where they had concealed themselves. "We must go to Marianne at once."

"Wait just one moment." Alex placed a restraining hand on her arm.

"Why?"

"Whose house do you suppose that is?"

"What difference does it make?"

"Probably none. Humour me for a moment."

Sighing with impatience, Estelle cast her eyes over the neat terraced house in question. It was arranged on three floors, with steps from the front garden leading to the basement, presumably housing the kitchens and servants' quarters. The house itself looked to be in an excellent state of repair. The windows were sparkling clean, and recently scrubbed steps led to a front door painted bright red. It sported a gleaming knocker in the shape of an anchor. The small front garden, a riot of colour, was as meticulously cared for as the rest of the premises. Her eyes roamed over the adjoining properties. They were similarly well-kept residences, typically occupied by the middle-classes, exuding an air of prim gentility. Her chief emotion was one of relief that Marianne had not been compelled to live in squalor.

"It seems to be a respectable area," she said when it became obvious that Alex was waiting for her to say something.

"Indeed, but does anything else strike you about the district?"

"Well, yes, now that you mention it." She frowned, taking a moment to formulate her thoughts. "They do not appear to be the type of places that would offer lodgings to a young man of limited means."

"Precisely. And so we must ask ourselves how someone in Porter's position, who presumably does not have independent funds, could afford to live in such an establishment, much less maintain your sister in similar style."

"Does it matter?" Estelle had had enough of this procrastination. "I wish to see my sister, Alex, not stand here debating the quality of her living arrangements."

"Naturally." He raised a brow at her incivility but did not remark upon it. "It was not my intention to frustrate you with idle speculations."

"Well then, let us get to it."

"Quite so. But before we do I was about to suggest that if Porter's parents could afford to article him to a solicitor, then they are very likely respectable people. The sort of respectable people who might inhabit just such a property, perhaps?"

"And if you are correct about that, then Marianne is living there suitably chaperoned." A slow smile of understanding spread across her features. As always his intuitiveness had taken her by surprise. She had been trying to convince herself she was not shocked at Marianne's living with Mr. Porter before they were married, always assuming of course that they had not eloped to Gretna Green. But Estelle did not consider that to be likely. And so she'd told herself that as long as her sister was happy it really was of no consequence what unconventional living arrangements she had made. Indeed, after her own activities of the previous night, Estelle was hardly in a position to sit in judgment upon anyone else. But the relief she now felt at the prospect of having got that wrong made her realize just how fearful she had been for her headstrong sister's reputation.

She turned towards Alex with a smile. "Thank you. That is a great comfort to me."

Her feelings towards Alex had been oscillating wildly since the previous night. At first she thought she was sufficiently mature to accept what had happened between them. But when he had gone to such pains to tell her not to read anything into it, she had not only been deeply disappointed but angry and upset too. She wanted to lash out and hurt him as much as he had hurt her. But by anticipating her concerns about Marianne—when she herself did not even know they existed—he had thrown her into confusion once again, and she no longer knew what to think.

Only one thing was apparent. By his actions he had proved he was not all bad. She decided to let him know he was forgiven for his previous transgressions by treating him to her most gracious smile.

"God's beard, Estelle!" Alex ground his teeth. "If you look at me like that again I swear I will not be responsible for my actions." He took her hand, turned it over and applied his lips to the bare skin on the inside of her wrist, just above the cuff of her glove. "Come, let us go and make ourselves known to your sister before I forget myself completely."

Still with her hand trapped in his, they crossed the street and Alex lifted the heavy brass knocker at number seventeen. Estelle watched it fall, heard the sound reverberating inside the house and wriggled with impatience. Her heart beat wildly as they waited for what seemed like an age before the door was opened by a uniformed maid.

"We are here to see your master," said Alex authoritatively.

"Who shall I say is calling, sir?" The girl stepped back and allowed them into the vestibule, looking a little awed by Alex's aristocratic bearing.

"I am Crawley."

"If you would just—"

"Molly, who is it?"

Estelle, standing behind Alex, let out a gasp of delight. She stepped round him in time to observe Marianne tripping lightly down the stairs, a covered bowl in one hand.

"Marianne!"

"Estelle?" The bowl clattered to the floor. It bounced the rest of the way down the stairs, smashing on the floor of the hall, its contents spilling over the toes of Alex's polished boots. "Estelle, is that you?" Marianne opened her eyes very wide, as though she did not quite believe what she was seeing. "Can it be possible that my prayers have been answered or am I simply dreaming again?"

"Yes, Marianne, it is me. I am come, my love."

Marianne hurtled down the remaining stairs, her face shining with happiness. Seemingly unaware of the crockery crunching beneath her feet, she flew into her sister's arms. Estelle hugged her close and when they eventually drew apart both of them had faces wet with tears.

"Oh, Estelle, how I have longed to see you. I knew how worried you would be about me. I wanted to write but Benjamin said—"

"Hush love, I am here now, that is all that matters."

"But how did you find me?"

"I will tell you everything later."

"And who is the gentlemen with you?" Marianne's gaze was now fastened upon Alex.

"Lord Crawley, may I present my sister, Marianne Winthrop."

"Lord Crawley?" Marianne dropped into a curtsey but her eyes were on her sister rather than the gentlemen in question.

"Indeed." Alex bowed. "I had the pleasure of making Miss Winthrop's acquaintance at Mrs. Cleethorpe's wedding."

"Marianne?" A door opened and Mr. Porter appeared. "What is going on?" He stopped in his tracks when he saw Estelle. "Oh, Mrs. Travis, you are here." He coloured as he bowed, not only looking as confused as Marianne but exceedingly embarrassed too.

"Mr. Porter." Estelle turned towards Alex. "Lord Crawley, may I make Mr. Porter known to you."

Alex acknowledged Mr. Porter with a slight inclination of his head and subjected his person to prolonged scrutiny.

"I bid you welcome to my mother's house, my lord." Porter still appeared flummoxed by Alex's presence but was regaining his composure with commendable speed. "And you too, Mrs. Travis, naturally."

"Thank you." Estelle spoke graciously, aware of his discomfort and intent upon putting him at his ease. Marianne was safe and obviously happy. After all Estelle's fears for her welfare, she was too relieved to care about anything else.

"Marianne would have had you here long before now, Mrs. Travis, and it is merely my cautious nature that prevented her from writing to you."

"I see."

"My father passed away last year but I promised him I would complete my articles with Nesbit, which I shall do in just a few months' time. I will then be able to take full responsibility for all of my obligations," he said with a significant glance at Marianne, "since I have been asked to remain with the firm."

"Benjamin is doing splendid work. Mr. Nesbit relies on him excessively and is quite unable to manage without him. That is why he has offered to employ him when he is out of his articles." Marianne spoke with pride in her voice.

"I am sure that must be so." Estelle smiled. "Mr. Travis was not a trusting sort of man but even he could not find fault with Mr. Porter's grasp of his business affairs."

"Is your mother at home?" asked Alex. He received a reply in the negative.

"Come this way." Marianne tugged at Estelle's hand and led her towards the stairs. "I have another surprise for you. Molly," she added over her shoulder, addressing the maid who had avidly been watching the entire scene unfold, "some tea for us on the top floor, if you please."

"Where are we going?" Estelle tripped lightly up the stairs behind her sister.

"Shush, be patient!" As they reached the landing on the top floor, Marianne stopped outside a closed door. "He was awake just now."

"Who was awake, darling?" asked Estelle. "Why are you speaking in riddles?"

"Because..." Marianne threw the door open with a theatrical flourish that was so typical of her that Estelle felt more tears spring to her eyes. Because they misted her vision it took her a moment to recognize the figure sitting up in a wide bed reading a book. He looked up with a smile on his lips; a smile that turned to disbelief when he espied her.

"Matthew!" Estelle hurtled herself towards her brother, who warded her off with a cautionary wave of his hand.

"Be careful, sis," he said, laughing. "I am still so weak that a strong puff of wind could knock me out right now."

"Whatever happened to you?" She bent to kiss his brow and frowned when she noticed how thin he was.

"Long story," he said cheerfully. "But, by God, it's devilish good to see you, Estelle. How are you? Sorry and all that about Travis."

"Thank you." She introduced Alex and they all sat down, Estelle holding Matthew's hand in one of her own and Marianne's in the other.

The maid appeared with a tray loaded with tea things and, leaving Marianne to pour, closed the door quietly behind her as she left.

"Well." Estelle's eyes roamed to first one sibling's face and then the other's. "Which of you will go first?"

"I will," said Marianne. "Estelle, I am so sorry I could not tell you where I was and that it was necessary for Benjamin to answer your letter dishonestly. But, you see, we could not be sure—"

"You could not be sure that I was not writing on behalf of Papa." Marianne's eyes widened but Estelle spoke again before she could interrupt. "It is perfectly all right, darling. After the insensitive manner in which I behaved the last time we met, I can scarce blame you for doubting me."

Marianne gaped in open astonishment. "So you *do* understand. I said she was sure to, did I not, Benjamin?"

"I should have trusted your judgment," said Mr. Porter, "and saved you both a deal of heartache."

"It is of no consequence." Estelle smiled her reassurance at Mr. Porter and leaned across to kiss her sister. "You were not at fault, either of you, and I have long wished for this opportunity to beg your pardon. I should have lent you a more sympathetic ear when you came to me for advice, Marianne."

"It is not your fault," said Marianne kindly. "It is in your nature to be dutiful and you could not help yourself."

"You came to pour your heart out and I refused to listen. No wonder you wanted nothing more to do with me."

"Not one day has gone by without Marianne agonizing over you, wishing you were here, Mrs. Travis," said Mr. Porter with transparent sincerity. "But I persuaded her that until she comes of age we could not risk it. If your father were to discover her whereabouts, well...we simply could not take that chance. If he were to find her here he would in all probability draw inappropriate conclusions, which could cost me my position at Nesbit's."

"Yes," said Estelle, "I quite see the difficulty."

"We did not know, when you wrote to me, whether you would feel duty bound to pass on any information I gave you to your father. And even if you did not, Marianne thought the servants very likely read your correspondence and might tell him." Estelle nodded in understanding. "I did not want to mislead you but did not see what else could be done."

He cleared his throat, colour heightening his complexion as he danced round the delicate subject of Marianne living beneath his roof. He was a very good-looking young man, his dark features the perfect foil for Marianne's delicate blond beauty, and they made a striking couple. Estelle knew him to be serious-minded enough to counter Marianne's capricious nature. She admired his diligent approach to his duties and his ambition to lend distinction to his chosen profession. It was also transparently obvious that he was wildly in love with Marianne, and she with him.

Mr. Porter ran his fingers round the inside of his high collar, looking acutely embarrassed. His eyes frequently darted towards Alex, who was doing his best to put him at his ease by pretending he was not there, but Mr. Porter obviously found his presence unnerving.

"Was there something you wished to say to Mrs. Travis?" he asked.

"Yes, indeed. You see, the thing is, Marianne not only worried about being forced into marriage but also feared for her safety, which is why she is here with me now."

"What! That's coming it a bit strong, Marianne," said Estelle, shocked. "I know you did not care for the idea of marriage to Mr. Cowper but surely—"

"No, Estelle, just listen to what Benjamin has to say before you make up your mind about anything. You will understand so much better after you have heard him."

"Her fears drove her here and I could not turn her away. No man of conscience could have done so, not if he knew what lay in wait for her if she was compelled to return home and when, well," he said, colouring, "when the man in question loved the lady to distraction but never thought that love would be returned."

Marianne beamed, her cheeks a becoming shade of pink. "How could you have been such a simpleton?"

"And so your mother took Marianne in and has acted as her chaperone ever since," said Alex, recalling the pair's attention to the delicate subject under debate.

"Quite so!" Mr. Porter flashed a brief smile of gratitude in Alex's direction. "Nothing of an inappropriate nature has occurred beneath this roof—that is what I wished to make known to you, Mrs. Travis. I complete my articles in three-months' time and Marianne comes of age a month after that. She has graciously consented to become my wife at that time," he added, pride and love shining from his eyes, "and will then become the mistress of this house. My mother wishes to reside with her sister in Scarborough, which she intends to do as soon as we are wed."

Estelle squeezed her sister's hand. "You are happy, my love, that much is obvious, and I am very glad for you."

"So you will not tell Papa?"

"Papa and I are no longer on speaking terms."

"What!" cried Matthew and Marianne in unison.

"Why not?" added Matthew. "I would have wagered what few possessions I can still call my own that you were too dutiful to ever defy him."

"That used to be the case but he has pushed me too far this time." She smiled at her brother. "Everyone has their limits, you know, even me." Briefly she outlined all that had happened since Mr. Travis's death. She told them of Susanna's intervention and gave an abbreviated account of her sojourn as an unemployed governess beneath Alex's roof.

"So he now wants *you* to marry Cowper," said Matthew. "My God, the man has not a scruple in his body."

"It does not altogether surprise me," Marianne said. "Cowper always preferred you."

"What makes you say that?"

"It was the main reason why I ran away. Not that I would ever have married Cowper, of course. Benjamin and I had decided that for propriety's sake I ought to pretend to go along with the scheme, but find reasons for the wedding not to take place until I came of age. Naturally, that was the point at which Benjamin would arrive on a white charger and spirit me away in the nick of time."

"What happened to change that plan?" asked Alex, when the betrothed couple lost themselves in one another's eyes and forget about the explanation which was being dragged from them with frustrating slowness.

"I overheard a conversation between Papa and Mr. Cowper." Marianne pulled a disagreeable face. "Well, to be honest, I did not actually overhear but suspected they were up to something and listened at the door to Papa's library."

"And what were they talking about?" asked Estelle.

"They were discussing me," Marianne said. "Cowper was complaining about my lack of docility. He thought it unreasonable that I would not even permit him to touch me, much less kiss me, and said how he would so much prefer to marry you. It seems you are much prettier, more compliant and know your place. Papa was going out of his way to placate him. I thought that rather odd because Papa seldom takes the trouble to be agreeable to anyone. He said marriages did not last forever, especially when the gentleman involved was older than his wife and fond of dangerous sports."

"My God!" Estelle's hand flew to her mouth. "Are you suggesting that they were actually plotting to kill Mr. Travis?"

"Yes, I believe they were. They spoke for some time about how it might be achieved, citing his love of the hunting field as the most likely place for an accident to take place. They mentioned the flighty new stallion he had just purchased and how unpredictable such creatures could be."

"And that is exactly how he died." Estelle's hands were trembling. "Do you really think they put their plan into action?"

"I really cannot say but it seems highly suspicious to me. I did not hear any more because I was discovered by Johnson. He hauled me into the study and told Papa I was listening to his conversation. I have never seen him half so angry before—or so apprehensive. Anyway, he thrashed me, then and there in front of Mr. Cowper," she said, her face flushed with embarrassment, "until I could not sit down and told me to forget all I had heard if I knew what was good for me."

"And as soon as I received Marianne's letter explaining what had transpired, I knew it would not be safe for her to stay in that house for a moment longer." Mr. Porter claimed his beloved's hand.

"So that is what you came to tell me about. And all I could do was advise you to be a dutiful daughter and marry Cowper."

"Do not be so hard on yourself, Estelle. I was to blame as well for losing my temper."

"Do either of you know why your father is so keen to welcome Cowper as a member of the family?" Alex asked. "After all, he can do little to raise the family's standing in society, which, unless I mistake the matter, has always been his primary objective."

"Indeed it has," said Estelle. "And the question of Cowper has bothered me for some time. What does he have that my father wants so badly, he is prepared to force one of us to marry him in order to obtain it?"

"I think I know."

All faces turned expectantly towards Matthew.

Chapter Thirteen

Alex could sense his presence was intimidating Porter, in spite of his efforts to put him at his ease. He had already satisfied himself that the young man was of good character, hard working and conscientious. Only his very obvious adoration for Estelle's sister had caused him to act in a rash manner and aid her escape from her tyrannical father. He shot defensive sideways glances in Alex's direction as he explained why he felt compelled to behave as he had. He addressed his comments to Estelle but it was evident he was equally anxious to gain Alex's approbation. But that was hardly to be wondered at. Porter must be aware that he could use his authority as a peer to remove Marianne from his care. Either that or report his interference to Nesbit, who would be compelled to dismiss him before he completed his articles.

By contributing little to the discussion, Alex hoped that Porter would become accustomed to his presence. He applauded his scruples and understood he had acted out of a sense of duty and honour.

Matthew was altogether another matter. He was not cowed by Alex's social standing and frequently scowled in his direction. He was still weak from the remnants of an illness, the cause of which he had yet to be disclosed. But his mind was not affected and he made no attempt to conceal the doubts he harboured about Alex's intentions towards his sister.

Recalling their activities of the previous evening, Alex conceded that Matthew had every right to be suspicious, and bore his scrutiny with forbearance.

Everyone exclaimed when Matthew voiced his belief that he knew what Cowper's hold over his father might be. They were now all talking at once, clamouring for an explanation, which it would be impossible to hear over the din.

"Do enlighten us, Matthew," said Estelle. "The question has been plaguing my mind since Father's visit."

"All in good time," said Alex. His tone caused everyone to look in his direction. "I think that first you ought to explain to your sister where you have been these three years and relieve her worries. We would also be glad to learn what has kept you confined to bed."

"Well, really, m'lord." Matthew sat a little straighter, bridling at the implied criticism. "I really do not see what authority—"

"Matthew, please." Estelle touched her brother's hand. "You have my assurance that you can trust Lord Crawley implicitly and say anything in front of him that you would say to me in private."

"That's as may be, Estelle, but this is family business."

"If it were not for Lord Crawley, Father would have found a way to extract me from Crawley Hall. I would by now be back in Hampshire, confined to my room until I agreed to marry Mr. Cowper. And the three of us would not have been reunited."

"Ah yes, well, since you put it like that, I suppose it can't do any harm." Matthew swallowed, not wholly satisfied, but when he looked at Alex again his expression was a little less severe. "I don't know how much my sister has told you about our family life, Lord Crawley, but she seems to have placed a vast amount of confidence in you." He lifted his shoulders. "I suppose there is little point trying to save face now."

"You can depend upon my discretion."

"Maybe so, but that don't make this any easier. Still, there's no getting away from it and the truth is that I ran away from my responsibilities because I wasn't man enough to face up to them." His features, as handsome as those of his sisters, were twisted in self-disgust.

Alex admired his courage, only able to guess at what it must have cost him to make such an admission.

"We do not blame you in the least," said Estelle. "Your situation was insupportable."

"I ran away too," Marianne reminded him.

"Thank you, girls, but I won't let you try to protect me. It ought to have been the other way round, and I regret leaving you to fend for yourselves more than you will ever know. I knew Father would bully you both worse than ever the moment I was gone. And Mother is no help. She thinks of no one but herself. So no matter how impossible Father's demands, I should have stayed to fight instead of bailing out and leaving you two at his mercy. Won't ever forgive myself for that."

"Why not simply tell us where you went and why?" suggested Alex patiently.

"I was getting to that." Matthew shifted his position in the bed and Estelle stood to plump the pillows behind his head until he appeared comfortable again. "You see, all I've ever wanted to do was work on the land. I wanted to obtain a position on a big estate somewhere, working beneath an experienced steward, learning my trade and coming up with modern ideas."

"An admirable ambition," said Alex with feeling, thinking of the outmoded plan for irrigating his lower pastures his steward had recently bored him with.

"But Father dismissed the notion out of hand. He wouldn't even let me explain my feelings, because he had other plans for me—to study art at university. He prides himself on being a connoisseur of the arts, don't you know, which is the biggest clanker imaginable. The only painting Father knows anything about is the sort that gets applied to buildings."

"And so you went to university?"

"Yes, and when I left college Father had me attending all his salons. He expected me to pass judgment on the men clamouring for his support."

"The responsibility must have weighed heavily."

"You don't know the half of it. It was only when he tried to marry me off without a thought for my own wishes that I decided I had had enough. It was finally time to be a man and stand up for myself—something I should have done long before."

"And so you went to Jamaica, I collect."

"Yes, a friend was on his way to his family's plantation and thought to find me a position there." Matthew shrugged. "It seemed like a godsend at the time. Even if it was hardly the type of work I had envisaged, at least it was a foolproof way to escape my father's domination."

"What happened to bring you home again in such a state of poor health?" asked Estelle. Her eyes lingered anxiously on her brother's emancipated body.

"Well, can't say as I exactly took to the life out there. Oh, it wasn't just the unforgiving climate." He sighed. "That unrelenting sun, you have no idea how it wears a body down. But I would have got used to that—everyone else seemed to. No, it was the sad state of the natives that I found hard to stomach. The wretched conditions they were compelled to live in are beyond description in feminine company. I was never more shocked. I never would have gone out there before abolition of the slave trade, you see, but now that the people were their own masters, I thought they would have a better lot."

"But you did not find it to be so?" Alex suggested.

"No, the plantations were still full of slaves, which I found quite unnerving. It wasn't what I expected at all. Had I properly understood the situation I never would have gone there. It was pretty confusing. The younger natives were keen for their freedom but the older workers seemed content with the status quo." Matthew paused. "You can have no idea how barbarically some of them were treated, and ours was considered to be one of the more compassionate overseers. Their living conditions were appalling."

"It is iniquitous!" Estelle cried passionately. "They deserve compassion. I daresay you would not treat your tenants with such scant respect, Alex."

"Certainly not." Alex's calm response gave no indication that he would have preferred it if she had not addressed him informally. He knew she had only done so because she was so impassioned by her brother's tale of injustice and temporarily forgot herself. Matthew had noticed the slip, as had Marianne. They exchanged a speaking look, their expressions speculative as they returned their attention to their sister.

"That is what I thought too," Matthew said. "It was very difficult watching the pathetic attempts of some of them to work when they were obviously afflicted with illness. But they had no choice. If they didn't work they knew the punishment would be brutal."

"Is that why you came home?" Alex asked.

"Not exactly. You see, there was one family I felt particular sympathy for. The father died of disease and left his wife and a whole string of children, none of whom were strong enough to work. I went to them one night under the cover of darkness and gave them some of my own supplies, hoping it would do something to restore their strength. What I discovered later, to my cost, is that the disease that had killed their father lived on in their hut, in the water which I stupidly sipped whilst there."

"Oh, Matthew, you could have died too!" Estelle was horrified.

"And I most likely would have done, had it not been for Porter here."

"Winthrop's letter saying he had returned to England reached Marianne just at the time she felt compelled to flee Hampshire," Porter said. "She so wanted to see him that I could not find it in my heart to deny her. We made our way to Dover and tracked him down at a boarding house. But he was delirious with fever and did not even recognize Marianne."

"I was never so frightened in my entire life," Marianne said. "But Benjamin was wonderful. He arranged everything. A doctor saw Matthew and said he was suffering from dysentery. Most people die of it, of course," she added, blithely unaware of her sister's ghostly pallor as she described in detail the wretched condition they had found Matthew in and continued to sing her fiancé's praises. "The doctor said Matthew only survived because he was young and well nourished. But had we not got to him when we did, I do not care to think about the consequences."

"We brought him back here as soon as he was well enough to travel and he has remained with us ever since. Every day he regains a little more strength." Benjamin spoke with becoming modesty but Alex knew he must have gone to a vast amount of trouble, and expense, to manage things so smoothly.

"That is because I have been nursing him back to health," said Marianne, unaware of Matthew pulling a face at her misguided efforts to make him comfortable. "He is allowed to get out of bed for a few hours every day now. However, he is still very weak and must not overexert himself."

"You have been through a lot, Winthrop," said Alex. "But now, if you are not too fatigued, perhaps you will explain to us why you consider Cowper to be of such importance to your father's schemes."

"He's the son of one of Father's earliest protégées who died in stricken circumstances, leaving the child with no one to care for him. Father took the child under his wing, hoping he would inherit his father's talent, but that did not prove to be the case. We still lived in the north at the time but moved to Hampshire shortly thereafter. Cowper remained in Leeds. Father arranged

157

for him to live with one of his building managers and to be educated there. When he finished school, Father made him learn about every aspect of his building projects and he soon took over a managerial role in that respect."

"Yes, I had ascertained that much from Mrs. Travis, but it does not explain why he is so anxious for Cowper to marry one of his daughters."

"I have been thinking about that," Matthew said. "Being confined to bed all day, a man gets a deal of time to think. Cowper is very useful to Father and completely loyal to him. He is not without wits either." He appeared fatigued by talking so much and paused to drink some water. "Father is wealthy, but has laid out vast amounts on young artists who have failed to live up to their promise."

"He is short of blunt?" Alex's brows shot upwards.

"That is my guess. Before I went away he was not averse to visiting the Patents Office if he chanced upon something which was not his but which might keep the coffers topped up."

"He steals other peoples' ideas?" Alex sat forward in his chair, sensing that they were finally getting to the crux of the matter.

"Exactly so. Or, to be more precise, Cowper does so on his behalf. He not only has access to all the inner circles in the building projects in Leeds, where great innovations are being made and fortunes established, but he also takes responsibility for Father's timber warehouse in Wapping. I daresay he picks up a lot of useful information from that source too, especially since he ends every day in a tavern. He is not without charm, when it suits him to display it. He is also a good listener and people tend to confide in him, especially when they are in drink."

"And you think he has discovered something of such import that he is withholding it from your father until he is wed to one of his daughters?"

"Yes, I do. Father is not the only one with social ambitions. I remember the first occasion when Cowper came to Hampshire and saw my sisters. Estelle was sixteen at the time and he was totally transfixed. He could not take his eyes from her."

"I had forgotten about that." Estelle shuddered. "The way he would not stop looking at me made me very uncomfortable and in the end I left the room."

"But you think whatever he is using to play your father at his own game came too late for him to claim Estelle. She was married to Travis by then."

"Yes, but I also think he wanted to claim what he considered to be his rightful place as my father's heir. Given that I had flown the coop, by marrying Marianne he would achieve that objective. I had enough dealings with the man to appreciate the way he thinks. He has a high opinion of himself and would consider that he had behaved much better than me and therefore deserved to be rewarded."

"Father said that if I married him he would make me his sole heir," Estelle said.

"Which is the same thing as making Cowper his heir," said Alex, "since your property would automatically become your husband's."

"Yes, it would."

"You think your father was so desperate for Cowper's discovery, Winthrop, that he would sacrifice one of his girls and also agree to change his will in order to obtain it?"

"Yes, that is precisely what I think."

"I wonder what it can be." Marianne frowned.

Alex ignored the interruption. "Your father was desperate to replenish his funds and knew of Cowper's preference for Mrs. Travis. And so when Miss Winthrop ran away, the two of them revived their plan to have her husband done away with."

"It is possible, although I hesitate to think so badly of Papa." Estelle appeared genuinely distressed. "But I do not see how we can prove it."

"We cannot, unless we can trick Cowper into admitting it."

"Then it is hopeless."

"Not necessarily." Alex rubbed his chin. "There might be a way."

"How?" asked four voices in unison.

"Ah, but no, if Cowper is in Leeds, then it will be impossible to arrange."

"He is not," Estelle said.

"How do you know?"

"Because when Father came to see me, he said that Mr. Cowper would be in London for several weeks. When I was reconciled to the idea of our union he was to invite him to the house to seal the agreement."

"Yuck!" Marianne pulled a face.

"Do you know where he resides when he is in London?"

"Yes," said Matthew. "He keeps permanent rooms in a house in New Market Street, convenient for Father's timber yard in Wapping."

"And do you suppose that is where he will be now if he is in London?"

"Most assuredly. And there is a tavern on the corner of the street which he visits at the end of each day. He is a creature of habit and his routine in that respect seldom varies."

"Good, that will serve our purpose well. All right, Porter, this is what I have in mind. In order to find out what Winthrop wants from him so badly, it will be necessary to draw Cowper out. And the best way to do that, I think, would be to set them against one another."

"How can that be achieved?"

Alex waved a hand at Estelle and she was immediately silent. "I suspect that whatever Cowper has, it is too detailed and too important to commit to memory, which means—"

"Which means he must have it written down somewhere," said Estelle.

"Exactly! And so all we have to do is figure out where."

"Can we not get into his rooms when he is not there and look for it?" Matthew perked up considerably at the prospect.

"I doubt that it is concealed there." Alex stood and looked out of the window, hands clasped behind his back. "If I were him I would either keep something that precious on my person at all times or, knowing how dangerous the areas he frequents can be, somewhere else that only he knows about."

"That is plausible," conceded Estelle.

"Porter, you have already done more than could be reasonably expected of one man for the sake of Miss Winthrop. However, if my plan is to succeed, I must ask you to consider doing yet more."

"Anything."

"Do not commit yourself until you have heard me out. My scheme is not without risk to your professional position, but that position is the reason we need you to carry it out. Were it otherwise, I would do it myself."

To an accompaniment of gasps of astonishment from his audience, Alex laid out his plan.

"But you cannot ask Mr. Porter to do that for the sake of my family," said Estelle.

"Do not forget that it will soon be my family too, Mrs. Travis. Besides, I would have this matter resolved for the sake of my future wife's peace of mind." He turned towards Alex, his expression resolute. "You can depend upon me, my lord, I will not fail you."

"I understand your concerns for Marianne." Estelle's eyes rested upon her sister's face. "But if you were to be caught in the deception, it would assuredly cost you your position at Nesbit's. You would not then be able to complete your articles and how would you support a wife?"

"If the deception is discovered I shall intercede," said Alex, "and assure Nesbit that Porter was acting under my direct and precise instructions."

"Well...I suppose—"

"You will have your part to play as well, m'dear."

"How so?"

"I doubt that Cowper will take your word that you are employed at Nesbit's, Porter. Or for any part of your story, come to that, and will want to see for himself that you are who you say you are."

"And so he will call at the office on some pretext to make sure I am there." Porter appeared unperturbed at the prospect.

"That is my anticipation. But even that will not convince him that you are privy to the information you claim to be. Do not forget that he is vastly loyal to Winthrop, looks upon him as a father figure and trusts him implicitly. That is why you will let slip that Mrs. Travis is due to call at your office at eleven on the following morning to sign the papers her father has prepared for her."

"You anticipate that he will come to Ramsgate and keep watch to see if I really do call?" Alex nodded. "And when I arrive he will have to believe Mr. Porter's account, or at the very least entertain severe doubts as to my father's true intentions." Estelle smiled widely and clapped her hands in delight. "That is brilliant, Alex!"

"Thank you," he responded, valiantly attempting to suppress his amusement.

"And when he is convinced you are telling the truth, his first reaction will be to recover his hidden papers, or at least check that they are still in place," said Matthew. "Then he will confront my father."

"That is my expectation."

"But I do not see how that will help our cause." Estelle frowned. "Unless we are a party to that confrontation."

"Precisely."

"But how can you know when and where Mr. Cowper will have it out with Papa?"

"You have hit upon our difficulty." Alex flashed a brief smile at Estelle. "And so we shall have to keep Cowper in sight at all times and adapt our plan in accordance with the direction of the wind."

"That sounds rather nebulous."

"The best plans often are."

"You can rely upon my cooperation," said Porter. "When do we start?"

"Tomorrow morning I will call to see Nesbit and inform him I require the services of his clerk for the rest of the day."

"Will he not require to know your business?" asked Estelle.

"No, he will readily acquiesce." Alex did not consider it necessary to say that his title would open that and many other doors. Nesbit would not presume to ask any awkward questions for fear of displeasing his aristocratic client. "That way, should our plan fail, the responsibility for Porter's actions will be mine, and I shall make it my business to square things with his employer."

"You look all done in, Matthew," said Estelle. "I believe we have worn you out with all our planning. We ought to leave you to rest."

"Nonsense! It has done me the power of good to see you, I never felt more rejuvenated." But his dropping eyelids told a different story. "I only wish there was more I could do to help." He fisted his hands in frustration. "Damn this fever!"

"There is one way you could make yourself useful, if you have a mind to," Alex said, anxious to ensure that Estelle's brother felt both involved and committed to the scheme.

"Name it."

"Well, you could keep your sisters entertained tomorrow whilst Porter and I are otherwise engaged."

Matthew rolled his eyes. "You don't ask much of a chap."

"We do not need a chaperone," Estelle protested.

Alex grinned and rose to his feet. "I was not for one moment suggesting that you do. I am merely being cautious. Your father will not have given you up and will still be actively searching for you. I do not think we were followed here but I am not about to underestimate the man and would feel better if I knew you were out of public view."

"Well, of course, Estelle must stay here with me tonight," said Marianne. "She can share my chamber and we will talk and laugh all night long. It will be quite like old times. But as to you, my lord, well...we only have—"

"No, Miss Winthrop, pray do not concern yourself on my account. Mrs. Travis and I have accommodation at the Albion in Broadstairs." Alex ignored the renewed speculative glances being exchanged between Estelle's relatives. "We shall return there now and I shall deliver Mrs. Travis to your care—" he nodded at Matthew, "—in the morning. Come." He extended a hand towards Estelle. "It is getting late and we ought to be gone."

Chapter Fourteen

The roads were choked with gigs, pony carts, wagons, and lads astride sturdy farm horses, all headed for the fair. Passage was slow and Alex was concentrating much of his attention upon his team to avoid a collision. Estelle was preoccupied and met his efforts to engage her in conversation with monosyllabic responses. She was delighted to be reunited with her siblings again and deep in thought about the revelations that had just been made.

They reached their destination before it occurred to her that Alex had smoothly taken control of matters—again. He had formulated a plan to uncover her father's nefarious activities. But that plan depended upon his participation for its success, since he was relying upon his social standing to absolve Porter from blame should something unforeseen cause them to fail. A gentleman of his elevated status deliberately inveigling himself in her affairs begged the obvious question. Why? She could not begin to imagine why, but fully intended to extract a satisfactory explanation from his lordship at the first opportunity.

Only half listening as he gave orders for supper to be served immediately, Estelle mounted the stairs and entered their chamber ahead of Alex, who held the door open for her.

"I have been thinking." She removed her gloves and bonnet and placed them on a table.

"So I apprehend, since you have barely spoken a word since leaving Porter's residence." He offered her a curling smile of such luminance as to temporarily send her thoughts on a sensual detour. "Have I done ought to offend you?"

"Not at all."

"Then perhaps you would care to share your thoughts with me?"

"With the greatest of pleasure. I thank you for being so willing to involve yourself in my family's affairs. However, upon reflection I am persuaded there is no necessity for you or Mr. Porter to inconvenience yourselves and that matters ought to be left as they are."

"I think Porter would give you an argument if you tried to stop him fighting on Marianne's behalf. In fact, he is already relishing the idea of besting your father and showing himself in an even more gratifying light to your sister."

"You approve of him then." She could not say why his opinion should matter to her but only knew that it did.

"I do indeed."

"I feel the same way. I approved when I first met him in my husband's house and nothing I saw today has changed that opinion."

"Well, there you are then."

"Yes, but I still do not see the need to involve either of you in our affairs. Mr. Porter will be qualified in a few months and my sister will come of age shortly thereafter. They will then be in a position to marry, and there is nothing my father will be able to do to prevent them. Why risk Mr. Porter's position unnecessarily?"

"You appear to have lost sight of the fact that it is not just your sister's reputation at risk here, Estelle. It is yours, and Matthew's, too."

"Mine is of no consequence."

"If you really believe what you say, then you cannot have considered the matter from society's point of view."

"Indeed I have." She bridled at the suggestion that she was too woolly-headed to reason the matter through. "But I do not give two figs for other people's opinion of me. I do not intend to remarry or be beholden to any man ever again. Instead I shall seek a position as a governess or companion, after I have seen Marianne settled and Matthew restored to health, naturally." She whirled away from him and unfastened her pelisse. "And I do not require society's approbation to follow such a path."

"What you say is true but you appear to have overlooked the fact that in order to gain employment, you will first require a character. If your father's activities were to be generally known, who would provide you with one?"

He followed her example by removing his hat and gloves and setting them on the table alongside her own. It was a strangely domestic action that caused regret to weigh heavily on her heart. He followed the direction of her eyes, raised his own, cool amusement reflected in them, almost as though he could sense the attraction she felt towards him on the rare occasions when she allowed it to creep beneath her guard. His superior response angered her, tamping down her regrets and reminding her that her silly infatuation was a lost cause. Lord Crawley must be accustomed to women flinging themselves at him and she had no intention of joining their ranks.

She put up her chin and averted her eyes in an effort to reclaim the moral high ground. "I daresay Miss Frobisher would offer me employment in her school, were I to approach her and explain my predicament."

Alex merely chuckled. "Possibly; if that is the sort of occupation you would find fulfilling. However, knowing what I do of your character, I seriously doubt it."

"You know nothing about me."

"I beg to differ." His grin was annoyingly smug. "No, m'dear, there is no help for it, I am afraid. We must resolve your difficulties with your father before you embark upon your search for a suitable occupation. If we do not, you will be tainted by association. The narrow-minded gentry will close ranks against you and you will be a lost cause." His expression, far from being full of condescending superiority as she half expected, was instead compassionate. "You are far too attractive for the comfort of many of the ladies who might otherwise have employed you. They would seize upon your father's public disgrace as an excuse to turn you away. In other words, your situation would become untenable and I would not have you exposed to such bigotry."

"Yes, but—"

"And Matthew's hopes of obtaining a position as a steward would be dashed too. No one would wish to employ a young man, however personable and enthusiastic, if his father's activities became fodder for the scandalmongers."

"All right, put like that, I do not see how I can prevent you from following your plan through, since you appear so determined. Thank you," she added, aware that her behaviour had been far from gracious when he was going out of his way to help her.

He responded with a courtly bow. "The pleasure is all mine."

"But that is what you intend to do, is it not?" she asked, moving away from him. "To expose my father's misdeeds, I mean."

"No, indeed. I have something else entirely in mind."

"Then what? Perhaps you would have the goodness to explain your thoughts, since the outcome of your actions is likely to impact upon my life, not yours."

A tap at the door heralded the arrival of their supper.

He chuckled at her fit of pique. "I will explain it all to you later, but let us eat first." He directed the maid to the table in front of the window and held a chair for Estelle until, with a rebellious toss of her head, she condescended to be seated.

"Now, what do we have here?" He lifted the covers and peered into a tureen. "I am famished. Ah, beef broth, if I am not much mistaken, and mutton stew. It smells delicious. Can I serve you, m'dear? A glass of wine to wash the dust from your throat, perhaps?"

Alex entertained her throughout the course of their meal with discourse wholly unconnected with her father. He spoke of his mother in affectionate terms and of the Crawley estate generally. He explained the improvements he planned to the tenants' cottages, asking her opinion about matters connected to the church, rolling his eyes as he explained about the new drainage system he was grappling with.

Estelle, who was acutely aware of the anticipatory atmosphere between them, said little. If Alex noticed her abstracted state he made no mention of it. She wondered if he knew when offering her the seat which faced directly into the room that the huge bed would fall into her sphere of vision every time she looked up from her plate, testing her determination to resist its temptations. She glanced at the compelling sophisticate seated across from her, his eyes fastened on her face with an expression of amused expectancy. His long fingers were linked round the stem of his glass and slid absently up and down its length in much the same way they had caressed her body the previous night.

She gulped and looked away. She could not in all conscience blame Alex for what had occurred between them since she had all but signified her willingness when she brazenly suggested they share the same bed. For the first time in her entire life she had put aside common sense and acted upon her impulses, enjoying her moment of quixotic madness and unable to regret it.

But it would not be repeated tonight. The landlord had anticipated yesterday that he might have another chamber vacant this evening. Estelle could not recall if Alex had asked him about it when they had returned earlier but would certainly remind him to do so. He had been at pains to make it clear to her this afternoon that their brief intimacies had no specific meaning for him. Well, no more did they for her. She would behave with dignity from this point onwards and had no intention of clinging.

"You were going to explain your strategy for dealing with my father and Mr. Cowper," Estelle reminded him as soon as the maid had taken away the remnants of their meal.

"That I was." He offered her his arm and led her to a comfortable chair in front of the fire. "If Cowper falls for the bait, he will assuredly either recover the papers he has stashed somewhere—"

"But what if it is not written down?"

"Then we are unlikely to succeed. However, I do not for a moment consider that anything that valuable would be trusted to one individual's memory."

"Then let us hope you are right."

"Yes, let us hope that."

"I can see your logic, I suppose." Estelle furrowed her brow and assumed a distracted expression to avoid meeting those compelling eyes. "And so he will recover the papers. And then what?"

"He will either recover the papers or at least check to see that they are still where he left them. I have sent for three trustworthy footmen from my London establishment to meet me in Wapping tomorrow. They will follow Porter to the meeting with Cowper and thereafter keep Cowper under constant surveillance."

"And so they will know if he has the papers with him and, if not, where they are hidden."

"I am confident that will be the case. And if he has them with him my men will, if circumstances permit, accost him and relieve him of the burden."

"But how will that help our cause? It will prevent my father from obtaining what is not rightfully his and, perhaps, remove his desire to see me married to Mr. Cowper. But it will not tell us if he had my husband killed."

"No, but I am hoping Cowper will volunteer that information himself."

"Hmm, I do not see how you can possibly achieve that end. Cowper is nobody's fool."

"Just trust me." He smiled at her. "I have not let you down yet, have I?"

"No, you have not." She made the concession and dropped her eyes, unprepared for the depth of feeling she thought she could see in his resourceful face.

"Well then." He turned towards the door.

"Where are you going?"

"The tap room."

"Oh." Was he trying to tell her that he had no desire to share a bed with her for a second night? Was her inexperience such that he could not bear the thought of repeating the act? She bridled. It was one thing deciding she did not wish to be seduced but quite another for him to reject her. "I see. Well, do not let me keep you from your brandy." She turned away so that he would not see the hurt in her eyes.

"What is it?"

"Nothing."

Leaning over her, he grasped her chin and tilted her head backwards. "Something is on your mind. Tell me what it is."

"Did you speak to the landlord about another room?"

"Yes, unfortunately there are still none available."

"How tiresome for you." She twisted her chin out of his grasp and stared at her lap. "The sofa will have to suffice for you tonight in that case."

"Is that what you want?"

"Yes."

"I don't believe you."

So angry was she by his insufferable arrogance that she forgot how dangerous it was to meet his gaze and lifted her eyes to his face.

"What a thing to say! You, sir, are the most presumptuous, self-opinionated, disrespectful gentleman it has ever been my misfortune to encounter. You can go and sleep in the stables with the rest of the animals as far as I am concerned."

She stood to face him, blazing with anger, even as her insides churned with a very different emotion. He wanted her! He was regarding her with elaborate circumspection but could not quite disguise the raw passion in his expression as he met her gaze and held it. There was a raffish smile on his lips but he did not speak. Obviously the decision was hers to make and she knew he would respect it.

She sighed, wracked with indecision. All this prevarication, pretending a disinterest she did not feel, suddenly seemed pointless. She was aware that another such opportunity would not arise. Whatever happened tomorrow, she would not be spending another night in the same chamber as Lord Crawley. She could not take back her actions of the previous night and suddenly the urge to repeat them threatened to overwhelm.

But that did not mean she would make matters easy for him. He deserved to pay for his presumption. He was still standing directly in front of her, watching her closely, and she suspected he gauged the exact moment when she reached her decision. With an extravagant sweep of her lashes she lifted her eyes to his rugged features and treated him to a sultry smile of capitulation.

"The tap room," she remarked. "It sounds compelling. Pray do not let me detain you."

"You, madam, must have been what God had in mind when he created Eve. Adam has my sympathies." His tortured expression became a tender caress. "Are you sure?"

She smiled in a beguiling manner. "Perfectly sure."

She spoke so quietly that the words were barely audible. But he must have heard them because he reached for her, drew her into those strong arms of his and kissed her. He kissed her with such burning passion that it robbed her of what little breath she had remaining.

She melted against his body, greedy for all he was offering, beyond caring about making him suffer. All she cared about now was the vortex of desire spangling through her in dizzying waves that left her gasping and desperate for more. He appeared to sense her need, expertly teasing and caressing until she cried out with the pleasure of it all. He was bringing her eager body to life with a speed that ought to have been indecent.

Well, if that's what it was, then indecency was vastly underrated. She abandoned herself to the exquisite shards of intense sensation cascading through her and willed the moment to last forever.

ᘓᘒ

Alex watched her as she slept, her lips swollen from his kisses. Her hair was a tangle of unruly curls spread beneath her naked body, and her silken limbs were still entwined with his. There was so much he had wished to say to her but having made such a ham fist of things the previous afternoon he had hesitated, in the end allowing his actions to speak for him. Now, his passion temporarily sated, he tried to decide precisely what it was that he *had* wanted to say. Unlike most of the women he dallied with, she appeared to have few expectations and did not require anything from him that he was not prepared to give. So trying to set boundaries for their relationship had perhaps been insulting.

What was he to do about her? What were these emotions she engendered, so alien to him that he was unable to put a name to them? And what was driving him to resolve her familial difficulties when he had many far more pressing matters awaiting his attention? He had already reunited her with her siblings and could walk away at any time with nothing to reproach himself for. He knew he would not do so but still could not say why that should be. By morning he was still none the wiser and had nothing but a dull headache to show for his cogitations.

They drove to Ramsgate seated closely together but separated by the unbridgeable divide of their individual thoughts. Alex cast frequent glances in Estelle's direction and would have given much to know what was running through her head. She appeared composed, a different creature to the wildly passionate siren who had woken in his arms a few hours previously. She had smiled at him in such a transparently sensual manner that his resulting passion was almost brutal. But did she now regret her impulsiveness? That was the burning question. To him it was vitally important that she should not.

Alex left the phaeton at the same mews as before, where the lads, who remembered his generosity, were quick to scamper up and take the horses' heads, deserting a gent who was in mid-rant about some misunderstanding. They walked the now familiar streets in uncomfortable silence. Alex was carrying Estelle's portmanteau, since she would be spending the night with her sister whilst he and Porter completed their business in town. They would not be able to do so and return to Ramsgate in daylight. Since it was Sunday on the morrow, Alex was spared the inconvenience of explaining Porter's absence to his employer and planned for them to return at their leisure the following morning.

As they reached number seventeen, the door was opened by Marianne, a vision in blue dimity, before they had even ascended the steps.

"Ah, there you are!" Marianne dropped a curtsey to him and hugged her sister. "Do come inside. Benjamin is already

A Reason to Rebel

gone to his work but Matthew has insisted on getting out of bed. He has dressed for the first time since arriving here."

"That is encouraging news," Estelle said.

They entered the front parlour where Matthew was seated beside the fire. He looked pale and worryingly thin but there was determination in his expression as he too greeted Estelle with a hug before offering Alex his hand.

"Glad to see you back on your feet, Winthrop. I say..." Alex's words trailed off as he eyed Matthew's neckcloth askance.

"I tied Matthew's neckcloth for him," said Marianne, "for he has quite lost the knack."

"Ahh, I see, that would explain it."

"It was to have been a Waterfall."

"You have given it a new slant, Miss Winthrop."

Marianne frowned critically at her handiwork. "It is kind of you to say so, but I am not entirely persuaded that I got the folds to fall exactly right."

Mrs. Porter, a genteel lady of refined manners, entered the room at that moment and bade the newcomers welcome, thus saving Alex the trouble of formulating a diplomatic response. Having been warned to expect Estelle, Mrs. Porter greeted her warmly and did not appear flustered to discover a viscount in her parlour. She welcomed Alex with the respect and deference due to his rank and, as predicted beforehand by Marianne, asked no awkward questions about the reason for his appearance.

Satisfied that the girls understood they must remain indoors, and charging Matthew with the task of ensuring they did so, Alex stood and prepared to take his leave.

"Take great care," said Estelle gently, her concerned expression making him regret that he could not bid her adieu in a more intimate fashion.

"And send Benjamin my love," added Marianne, misty-eyed. "I do not for one moment doubt that he will save the day, but you must not permit him to be reckless."

"Heaven forbid!" Alex flashed a smile at Estelle as he left the room.

Chapter Fifteen

The hours passed with frustrating slowness. Estelle, normally the most patient of creatures, was convinced that the hands on the long case clock in Mrs. Porter's front parlour must be moving backwards. Its hollow ticking sounded unnaturally loud, intruding upon the dilatory conversation she and her siblings were conducting. She found her attention wandering and her eyes constantly being drawn towards the timepiece. Her restless state affected Marianne too, and by the following morning, Matthew complained he had all but exhausted himself in his struggle to engage the attention of both his sisters for more than two minutes at a time.

"I might just as well have remained in Jamaica for all the attention you two have to spare for me," he grumbled.

Estelle apologized for her preoccupation but did not attempt to explain it, scarce understanding it herself. It was all right for Marianne—she was engaged to be married to Benjamin, which afforded her the right to openly voice her concerns for his welfare.

Estelle tapped her fingers impatiently on the arm of her chair and disciplined herself to attend to Matthew. Oh, how she wished she could follow her sister's example and publicly express her fears in respect of a certain gentleman! Thoughts of his smouldering brown eyes and somnolent smile, passionate kisses and questing hands crowded and jostled for position in her mind.

She was getting more worried about his failure to return as the minutes ticked by with such agonizing slowness that she wanted to scream with frustration. Aware of Matthew's censorious gaze resting upon her, she assumed a façade of neutrality, tamped down her impatience and kept her fears to herself.

"Was that a carriage I heard?" she asked a few moments later, hope flaring as she lifted her head and cocked it to one side.

"Since there is a road on the other side of that window, it is not beyond the bounds of possibility," said Matthew, whose patience was wearing increasingly thin. "It is doubtless another neighbour following Mrs. Porter's example and heading for church. Now come, Estelle," he said as he dealt the cards, "stop imagining things and pay attention to the game, if you please, or I might as well return to my bed."

"I was only remarking upon the possibility of an unexpected visitor calling. Obviously it cannot be Mr. Porter or Lord Crawley returning, it is far too soon to expect them."

"Then stop fussing so. We know they intended to pass the night at Lord Crawley's establishment in town, and if anything had occurred to detain them, his lordship would have sent word. They won't get here for another hour or more yet. Even if they left before cockcrow they could hardly be expected to cover the distance any faster than that."

"You are wrong!" Marianne, who felt no necessity to exercise restraint, had pulled the curtains aside and was craning her neck to gain a view of the front steps. "It is them! They are here already."

She rushed off to open the front door, sprigged muslin skirts swirling in her wake.

"Thank the Lord for small mercies!" said Matthew.

Marianne and Benjamin dallied in the vestibule, wrapped in one another's arms. Alex strode straight into the parlour without divesting himself of his outdoor garments. He paused as he reached Estelle's chair, his eyes searching her face, his hand briefly brushing her shoulder.

"You made good time," she said. "We did not expect you for some time yet."

"We set out early and my team was keen to stretch their legs. We thought you might be anxious."

"You don't know the half of it." Matthew rolled his eyes.

"It is difficult to remain in ignorance whilst others take all the risks," said Estelle with dignity. She was a trifle miffed now, feeling Alex had no business looking so disgustingly full of himself when she had imagined all manner of dire misfortunes befalling him. "How did you fare?"

"The seed has been planted." His voice sounded as tired as he himself, upon closer examination, appeared to be. "We can only wait now and see what we have set in motion, for the next move must be Cowper's."

"Tell me everything that happened. I must know it all."

"Naturally, but we should let Porter relate the particulars. He showed great courage and the story is his to tell."

"Yes, of course."

Mr. Porter and Marianne eventually entered the room, hand in hand. Matthew and Estelle exchanged an indulgent glance. The way they were behaving, one might be excused for imagining they had been separated for weeks. Marianne, belatedly appearing to recall they were not alone and that she had social obligations, rang for refreshments and some time was spent making the travellers comfortable. Estelle curbed her impatience and was eventually rewarded when Mr. Porter cleared his throat and the story started to unfold.

"We found the tavern that Cowper frequents, just as you said we would," he said, causing Estelle to wonder why that should surprise him. Did he imagine that taverns got up and changed their location in the middle of the night? She smiled at the notion but said nothing. "I could not see that Cowper was there at first, never having met the man and only having your description to go by. The establishment was very dimly lit. But I persevered and eventually located him talking to two very rough-looking men whom I did not at all like the look of."

"I hope you did not do anything rash," cried Marianne.

"No, my dear, I merely purchased a tankard of ale and positioned myself so that Cowper was clearly in my sights. His two companions left after what seemed like an age and I seized the opportunity to stroll up to his table and seated myself across from him, uninvited."

"Gosh, how daring!" This, of course, from Marianne, whose eyes were round with admiration. "Did he take exception to that?"

"He looked at me but did not speak and so I had to take the initiative. I did not see any reason to procrastinate—after all, his companions might have returned at any time. And so I merely remarked that I was looking for a cove called Cowper and was I to understand that I had found him? He looked wary and asked who it was that wanted to know. I could see him regarding me closely when I mentioned his name and I don't mind admitting that it quite unsettled me for a moment. There is something disquieting about his eyes and I did not enjoy being the subject of such close scrutiny."

"I am sure I should have been terrified." Marianne reclaimed her beloved's hand, her face shining with pride.

"Well, I don't know about that. I suppose I just thought about you and your sister when my courage was in danger of failing me. Anyway, I remembered Lord Crawley's advice. I was to play it cautiously and not give away information easily. So I said that the man I sought was a colleague of Joseph Winthrop and if I could only find him I might well be able to supply him with information to his advantage."

"Gosh, how did he respond to that?" asked his faithful admirer.

"He said he was Cowper and wanted to know what business I had with him. I took a long draught of my ale and took my time replying. Then I told him what Lord Crawley and I had agreed between us. I was in articles at Nesbit and Jones in Ramsgate and that Winthrop had called a few days previously to consult with our senior partner."

"I'll wager that got his attention," said Matthew.

"No, I was discouraged at first because he did not react at all. But Lord Crawley had predicted he might play his cards close to his chest. I said that if what I had to tell him was of no interest I wouldn't waste any more of his time, or mine, and made to move away. But he stopped me by saying, real casual like, that as I had made a point of finding him he might as well hear what was on my mind. Well, I knew I had him then and said that an articled clerk didn't make much money, and I felt sure that what I had to tell him about Winthrop must be worth something to him."

"And he said he could not know that unless you told him more," ventured Estelle.

"Precisely. Well, I told him that I was not that green, that I had dealt with his type before, and information did not come cheap. He looked at me for such a long time then, with such a queer expression on his face, that I felt quite chilled to the bone by it."

"Oh!" Marianne paled and clutched his hand even tighter. "He does have the most terrifying eyes. They always gave me the shivers."

"But I stood my ground," Mr. Porter informed his rapt audience, appearing to positively bask in Marianne's wide-eyed adoration. Estelle, suspecting him to be buoyed by his daring feat, was unable to condemn him for making the most of it. "I told him I had been sent to town by my employer on an errand and, having overheard that Cowper was very likely being duped by Winthrop, thought I might take the opportunity to seek him out. He wanted to know how I had found him but, again, Lord Crawley had anticipated that question. I told him I had overheard Winthrop saying he had chosen a Ramsgate solicitor to transact his business because it was close to where his daughter was currently residing. It was also a long way away from Leeds, and from Wapping, where Cowper was currently in residence in New Market Street."

"How clever!"

Mr. Porter's face glowed and his efforts to appear modest fooled no one except Marianne.

"I explained I had time to kill before returning to Ramsgate in the morning and thought I might as well try to give Cowper a helping hand. He was no longer feigning disinterest by that point and wanted to know what more I could tell him. Now," he said, leaning forward, his expression intent, "this was the tricky part. I said that I would not say much more unless he made it worth my while, at which point he pretended to lose interest. I said I could understand he may not believe I was who I said I was, what with so many rum'uns being about nowadays, but if he doubted me he could check for himself easily enough." He paused before delivering his *coup de grace*. "I then mentioned, as though it was an afterthought, that I understood Mrs. Travis had gone missing, along with her sister. He did not respond but I had his complete attention again, I could see that at once."

"What did you do then, Benjamin?"

"I said I was surprised Winthrop had not informed him they were both safe and well, speculating aloud as to his reasons for withholding that information from his close associate. He responded by asking me, as we had hoped he would, if I had seen both of the ladies. He tried to make the enquiry sound casual but I had the measure of him by then and knew it was a sham. It was more important to him than anything. He really wanted to know." Marianne stared at her intended with a besotted expression and sighed at this further display of his heroic qualities. "That is when I told him that both ladies would be calling to see my superior at eleven o'clock tomorrow morning."

"The devil you did, Porter!" cried Matthew. "Both ladies? We did not agree to that."

"I did," said Marianne. "Benjamin mentioned the matter to me before departing for work yesterday. It was Lord Crawley's suggestion and naturally I agreed at once."

"Why was I not consulted?"

"Your pardon, Winthrop," said Alex. "I intended to consult you but in all the rush to get away it clean slipped my mind. But the fact of the matter is that we want Cowper to believe that neither sister ran away and that they have both been acting according to their father's dictate all this while. Porter obliquely implied that Miss Winthrop was whisked away from him because he was starting to insist upon fixing a wedding date. Winthrop hoped to be held innocent in respect of her desertion so that he, Cowper, would hand over whatever it is that Winthrop so covets."

"Which is when I clammed up unless he made it worth my while to stay, and he dug deep in his pocket without quibbling," said Porter, resuming his story. "I then implied that I knew of the subsequent plot to do away with Travis. Winthrop was anxious to relieve his conscience in that respect and as much as admitted it to his solicitor, placing the blame entirely at Cowper's door."

"But that is brilliant!" cried Estelle. "He is bound to believe Mr. Porter and will not be able to help recovering his papers and confronting my father."

"That is my expectation." Eyes half-closed, Alex leaned back in his chair, one booted leg resting on his opposite knee. "We know from the men whom I have keeping watch over Cowper that he did nothing unusual after seeing Porter yesterday. He merely stayed in the tavern for another hour and then returned to his lodgings, remaining there all night. If he has accepted the bait then we expect him to make for Ramsgate sometime today. He cannot risk being delayed and not observing the ladies attending the solicitor's office tomorrow.

Once he sees them for himself he will have to believe that Porter told the truth in all other respects as well."

"By gad, sir, I do believe, with your assistance, we will get to the bottom of this farrago before any of us are much older." Matthew's face was flushed with admiration. Alex acknowledged the compliment with an inclination of his head and continued speaking.

"Porter has already hinted that Winthrop, having disinherited his only son, is putting his affairs in order and drawing up papers to split his fortune equally between his two daughters," said Alex. "A reward for doing all he asked of them."

"Whereas Cowper was expecting to marry Estelle and gain it all," said Marianne.

"Yes, and now he will suspect Winthrop had never intended him to marry either of his daughters and did not mean to reward him financially either. Not only that, but he has implied to a solicitor that he alone, Cowper that is, was guilty of murdering Travis."

"Cowper will be furious. He has a fearful temper and will not be able to resist confronting our father with the information he has against him," said Matthew confidently. "But, hang on, how will that help us if we are not there to hear it?"

"Oh, but we will be there," said Alex. "My spies tell me that your father recently returned to Hampshire. That does not mean he is no longer looking for you, Estelle, merely that he has assigned the task to others. And so Cowper will most likely recover his papers and head straight for Hampshire, demanding explanations." Alex paused, his expression set in stone. "But I, and some of my men, will be there to listen to their exchange."

"How will you manage that?" asked Matthew, who was looking rather awed.

"That is indeed the question, and I was rather hoping for your help in that respect. Where does your father traditionally hold his business meetings? Is there more than one method to gain access to that room? I need you to remember all you can

A Reason to Rebel

about the layout of the estate you grew up on. Few secrets escape the notice of small boys."

"The summerhouse," said Estelle and Marianne together.

"I beg your pardon?"

"Of course!" Matthew thumped his thigh in excitement. "The summerhouse is built directly over the ice house."

"And there is a trapdoor leading to steps and then to the passageway," said Estelle. "Marianne and I found it when we were children."

"Ah, I see."

"It was a useful means of escaping from the house unseen."

"Where does it lead to in the house?"

"The cellars. There is a stout door from the cellar to the steps up to the kitchen but it is often locked."

"That should not cause much of a problem. Can you draw a diagram of the exact location of the trapdoor, Winthrop?"

Estelle bridled. She knew the passageway better than any of them and it was she who had just supplied Alex with the information about it. But it was as if she had not spoken. He was ignoring her and addressing all of his questions directly to her brother.

"No need for drawings," said Matthew, "since I shall accompany you."

"Out of the question. Sorry, Winthrop, but you're not fit enough. If there is trouble you would be a liability."

"Not necessarily, I can still—"

"You've done naught but sit in a chair for the past two days and yet you look fagged out," said Alex, not unkindly.

"Damn it, this is my family. It ought to be my responsibility."

"I am sound in wind and limb," said Mr. Porter. "If you will pretend need of my services to my employer, I will accompany you."

"It could be dangerous and it is not your fight."

"It is more my concern than it is yours." Steely determination underlined his tone. It was as though he was reluctant to surrender his newfound taste for adventure, which lent him the courage to challenge Alex's plan. "Marianne's family will soon be united in marriage to mine and you cannot prevent me from playing my part in curbing her father's unlawful activities."

"Very well, since you put it like that, I welcome your assistance, Porter."

"And I shall come too," said Estelle. "I can guide you to the passageway."

"Absolutely not!"

"I beg your pardon."

"You and your sister will attend Nesbit's office tomorrow morning, which will require fortitude enough on both your parts. I have contrived to put every protection in place but the outing is still not without danger. I shall send one of my footmen to escort you. I discovered that your father's retainers wear a plain livery of green coats and green and gold waistcoats, easy to obtain. My man will be dressed accordingly, accompany you to the solicitor's in an anonymous cab and see you safely back here. And then Matthew will keep you entertained until we return. Is that quite clear?"

"No, it is far from clear. I would have a word with you in private, my lord."

"Not now, Mrs. Travis." Alex dismissed her objections with a casual flap of his hand. "The matter is not open to debate. You *will* do as I ask and can have nothing more to say to me, either here or in private."

"Oh can I not!"

"If you wish to help," he said, apparently unmoved by her anger, "draw me a diagram of the summerhouse, the best way to approach it from the road and the direction the passageway takes once I have located it."

Estelle, infuriated with his dictatorial attitude, stood to confront him, hands on hips as the anger churned away inside of her. She was more than ready to put him right on a few basic facts. Faced with this harpy towering over his chair, blistering rage sparking in her eyes, Alex had no option but to stand also.

"This is my fight. I am the one who will be forced into marrying the vile man if we cannot find a way to prevent it and I will not be left out of things."

"You will do as I say, madam."

They faced one another like two prize fighters, each waiting for the other to pounce. He still looked perfectly composed, as though he did not have the slightest doubt that he would prevail and her objections were of no consequence. The atmosphere seemed to vibrate with his presence. Estelle was briefly overwhelmed by the attraction she felt towards this arrogant, annoyingly disrespectful, formidably alluring and utterly compelling male who, when he chose, could also be relentlessly gallant and persuasively convincing.

"I shall do precisely as I please." She tossed her head and blinked back tears of frustration.

"You will do as I have requested or I will have Matthew lock you in your chamber as soon as you have completed your errand in the morning."

"You would not dare!" She threw the words at him, forgetting about their audience, who were enthralled by the exchange.

"I would not recommend that you put that theory to the test." His expression softened into a tender caress. She blushed as she felt herself reacting to it deep in her innermost core. "I cannot bring myself to deliberately put you in danger's path," he said so softly that she scarce heard the words.

"Do you consider me to be such a goose that I am incapable of facing my father without swooning? Is that what so bothers you?"

"I think no such thing. Your courage is not in question," he assured her passionately. "But you appear to have lost sight of the fact that there is considerable danger involved. If something goes amiss you would finish up precisely where your father wishes you to be, which is back under his control."

"I suppose you are right." Estelle felt the air leaving her lungs and the fight draining from her body. "But I must face him, Alex, can you not see that?" She changed tack, her mood swinging from bellicose to passionately persuasive, her eyes fastened upon his profile as she pleaded for his understanding. "I cannot live the rest of my life wondering if I might one day encounter him or how he might manipulate me if he finds out where I am living. He must see with his own eyes that I no longer fear him, will not be controlled by him and intend to live my life as I see fit, without reference to him."

"If my plan succeeds you will never have to see him again and so your fears are groundless."

"What do you intend then, sir?" asked Matthew, his words breaking the tense atmosphere between the combatants.

Estelle dropped her eyes and looked away, embarrassed by the passion which had crept into her expression. It was a passion which had little to do with her fear of her father.

"Ah yes, perhaps if I explain that, you will better understand the impossibility of your attending, Estelle."

"Anything is possible, I suppose." She moved away from him and resumed her seat.

Chuckling, Alex leaned against the mantle. "You and I, Porter, plus two of my best men, will reconnoitre the estate tomorrow morning, whilst Estelle and Marianne are acting out their part. We must be sure we know how to get in unobserved."

"We can give you a lot of help there," said Matthew. "There is a seldom-used cart track on the northern part of the estate that leads to the back of the woods and on to the garden. You will be able to see the summerhouse from the edge of the woods. Crossing the expanse of open lawn in daylight will be the difficult part."

"Hmm, that may prove to be unnecessary. As long as we can see in daylight what we are aiming for it will have to serve."

"How can you be sure that Cowper will not arrive in daylight?" asked Estelle, drawn into the conversation in spite of her determination to remain aloof.

"I cannot be entirely sure about anything but it is my expectation. Once he sees you and Marianne tomorrow I suspect he will return to London to collect the all-important papers, or at the very least, ensure they are still where they ought to be. He will then go direct to Hampshire to confront your father. He will not be able to travel to Ramsgate today on the mail coach because it does not run on a Sunday and so I anticipate that he will hire either a curricle or a saddle horse, probably the latter. He will not be able to cover the distances between Ramsgate, London and Hampshire whilst it is still light, even if he abandons the horse and travels by coach."

"Yes, that is true." Estelle was reluctantly impressed by his meticulous attention to detail.

"I expect him to arrive in Hampshire between nine and ten o'clock tomorrow evening. But we will be ready for him. He will arrive at the front drive to the house and when he does, we will know it from my man stationed there and be ready to move."

"You will not have much time to act. Would you not be better off if you were already inside the house?"

"Yes, but it is too dangerous. We would be bound to be discovered. I agree that time will be of the essence once we know Cowper has arrived, but it ought to be possible to gain access to the house provided we have no setbacks. We will need to get into the summerhouse, locate the trapdoor, follow the passage to the cellars, get out of the cellar and into the kitchens unobserved—"

"They should be empty by that time of night. My parents dine early."

"Good. Winthrop, we will need a map of the internal layout of the house. If your father is likely to entertain Cowper in his study, then we need to get to an adjoining room unobserved. What is the likelihood of that?"

"Our mother will retire to her sitting room on the first floor immediately after dinner and will not leave it," said Matthew with confidence, making a gesture with his hand that implied she would be well in her cups by that point. "Father will be in his study and the morning room adjoins it. There will very likely only be the butler and one footman about. He does not keep a large staff unless he is entertaining."

"Well, provided we can avoid them we should get to the morning room unobserved, just so long as we remember which room is where and do not mistake one for the other."

"When you emerge through the green baize door into the vestibule you require the second door on the left, immediately opposite you," said Estelle.

"Thank you, we shall remember that."

"And you ought to be able to overhear what is being said easily enough." Matthew grimaced. "My father always bellows like a bull, even when he is not in a bad mood. If Cowper is also angry I daresay their exchange will be more of a shouting match."

"That is what I am counting on."

"There is a door that adjoins the two rooms, covered by a thick curtain on my father's side." Estelle adjusted her skirts and did not look at Alex as she spoke. She suspected her face would betray the fear that beset her at the thought of her protector invading her father's study. It would not do to reveal such weakness. "He complained of draughts reaching him through it but is too mean to order a bigger fire. You could open the door a little behind the shield of the curtain and he very likely would not notice."

"Our plan appears more likely to succeed by the minute. And since you are determined to come along, Porter, you can do something useful."

"What do you have in mind?"

"Although I am a magistrate, Winthrop knows me and will appreciate that I have no jurisdiction in Hampshire. And so I was planning to have one of my men pose as a magistrate with the appropriate authority but you could more usefully fulfil that role, Porter. When the men admit to their misdeeds, we will reveal ourselves and threaten to take them in charge."

"Is that what you will actually do?" Estelle had not stopped to consider the consequences for her father and his murderous co-conspirator until that point.

"It is what I ought to do but I do not think that would benefit the three of you." He indicated Estelle and her siblings with his eyes.

"Perhaps not." Matthew's expression was resolute. "But if they really did arrange to have Travis murdered and are stealing, I do not think they should be allowed to profit from their crimes."

"No more do I." Alex's expression turned pensive. "What matters to your father more than just about anything? Why is he so determined to have control over you all and make you do as he wishes?"

"Social standing and his position as a patron of the arts," said Estelle promptly.

"Exactly! And that is what I intend to take away from him. When we have heard enough of their exchange, we will show ourselves. I will remind them who I am and introduce Porter as a magistrate with the authority to report all he has heard and have them both taken in charge."

"But Winthrop could argue that we were in his house without his permission," reasoned Porter, "and therefore have no authority."

"He could but I doubt that he will. We shall recover the secret they were attempting to steal, by force if necessary, provided Cowper has it about his person. If he has left it where it was my man who is following him will have already uncovered it and got word to me to that effect."

"You appear to have thought of everything." Estelle was unable to keep a grudging note of admiration from entering her voice.

"Thank you." He offered her a courtly bow. "And once we have uncovered their secret I shall make them aware that we know they murdered Travis. It will be clear to them by then that the only future they have to look forward to is the end of a hangman's rope." Estelle shivered. "Don't worry." He placed a hand on her shoulder, his thumb tracing patterns on it beneath the cover of his palm. "It will not come to that. Once they have had an opportunity to reflect upon their situation, I will not have to exert much pressure to make them both sign a full confession. After that I will give them two days to leave the country for ever. The Hampshire estate will then be yours, Winthrop."

"I say!" Matthew's face lit up with pleasure.

"I will tell them that if they ever show their faces in England again I will pass their confessions to the appropriate authorities."

"Thank you," said Estelle. "They do not deserve such compassion."

"No," he whispered so that only she could hear him, "perhaps they do not. But you most assuredly do."

Chapter Sixteen

Alex remained at number seventeen for the rest of the day, alternately refining his plans for the morrow with Mr. Porter and quizzing Matthew and Estelle on the particulars of Farleigh Chase. They drew sketches of the layout at his request, and from them he was able to anticipate potential hurdles which would not even have occurred to Estelle. She was still vexed with him for excluding her from the final confrontation with her father, even if she did privately concede that it was not possible for her to be in two places at once. But more than that, she resented the high-handed manner in which Alex dictated her movements.

She observed him deep in conversation with Mr. Porter and her brother. His brown curls spilled over a brow knotted in concentration, and a vein was pulsing in his temple as he listened to what was being said. Her annoyance slipped away, replaced with a torrent of gratitude for all he was doing for her family, filling her with a sense of well-being. He laughed suddenly at some remark Matthew addressed to him and his features settled into the softer expression he more habitually wore. The manner in which his brown eyes flashed with amusement caused a sharp pang of regret to lance through her. She hastily averted her gaze lest he sensed her watching him and correctly interpreted her thoughts.

Too late! He turned his head just at that precise moment, obviously aware of her scrutiny, and offered her a smile that could have melted stone. She blushed deeply but could not tear her eyes away from his and boldly held his gaze.

Alex declined Mrs. Porter's invitation to dine and left number seventeen in the late afternoon. He was bound for the Albion, where he expected one of his men to be waiting to report to him. Estelle tamped down all thoughts of returning there with him and made do with accompanying him to the door.

"Thank you for all the trouble you are taking," she said, shy suddenly and sounding ridiculously formal. "I want you to know that all three of us are deeply grateful. We never would have been able to manage anything like this unaided."

"You are entirely welcome." He tilted her chin with his forefinger until she was forced to meet his eye. "Have courage, Estelle, we will prevail."

"I do not for a moment doubt it, sir. I have complete faith in your abilities."

"Then what is it? What troubles you?"

What indeed? How to tell him that her thoughts were not currently occupied with the difficulties that would face them all on the morrow? Instead she was anticipating the heartache she would have to endure when she was obliged to say goodbye to him forever.

Estelle was a realist. Susanna might have made an advantageous marriage but lightning seldom struck twice. She might have lost her heart to Lord Crawley—well, there was no *might* about it. But even if she was not so far below him socially, the fact that her father was an amoral scapegrace made the silly notions which refused to budge from her head even more unrealistic. She really she ought to know better. She was the sensible member of the family who did not nurture implausible dreams.

Besides, even if all those matters could be set aside, there were still Lady Crawley's feelings to consider. She was a stickler for maintaining standards. Had she not already told Estelle as much when speculating about the suitability of certain ladies as

Alex's consort? She was a compassionate soul who felt the hardships of others most keenly. But that did not alter the fact that she set considerable stock by her family's social position and would not stand meekly aside and permit her son to weaken it by making an unsuitable alliance.

Enough! Estelle dredged up a timeless smile, turning her head to avoid further contact with Alex's hand.

"Nothing concerns me, other than the fact that you are going to such a vast amount of trouble for us all that I know not how to thank you for it."

"I daresay we shall think of a way, once this is all over." His words were accompanied by a raffish smile that made her feel weak at the knees.

"Is everything just a jest to you, Alex?" she asked him more sharply than she had intended. "Is that why you are doing this? You are bored, did not care for the thought of Lady Jacob's party and seized upon this as a convenient excuse to leave Crawley Hall?"

"Do you really hold me in such low esteem?" He lifted a haughty brow, took her hand and raised it to his lips, only to think the better of it. With a quick glance around the vestibule to ensure no one was observing them, he dropped a delicate kiss on her lips instead, causing her senses to reel with the intensity of the passion she could sense in the gesture.

Ashamed of her outburst, Estelle attempted to formulate an apology. "I did not mean to imply—"

"I know you are disappointed not to be more involved, but you are already fulfilling a vital role by showing yourself in public. I need you to give me your word that you will not do anything rash tomorrow, Estelle. You must promise me that you will call at Nesbit's office and then return directly to this house, where you will remain in your brother's care."

"It is hardly likely that I will be able to do anything more, seeing that I am to be so closely guarded."

"Nevertheless, I still require your promise." He looked down at her, a severe expression in his eye. "If anything were to happen to you, I do not think I could—"

"Oh, very well, I give you my word that I will always conduct myself with your elaborately overprotective instructions in mind. There, satisfied?"

He chuckled. "Thank you, you have set my mind at rest. And when this is over—"

"There is just one thing more we need to resolve before you leave, sir."

Mr. Porter joined them from the front parlour, causing them to jump guiltily apart. Alex transferred the whole of his attention to their interlocutor and she did not see him again that day.

C380

Estelle dressed in her russet travelling attire the following morning for the visit to the solicitor's office. Marianne remarked how well it became her.

"Marriage to that disagreeable old man has done nothing to diminish your beauty," she said, as the sisters finished their toilette.

"Why thank you, Marianne. And being in love has enhanced your own appearance, my love. There is radiance to your complexion and a becoming sparkle in your eye."

"Do you not consider Benjamin to be the handsomest, bravest, cleverest man in the entire world?"

"Indeed I do." Estelle hugged her sister. "It gladdens my heart, after all we have been compelled to endure, to see you so happy."

"Thank you." Marianne grinned, a calculating expression in her eye. "And what of you and the dashing Lord Crawley? He is enamoured of you, I think."

"He is no such thing! He is merely being gentlemanly and doing a service for his best friend's wife."

"Oh, is that why he is so inconveniencing himself? I was wondering."

"Michael Cleethorpe and Lord Crawley are virtually inseparable and, with Susanna being in a delicate condition, Michael does not wish her to be worried about us."

"Ah, that would explain it then."

"Marianne, he is all but engaged to another lady."

"Yes, darling, if you say so."

"Oh!" Estelle threw her hairbrush at her sister. "You are as bad as Susanna. Sometimes there is no talking to either of you. Come along, we shall be late."

They descended the stairs and found Bradley, the footman whom Alex had charged with their care, awaiting them. He was young and reassuringly strong looking, with a cheerful disposition and ready smile. His makeshift livery of green and gold was so like that worn by their father's retainers that even the sisters, who were accustomed to seeing it every day, had difficulty detecting the differences.

"You look very convincing, Bradley," said Estelle.

"Thank you, ma'am. Let us hope that it fools the villains, if they are watching us. Are you ready, ladies?"

Upon learning that they were perfectly ready, Bradley opened the door and looked cautiously up and down the road before ushering them into the cab stationed immediately in front of the door.

"I understand from Lord Crawley that you anticipate being in the solicitor's office for upwards of half an hour," said Bradley.

"That is our expectation." Estelle inclined her head in agreement.

The cab slowed as they neared their destination. "One moment, if you please, ladies." Bradley leapt from the conveyance before it came to a complete halt and scanned the road carefully in both directions. Seeing nothing to excite his suspicions he handed each lady down from the carriage. He escorted them to the door and opened it for them.

"Thank you," said Estelle.

"I shall station myself outside here, ma'am, and be waiting for you. I shall keep a sharp lookout but if anything inside don't look right, just call and I'll come running."

"That is a reassuring thought, Bradley, but I do not anticipate that we shall encounter any difficulties."

"Let's hope not."

Stepping into the anti-room a clerk bowed to the ladies and asked them their business.

"Oh no!" Marianne looked genuinely distressed when they were told that Mr. Nesbit was not expecting them and, indeed, was not in the office at all. "And we have come so far. What are we to do, Estelle?"

Marianne produced a handkerchief and dabbed at her eyes. Estelle knew her sister's tears were the product of laughter rather than distress and kicked her shin. She was grossly overacting but the flustered clerk did not appear to notice. In fact he seemed quite moved by Marianne's wretchedness. He conducted the ladies to a small anteroom and invited them to sit down.

"Perhaps you would care for some tea, ladies, whilst we sort out this unfortunate misunderstanding."

"Thank you. That would be most welcome."

"What if Mr. Cowper is watching us and tries to come in here?" asked Marianne anxiously when the clerk disappeared to arrange their tea.

"Lord Crawley does not think that likely. And remember, we are supposed to be hiding from him at our father's behest. If he doubted that, he might try to follow us, or find a way to grab at least one of us. But by coming here, we will confirm Mr. Porter's claim that we are in the scheme with our father. And so rather than confronting us he will go directly to him with his complaints."

Before Marianne could respond the clerk reappeared with their tea. He was followed by an older gentleman.

"Good morning, ladies." He bowed. "I am Mr. Grant. I regret that you have been inconvenienced but doubtless I can be of service to you in Mr. Nesbit's stead. Indeed, it would be an honour."

"Oh no, sir. I thank you but our father said we were to deal only with Mr. Nesbit." Estelle noticed the downturn in Mr. Grant's expression and treated him to her sweetest smile. "Were it up to us, of course, we would not hesitate to place our trust in you. But as it is—"

"I perfectly understand. Pray do not distress yourselves. Please partake of these refreshments and we will arrange an alternative time for you to see Mr. Nesbit."

"How kind you are, sir."

The ladies emerged, as planned, almost exactly half an hour later.

"That went perfectly to plan," said Estelle as Bradley assisted them into the cab.

"Couldn't be more pleased, ma'am."

He closed the door and signalled to the cabbie to drive on by banging on the roof. So buoyed with success were they that the ladies did not look properly at Bradley, whose face was partially concealed by the brim of his hat, until the cab had lurched away from the pavement. Only then did something coarse in his tone make Estelle glance up suspiciously.

"No!" The feelings of mild euphoria at having conducted their part in the scheme so successfully abruptly gave way to despair.

"Afternoon, Mrs. Travis," said Johnson, her father's right-hand man. He doffed his hat in a mock salute. "Your father will be right pleased with me—two for the price of one. He weren't expecting that."

Wendy Soliman

ᗯᏸᎤ

Upon leaving number seventeen on Sunday evening, Alex walked briskly to the hotel where he had left his phaeton and drove back to the Albion at a leisurely pace. But he was unable to shake off the feeling of unease which had gripped him the moment he left Estelle in her brother's care. He went over the plan countless times in his head, unable to account for the fact that he was only beset with concerns when he considered her part in it. The rational part of his brain told him he had nothing to fear. He had considered all eventualities and made contingency plans for every one of them. But he clearly wasn't in a rational frame of mind and such assurances did little to quell his anxieties.

The girls were required to appear in public only when entering and leaving the cab. Under the watchful eye of Bradley, one of his most dependable servants, nothing could possibly go wrong. When Alex first encountered him at a mill, Bradley had been an angry young man with a grudge against a world that had done him few favours. He was attempting to make a living as a bruiser, all courage and strength, his lack of technique and fiery temper being responsible for the many vicious beatings he had already endured. Alex had sensed something in the battered and bloodied youth that night and, aware that he would be dead within a year if he carried on in such a fashion, compulsively offered him employment. In return he had enjoyed Bradley's unswerving loyalty ever since. Bradley would not be found wanting, Alex assured himself for the fiftieth time.

But the feeling of unease still refused to go away.

What was it about Estelle that so compelled him? She was a beauty, that was undeniable, but so were countless other women of his acquaintance. He had watched with fascination this past week as she slowly emerged from beneath the burden of her sense of duty to spread her wings and allow her independent spirit to flower. But that was nothing to the

200

manner in which she shed her inhibitions when they shared a bed together. He became aroused at the mere thought of it. He chuckled at her prim attempts to deny her need for him, only to abandon them with a speed that defied any true conviction. Such unbridled passion and profound sensuality were a rarity in his extensive experience. But did they account for the protectiveness he now entertained towards the chit? It hardly seemed likely. But the only other explanation he could think of was equally impossible, and at first he refused to even consider it.

Alex was prepared to enter into matrimony now that his father had passed on and he had succeeded him as Viscount Crawley. It was his duty to produce an heir and ensure the succession. His mother's attempts to remind him of the fact by parading a succession of suitable young ladies before him was diverting. He found them all charming, even if they did little to stimulate his intellect, and did not much care which one finally became his viscountess. He was almost willing to let his mother make the final selection on his behalf. After all, she would likely spend more time in his eventual wife's company than he himself expected to, and so the two ladies ought to enjoy one another's society.

He was a realist. He did not believe in undying love, which was why he had tried so hard to dissuade Michael from uniting with Susanna, convinced he would recover from his infatuation and regret his impetuosity. But now?

Was that it? Could the unknown emotion he entertained towards Estelle—the one that was causing him such anguish—really be love? He jerked his team to a clumsy halt, for once mindless of their mouths, as the thought hit him with all the force of one of Bradley's haymakers. Could it really be?

When Susanna had asked him to describe the qualities he most sought in a wife, he had teased her about it, but in reality he could not tell her because he did not know the answer himself. But he did now. His face broke into an unrestrained smile as he acknowledged this unexpected truth. The lady he wished to share his life with was currently engaged in a battle for independence, determined to disengage from a monster of a father who would not hesitate to use any means at his disposal to bend her to his will. Alex hardened his expression even as his determination to keep her safe increased tenfold. His anxieties returned and now that he understood the reason for them, he knew there was nothing he would not do to keep the woman he loved safe.

Upon arrival at the Albion, Alex was confronted by two of the men who had been keeping watch over Cowper.

"He hired a nag and rode down here today, m'lord."

"As we expected then."

"Yeah, except he ain't much of a horseman and I reckon he'll be pretty sore tomorrow."

Alex chuckled. "Where has he put up for the night?"

"A rundown tavern on the wharf. Cheap looking and not at all respectable."

"He should feel right at home then. Has John Coachman arrived with the chaise and four as I instructed?"

"Aye, m'lord."

"Good." Alex had decided that his requirement for fast, reliable transportation now transcended the need for stealth. He was convinced that Winthrop did not know his children were in Ramsgate. It was a calculated risk he was prepared to take that his own presence, and therefore theirs, might be given away by his carriage. By the time Winthrop heard of it he would be too preoccupied with very different concerns to be able to do anything about it. "Get John to take Mr. Cleethorpe's phaeton back to Fairlands in the morning and I will drive the chaise to Hampshire myself."

"Very good, m'lord." The man made to leave the room.

"Oh, and Simmonds."

"M'lord?" The man paused, his hand on the door latch, a look of enquiry on his face.

"Any news to report from Bradley?"

"No, m'lord, were you expecting any?"

Alex, who no longer knew what he was expecting, made no reply and dismissed his servant with a wave of his hand.

The following morning Alex and Porter made an early start. Alex left a message for Porter's employers to the effect that he still required the services of their clerk. He could not afford to delay by waiting to speak to them in person. He drove them both to the village of Farnham, a few miles away from Estelle's family home. They arrived in the late afternoon and put up at the inn there.

"Now we wait for word from Ramsgate," said Alex, who suspected that his expression must be as bleak as he felt at that moment, in spite of his best efforts to portray an appearance of calm. "We need to know what Cowper has done before we reconnoitre."

"All right." Porter paced the room, consulting his pocket watch every few minutes and then peering out of the window in search of Alex's men. "The ladies must have done their part. Let us hope they were convincing."

"I do not doubt that they were."

"I hate this waiting and being idle." Porter had been saying the same thing every two minutes and was driving Alex demented. But he made allowances for a man in love, knowing for himself now what agonies he was suffering, and did not take him to task. "The time passes so slow."

"Make the most of it. We will soon be fully occupied." There was a knock at the door. "Ah good, that will be supper." Alex stood and opened the door himself.

But it was not a maid with their meal. Instead Alex gaped and then emitted a strangled oath as he opened the door wider. Matthew and a bloodied Bradley staggered into the room.

"We came at once," gasped Matthew, who looked ready to collapse with fatigue from the strain placed upon his weakened body by their hasty journey.

"What has happened?"

But he already knew. The lead weight pulling his heart into his boots could only mean one thing, so he was not surprised when Matthew confirmed his worst fears.

"The girls have been abducted."

Chapter Seventeen

The cab stopped in a remote spot some distance from the solicitor's office. Estelle shook off Johnson's hand and alighted from the vehicle without his assistance. She looked about her, any hopes for calling for assistance quickly evaporating. There was not a soul in sight. But that did not mean she intended to surrender without a struggle.

"Help us!" she hissed, tugging at the cabbie's coat and casting an imploring look in his direction. "We are being taken against our will."

The jarvey, engaged in scratching his ear, turned slowly towards her and contemplated her with total disinterest. "Don't look like no abduction to me," he said, clearly having little truck with female histrionics. "You arrived with this gent and seemed comfortable enough then."

"She gets fanciful notions in her head sometimes," said Johnson, breaking in on the conversation. "Pretty as a picture," he added in an undertone, "but not quite all there."

The jarvey nodded his understanding and caught the coin Johnson threw to him. Turning his conveyance, he whipped up his horse and was gone. Estelle clutched Marianne's hand, watching the dust kicked up by the wheels of his cab with a feeling of impending doom. She could feel her sister's entire body trembling, just as her own vibrated with impotent rage, but knew it was important not to reveal the extent of their fear to her father's despised henchman.

"This way ladies, if you please."

Johnson bowed low but his eyes did not once leave them. Even if they attempted to run, they would not get five paces before he overpowered them. With the utmost reluctance, she motioned Marianne to enter their father's waiting chaise and climbed in behind her. The conveyance moved away immediately and they were soon being jolted about at a breakneck pace bound, she had no doubt, for Farleigh Chase. Johnson sat opposite them, making no effort to hide his smug satisfaction. Pretending to straighten Marianne's bonnet, Estelle took the opportunity to whisper in her ear.

"Follow my lead. Do not let him see your fear."

Marianne, eyes round with anguish, lifted her chin and nodded just once.

Estelle's mind was whirling faster than the road sped by beneath the wheels, frantically trying to formulate a plan to regain their freedom. They could hardly rely on Alex to extricate them since it was not safe to assume that word of their abduction would reach him in time. If Bradley had been badly hurt and could not get to number seventeen, then it would take Matthew time to realize something was amiss. Besides, in his weakened state, how would he contrive to raise the alarm? And if Alex launched his assault without being aware that she and Marianne were already in the house, it would give her father the ultimate advantage.

Estelle wondered how she had ever supposed she would succeed in escaping her father's ubiquitous clutches. If she only had herself to worry about, then in all probability she would have eventually bowed to his will, but she now had her sister's happiness to consider and that was altogether another matter.

Marianne stopped trembling and rested her head on Estelle's shoulder, refusing to give Johnson the satisfaction of looking in his direction. Like Estelle, she was pretending not to notice the crude manner in which his eyes raked over their bodies.

"The master will be right pleased with me for bringing you two back." Johnson chuckled. "Shouldn't wonder if he don't offer me a handsome reward."

"I would advise against such speculation, Johnson," said Estelle, "since we shall not remain at the Chase for long."

"I sure do hope you continue to go against him. If you do that he'll likely wash his hands of you and then you'll be mine." He made smacking noises of approval with his lips.

Estelle made no attempt to hide her revulsion. "If that is what you imagine, it is not me who is light in the attic."

Johnson bridled at the insult, just as she had known he would, and silence once again reined in the carriage. Estelle allowed her thoughts to wander. Of late she had discovered a taste for fighting back, which showed no immediate signs of abating. She would *not* be intimidated into doing as her father wished. However unpalatable his punishments, she would take them, without giving him the satisfaction of showing any emotion, and wait until he relaxed his guard.

As soon as they arrived at Farleigh Chase, the girls were ushered straight into their father's study. Estelle shook Johnson's loathsome hand from her shoulder and walked into the room, head held high as though she was doing so from choice.

Her father looked up, his temporary expression of surprise at seeing not one but both of his daughters standing before him quickly replaced by one of calculating satisfaction. "You have exceeded my expectations, Johnson. Well done indeed! I will see you suitably rewarded later."

"Very good, sir." Johnson moved towards the door, casting a predatory look towards Estelle as he did so.

"Well," demanded their father as soon as they were alone. "What have you both to say for yourselves?"

"What would you have us say, Father?" asked Estelle.

Wendy Soliman

"You would do well to remember where you are and to whom you are speaking, my girl. You are no longer in a position to feign independence."

Estelle looked about her with an expression of disinterest which she knew would give her father pause. "I am hardly likely to forget either of those factors, unfortunately."

"Where have you been?"

"I am of age, Father, and my whereabouts are no concern of yours."

"By God, girl, I don't know who has been putting such undutiful notions into your head but I shall soon knock them out of you."

"Violence, Father?" Estelle raised a brow in a manner intended to intimidate. It was a ploy she had observed Alex use to advantage. "Is that still your answer to everything?"

"You forget yourself, Estelle!" Her father's fleshy jowls were red with anger. "However, provided you can assure me that you will, both of you, behave in accordance with my wishes in future, we shall say no more about it. Cowper can take his pick now. I do not doubt that you will be his choice, Estelle, in which case I shall find someone else for Marianne."

"I shall not marry anyone of your choosing!" Marianne spoke for the first time since confronting her father, her eyes sparkling with defiance. "And there is no use you thinking I shall. There is nothing you can do to make me."

"Be quiet, girl, and speak when spoken to." He looked Marianne up and down in much the same insolent fashion as Johnson had done. "You are an attractive chit and if you would only learn to curb your tongue, you could be a great asset to your family."

"I will not be quiet and you can do nothing to compel me. All your bullying and threats will have no effect upon me."

He slapped her face. Marianne cried out and cradled her flaming cheek with her hand. He then rang the bell, which was answered so quickly by Martha that she could only have been

208

waiting in the hall to the summoned. She had a malicious glint in her eye as she dropped an ironic curtsey to her mistress.

"Take them up to the nursery and lock them in," said her father. "If they wish to behave like badly behaved children then that is how they will be treated until such time as they remember where their duty lies."

"This way, ladies," said Martha, cackling.

"Keep your hands off me." Estelle shook her shoulder free of Martha's claw-like hand, lifted her skirts and mounted the stairs with as much dignity as she could muster. Aware that half the servants seemed to have made excuses to be in the hall and observe their fall from grace, she willed Marianne to follow her example.

Upon reaching the nursery Martha sullenly offered them both a drink of tea, which had just been brought up by a maid.

"Nice accommodation," Martha taunted. The austere room smelt musty from disuse and did not even have a fire lit to take the chill out of the air. "For two such fine ladies, that is. Just goes to show, you never know when you're well off until it's too late." She poured a cup of tea and handed it to Marianne, who drank deeply.

"Be silent, Martha," Estelle said in a tone she had always wanted to use with her maid but had never dared to in the past. It worked, albeit briefly, as Martha glared at her with a mixture of surprise and hostility.

"No need to get so uppity, miss, not if you know what's good for you. I shall be your only contact with the outside world until you come to your senses and do as your father tells you, so it don't do to get on my wrong side."

"I don't feel well," said Marianne.

Estelle turned to her sister with concern. "What is it, darling?"

"I don't know. I..."

The cup fell from her grasp and Estelle only just managed to catch her before she crumpled to the floor. Half-dragging

Marianne's inert form, she managed to get her to the closer of the two beds.

"Help me!"

Martha took her time coming across to lift Marianne's legs and lay her on the bed.

"What have you done to her?"

"Just something to make her sleep."

"How dare you! You have gone too far this time. My father shall hear of this."

"It was your father's orders. Don't blame me, 'cause unlike some I could name, I only do what I'm told. She'll sleep like a baby for hours and wake none the worse for the experience."

"Why her? Was I destined for the same treatment?"

"No, as far as I know he wants to talk to you without her influencing you."

"He could have just sent for me alone."

"And you would have come back here and she would have persuaded you to rebellion. No, I can see his reasoning. You were always willing to do as you were told until you got back with her, and certain others I could name."

"You forget yourself, Martha."

The old woman chuckled. "Nah, I've always known who I am. But can you say the same, your majesty?" She turned to leave the room. "Help yourself to tea, there ain't anything in the pot, it was just in her cup. Oh, and don't get any fancy ideas, there's no way out of here. It's a clear drop out of that window. You'd break yer neck if you tried it. The door'll be locked and 'tis only me as has the key." She let herself out. "Sweet dreams, m'lady." Cackling, she took herself off down the corridor.

Having no wish to dwell upon her desperate straits, Estelle busied herself by removing Marianne's bonnet, gloves, pelisse and boots. She tucked the covers up to her chin and made her as comfortable as she could. The coldness of the room was starting to get through to Estelle and she wrapped her arms round her torso in a futile attempt to keep herself warm. There was nothing to read, no form of occupation and nothing for her to do except think. She poured a half cup of now lukewarm tea and sipped cautiously at it. When she experienced no ill-effects she refilled her cup, aware that she would require all the strength she could muster if she was to somehow prevail.

Feeling refreshed, she stripped off her outer garments and lay beneath the covers on the adjoining bed. If she was a little warmer, perhaps she would be able to think more coherently. It did indeed appear hopeless and she was discouraged at the thought of being trapped in this hateful room, at the mercy of her father's mercurial whim. Had he confined them to the room they had shared as girls on the first floor, escape would have been comparatively easy. But he had obviously learned to be cautious.

She was unsure how long she had lain there, pondering upon the futility of their situation, when she heard a key in the door and assumed it to be Martha. But instead her father's bulky figure loomed large over her.

"Are you awake, Estelle?"

She did not want to have anything to do to him. She certainly had nothing to say to him that he would want to hear, but she knew he would not go away until he had said what he had come to say. Reluctantly she turned her head in his direction.

"I am awake. How could I possibly sleep in this chill?"

"That is easily resolved. All that is required is that you give me your word you will marry Cowper when your period of mourning expires, and every comfort at my disposal will be yours to enjoy."

"What is to prevent me from giving you my word and then reneging?"

Her father waved away the suggestion. "I know you too well to be concerned on that score. You might well have developed a temporary rebellious streak, which is partly my fault, I can see

211

that now. It was insensitive of me to spring my plans on you in the manner I did when you were still lamenting the loss of your child. Not all women possess your mother's stoic nature and I should have taken that into account."

Estelle gaped at her father. He *never* admitted to being in the wrong, and this was as close to an apology as she had ever known him to come.

"However, your word is your bond," he said, looking alarmingly self-assured, "and once given you would never retract it, no matter that you might give it under duress."

"And if I do not do as you ask, I too will be drugged and imprisoned against my will, I suppose." Her eyes swivelled to take in the inert form of her sister. Anger at his treatment of her rekindled her temper.

"She will be none the worse for the experience and perhaps it will teach her a little respect."

"You are a monster!"

"And you owe me an answer. What is it to be?"

"You already have my answer. I gave it to you when you came to Hertfordshire and nothing has changed. I will not marry that man."

"This is becoming tiresome," said Winthrop with a heavy sigh.

"I do not understand your obsession with Mr. Cowper. What does he have that you covet enough to sacrifice one of us?"

She was watching her father closely and thought she saw a mixture of surprise and alarm flare briefly in his eyes.

"That is not for you to concern yourself with." But he did not bother to deny the assertion. "Now, I ask you one last time, will you do as I ask?"

"No, never. I would die first!"

"And there is nothing I can say to persuade you?"

"Nothing at all."

"Think of the duty you owe to me as your father. Everything I have done to amass a fortune has been done for the three of you. And what thanks do I get for the sacrifices I have made, eh? Answer me that if you can?"

"You speak of the duty and honour due to you from your children, Father, but what of the love and understanding you ought to show to us? Do you rejoice in making us unhappy, turning us against you and driving us away, one by one?" Her voiced softened. "It should not be so, Papa."

"Stuff and nonsense, child. I live in the real world, which is harsh and unforgiving, and has no place for sentiment." He glanced at Marianne. "If I were to allow your sister to choose her own husband, would you then be more receptive to my suggestion? You claim to love Marianne and want only what is best for her. Prove to me that you mean it."

"No, Father, I would not consider it, not even then." Estelle knew that, unlike her, her father's word was most definitely not his bond. He would say anything, make all manner of promises he had no intention of keeping, just to get his way.

"What has happened to you, Estelle? Who has turned your head to the extent that you no longer remember your responsibilities?"

"No one. I have merely got to the age where I know my own mind."

"No, it is something more than that, I should have seen it before now. There is something different about you. You have changed in a more fundamental way." He regarded her pensively. "Is it that Crawley man?"

"No," she said a little too quickly.

"It is! That's it." His countenance was puce with rage. "Damn me, I knew it had to be something of that nature—I just knew it. Estelle, I credited you with more sense. The man is pretending an affection simply to get what he wants from you, nothing more."

213

"You know nothing about the matter, sir. Do not judge others by your own miserable standards."

"Ah, so he *has* got you thinking the impossible. He has befriended you for one reason and one reason only. God alone knows, I am ambitious for my ungrateful children, but even I know that aristocrats of his ilk use women like you for one purpose. They do not marry them, Estelle. Not ever."

"You are making the mistake of supposing that I wish to be married again, which I most emphatically do not." She smiled, intent upon a modicum of revenge. "Perhaps I am simply content to enjoy his protection."

"Has he dared to touch you?" When she refused to answer, he slapped her face hard, just as he had done Marianne's earlier. "You jade! The women walking the streets ply their trade out of necessity, but you...you have never wanted for anything. And yet you have always pretended a superiority and looked down upon your father. But now I find you have lifted your skirts for the first man who smiles at you. You disgust me!" Spittle dribbled down his chin but he did not appear to notice. "I suppose he was setting you up as his mistress, which is what you were doing in that solicitor's office today. Well, you can forget all about that. You will not be leaving this house, or going anywhere unescorted, until you agree to marry Cowper."

"Which I will never do," she retorted, as angry now as he was. "You can rant and rail, threaten and cajole in your usual brutish manner, but nothing will make me agree to your terms." She smiled, unafraid of him for the first time in her life, and revelled in the feeling of liberation as she stood up to him. "You see, I am aware now of what I would be missing should I ever again allow another man to touch me."

She expected him to explode with anger but instead he simply shook his head. And then, with a dexterity unusual for such a large man, he grabbed her arm and pushed her face down on the bed. Lifting her skirts, he used every ounce of his considerable strength as he smacked her bare backside. The pain was excruciating but she bit on the counterpane beneath her, refusing to give him the satisfaction of hearing her cry out.

"So, you think you know enough of the world to be able to defy me, do you?" *Smack.* The sound of his hand brutalizing her bare flesh echoed round the room. "You imagine I am not awake enough on all suits to get the better of a mere slip of a girl?" *Smack.* "If you continue your act of bravado, you will receive this punishment and worse on a daily basis until you do as I wish." *Smack.* He paused, breathing hard from his exertions. "You will have naught but bread and water to sustain you. I will take your sister away from you and you will see no one except Martha and me until you come to your senses. Is that clearly understood?" When she did not answer him he hit her harder still. "Answer me when I speak to you, girl, or you will live to regret it."

"Yes."

"Yes what? I cannot hear you, Estelle."

"Yes, sir."

"And you will think on what I have said to you? Think of the benefits to your sister if you make this small sacrifice?"

She nodded, not trusting herself to speak.

"Very well. I will leave you to reflect. But just remember this, Estelle. If you do not do as I ask, then you are no use to me and I might just as well give you to Johnson. God alone knows he desires you, as any man in his right mind would, and he deserves a reward—because unlike you and your siblings, he understands the meaning of loyalty."

With a final vicious flurry of his open palm, he released his hold on her. Estelle turned her head and looked at him contemptuously, annoyed because tears had sprung to her eyes even though she stubbornly refused to allow them to fall.

What she saw in her father's gaze shocked and disturbed her far more than the thrashing he had just administered. His eyes were glued to her, his breath was coming in short gasps and his face was purple—with excitement rather than rage. He had enjoyed hitting her and could, had he so wished, have done anything else with her that took his fancy. He knew it and wanted her to know it too. He wanted her to understand that he had complete authority over every aspect of her life.

Estelle shuddered with disgust, and real fear, and was the first to look away.

Chapter Eighteen

"My God, Marianne!" Porter clutched his head in his hands and fell despondently into a chair. "He will kill her for sure. What in God's name have we set in motion?"

Alex hid his dismay a little better as the full extent of his folly hit him. He resisted the urge to punch his fist through the wainscoting only by exercising the severest restraint. How could he not have anticipated something like this, he who had worried over every other detail of their plan? He had had an uneasy feeling about Estelle since leaving her yesterday. He ought to have set six men to guard the ladies, not a mere one. He was an arrogant fool who could not be trusted to lace his own boots, much less meddle in other people's lives.

"Tell me all that happened, Bradley." His voice betrayed none of his inner turmoil. If he was to rescue the girls, he must put his emotions aside and focus dispassionately upon finding the best way to go about it.

"Well, I took the ladies to the solicitor's office and everything went according to plan. Once they were inside, I stationed myself at the door and kept a sharp lookout but didn't see anything to arouse my suspicions. Then, just as I was starting to think it was time for the ladies to reappear, some cove barged into me. He apologized for being clumsy and in the second I took my eyes off the door something hard bashed the back of my head." He shrugged and looked acutely embarrassed at having been so easily duped. "Beg pardon, m'lord. I should have realized at once that it was a sham."

"Never mind that now, just tell me everything you can remember."

"Well, the next thing I knew I was waking up several streets away with a headache. There was a crowd of people gathered round me, gawping and asking if I was all right."

"I suppose no one else saw what happened."

"Nah, like I said, they had moved me away from the solicitor's door and must have substituted someone else in my place. I wasn't unconscious for long but as soon as I regained my senses and staggered back to Nesbit's office, the cab had long gone, with the ladies in it."

"And you are sure nothing is broken in that head of yours?" Alex was aware that his retainer had only been injured because he was following his ill-thought-out orders.

"Yeah, they hit me a right cruncher and no mistake, but luckily I've got a tough skull. If that wasn't the case, I'd never have survived all the facers I've received in my time." He looked angry and upset. "The only real damage is to my pride, m'lord. You entrusted me with the ladies' care and I failed you."

"Not your fault, Bradley."

"Who has them, do you suppose?" asked Porter.

"Their father, in all probability. They are most likely already at Farleigh Chase."

"That is what I thought too," said Matthew. "Which is why I said to Bradley that we ought to come here directly and let you know what had happened."

"Good thing you did." Alex stroked his chin in thoughtful contemplation. "It changes things, of course."

"Yes, it gives Father the edge."

"You do not suppose that Cowper has taken them then?" said Porter.

"Doubtful, because this time yesterday he did not even know for sure that they were in Ramsgate. We know he travelled there alone on horseback and he simply would not have had time to organize their abduction. Besides, I doubt if he possesses sufficient wits to devise such a scheme. No, when he saw them in Ramsgate he would have believed them to be in league with their father. He also would have had to accept that neither of them ever had any real intention of marrying him when Winthrop was supposed to be promoting the matches."

"Which would infuriate him," said Matthew.

"Quite. But it would also make him appreciate that he had little chance of inducing either of them through force. He must now be thinking that the only way to bring a wedding about is by confronting Winthrop and putting more pressure on him."

"Yes, that is true." Porter appeared to have recovered from the initial shock and regained a modicum of composure. "Unless he imagined the threat to their reputations might persuade one to sacrifice herself for the sake of the other."

"No, Winthrop has them," said Alex with determination. "I would wager my fortune on the fact."

"But how did he know where they were?" asked Matthew.

"How indeed? I know for a fact that he did not follow us from Crawley Hall and so how the devil..." Alex thumped his thigh with a clenched fist and swore. "God's teeth, I have been a knucklehead! I was getting so carried away with devising a plan to confront Winthrop that I forgot to be cautious."

"I do not see how," said Matthew with a perplexed frown. "You considered every eventuality."

"No, I did not. Winthrop suspected I knew where Estelle was and surmised that she was either hiding at Crawley Hall or with me somewhere else. And so what would you do if you were him, gentlemen?"

"Have you followed," suggested Porter tentatively.

"Exactly, but as he had no idea where I was, he did the next best thing and kept a watch on Crawley Hall. He hoped

Estelle would learn he had quit the local inn and would show herself, enabling him to spirit her away. Failing that, he was depending upon me to lead him to her, which is precisely what I did."

"No, you didn't," said Matthew, "because she wasn't at Crawley Hall."

"No more was she, but don't forget I have an establishment in London as well."

"Of course, now I know how they did it," said Porter. "We stayed at your house after I confronted Cowper, so Winthrop's spy must have followed us when we returned to Ramsgate."

"Indeed. Damn it, how could I have been so careless?"

"Do not be so hard on yourself, my lord." Matthew had regained a little colour now. "You were not to have known."

"No, but I should have anticipated the possibility. It is just what I would have done in Winthrop's place. I have been a blind, arrogant fool, too full of my glorious plans to see what was before my very nose."

"If they followed us back to Ramsgate, they must have known the ladies were at my mother's house," said Benjamin, unable to keep the concern from his voice.

"I think not. You will recall that we delivered my equipage to the mews at the Royal Oak and took a cab back to your premises, precisely to ensure that we were not followed. It would be difficult to follow a cab without detection on a relatively quiet Sunday morning and no one attempted it because I was watching."

"Yes, I recall that you were on your guard the whole time."

"But they still would not have known whether we had any connection with the ladies. They must have simply spread your description about and asked anyone who would talk to them if you were known locally."

"And if they made enquiries in the tap room at the Royal Oak, they would soon have learned where I am employed," said

Benjamin. "Fortunately they would not have found out where I reside through that means."

"Well," said Alex, "that clears up that part of the mystery."

There was a tap at the door. Another of Alex's men reported that Cowper had returned to Wapping, called at a solicitor's office and emerged with a bundle of papers.

"But we were unable to approach him, m'lord." The man shuffled his feet in embarrassment. "He had a hired post chaise waiting right outside the door and got into it before we could get to him."

"Damn it!" Alex raked his fingers through his hair in frustration. "Things just keep getting better and better."

"Does it matter?" asked Matthew. "We knew there was a possibility of not obtaining the papers in advance."

"True, but I should have liked to know what they contain." He turned to face his man again. "Do you know where he went in the chaise?"

"Yes, m'lord, we heard him direct the driver to take him to Hampshire with all due dispatch."

"So what do we do now?" asked Benjamin.

"We go to Farleigh Chase, of course," said Alex with an air of grim determination, "and rescue the ladies."

C8Ю

Estelle did not move for a long time after her father left her, locking the door behind him, and only eventually did so when Marianne mumbled in her sleep. She winced with the pain that simply moving her legs occasioned, feeling deeply humiliated as a consequence of her thrashing. But far from persuading her to her father's point of view, it had only made her more determined than ever to find a way to escape.

Marianne turned on her side and showed no immediate signs of waking. Reassured that she was not in any discomfort,

Estelle patted her cheek and left her to her slumbers. Just for a moment she wished that she too was unconscious and could postpone facing the grim reality of their situation.

She wondered how to assess the damage her father had inflicted upon her but did not have the strength to attempt it. There was no means of washing herself in this barren room and she would die before she asked Martha to attend to the matter. Lying face down on her bed, her mind whirling with unrealistic escape plans, she must have dozed.

The sound of Marianne's weak voice calling for her took some time to penetrate her sleep-fuelled brain. She had only just managed to stand and go to her sister when a key sounded in the lock. Martha entered the room carrying a tray laden with bread and water.

Estelle haughtily declined but, judging from the croaking nature of her sister's voice, Marianne was sorely in need of water. She sipped delicately at a sample from the jug to satisfy herself that it was safe before pouring her sister a glass. Marianne took just two sips before promptly passing out again.

"You witch, you have done it to her again! Why?"

For the first time in her life, Estelle lost her temper with another human being. Ignoring the pain from her beating, she sprang at the maid like a wildcat, memories of all the humiliations she had suffered at this woman's hands lending her superhuman strength. Taken by surprise, Martha, who although older than Estelle was a lot stronger, fell to the ground, banging her head on the hard boards. She blinked and looked up at her attacker with a vacant, dazed expression. Thinking she had triumphed, Estelle made the mistake of releasing her hold on the woman's arms as she tried to decide what to do next.

Martha, with a feral scream of rage, took immediate advantage of Estelle's vacillation. Punching Estelle's side hard enough to take her breath away, she struggled to regain her feet. Estelle responded instinctively and snaked out a hand, grabbing Martha's ankle and bringing her to the floor, where she landed heavily and did not immediately move. Making the most of her brief advantage, Estelle grabbed the glass which Marianne had just drunk from and, forcing her captive's mouth open, tried to pour its contents down her throat.

"Don't!" Martha twisted her head violently from side to side. "For the love of God, I was only doing what I was told."

"And enjoying it far too much. Just see how you like it, you spiteful bawd!"

Martha struggled like a demon, kicking and gouging at any part of Estelle's body she could reach. Estelle held her down by sitting on her and again prized her mouth open, narrowly avoiding her gnashing teeth. Martha repeatedly spat out the contaminated water but obviously could not avoid swallowing enough to be effective. Her struggles became weaker and she quickly lost consciousness.

Estelle, grunting with satisfaction, dragged her hated maid towards the other bed. She tied her hands firmly with a pillow case, gagged her mouth by the same means, and secured her bound hands to the bed head, making no attempt to be gentle. If one sip of the potion was guaranteed to knock Marianne out for hours, then the same must be true of Martha, and she would not wake up until morning. But Estelle did not intend to take any chances. Besides, she was rather enjoying extracting a modicum of revenge for all the insults and degradations she had been compelled to endure at the woman's hands over the past year.

She hastily formulated a plan and stripped Martha of her uniform, donning the plain cap and hoping it would keep her wayward curls in check. The woollen skirt was far too large but would have to serve. The white apron effectively covered the bodice of her travelling gown. Taking the key to the room from the pocket of the skirt, she slipped quietly from the room, carrying the tray which had borne their supper in front of her. She had no idea what time it could be but judged that it must be after dinner, in which case few servants would still be about.

She remembered at the last minute to take the back stairs and discovered she was in luck. The butler, Dowling, was in his pantry working his way through what looked to be a decanter of her father's best brandy. Estelle did not think he saw her but even if he did happen to glance up, he would only observe the back of her head as she passed the high pantry window. She was about the same height as Martha and he would assume it was she.

Cook nodded to her as they passed one another in the narrow passageway to the kitchen. Estelle's heart leapt to her throat when the woman paused to speak with her. Fortunately cook's eyesight was not as good as it had once been and in the dimness of the passage she saw merely what she expected to see, which was Martha in her maid's uniform returning used crockery to the kitchen.

"Any problems?" she asked.

"No, none," said Estelle in a deep, surly voice, hoping she had made it sound vaguely like Martha's. She kept her head lowered and turned slightly away.

"Good night then. There is just Mr. Dowling left in his pantry and he is well into his cups." Cook rolled her eyes expressively. "The master has a visitor. Mr. Cowper already come to chase one of the girls, I shouldn't wonder. Mr. Dowling showed him in just a few minutes ago and has been told he's not needed any more tonight. Goings on that the master doesn't want any of us to overhear, I shouldn't wonder," she said, with a significant nod in the direction of the green baize door and her employer's study beyond it. She said goodnight again and shuffled off to her own quarters.

Estelle thought quickly. If Cowper was here already, there was no time to spare. She unbolted the door to the cellar, wondering if Alex was here yet, but rather doubting he would have troubled to re-bolt the door if he was. Her thoughts then turned to the problem of Mr. Dowling. He might be jug-bitten but even he was hardly likely to overlook a posse of strangers traipsing through the kitchen, however stealthily they might endeavour to move. There was no help for it. She would just have to incapacitate him.

She grabbed the first weapon that came to hand, a sturdy copper-bottomed pan. It was so heavy, it required both of her hands to raise it above her head. She crept up behind the drowsy Dowling. Steeling herself to do what had to be done, she wondered how much pressure it would require.

Before she could make up her mind, a strong hand gripped her wrist and another clamped over her mouth to prevent her from screaming. She was dragged backwards by what she presumed was one of her father's men.

She slumped against her attacker, her energy spent. She was trying to decide whether to make one final bid for freedom by biting the hand that covered her mouth when a voice she would have known anywhere whispered softly in her ear.

"Estelle, what in the name of Hades were you about to do with that pan?"

Chapter Nineteen

"Alex!"

Estelle flung her arms round his neck. She was so relieved to see him that she did not care what the others pouring through the cellar door thought of her unorthodox behaviour.

Alex indicated the butler with his eyes. Bradley and another of his men stealthily approached him from behind, binding and gagging the intoxicated servant before he had time to blink his eyes and demand an explanation for this intrusion into his sacred domain.

"Are you all right?" Alex held Estelle at arm's length and examined her face.

"Yes, I thank you, we are unharmed."

"And Marianne?" Mr. Porter's eyes scanned the room as though expecting her to materialize from some dim recess and hurtle herself into his arms.

"She is upstairs, unharmed but asleep. My father ordered a sleeping draught to be administered to her."

"I must go to her."

"Not now, Porter." Alex's authoritative tone stopped him in his tracks. "She is safe and better off out of this. Leave her be until we have seen to the rest of the business. Is Cowper here, do you know?"

"He arrived a few minutes ago."

"Then there is no time to lose. Was it you who unlocked the cellar door?"

"Yes, I thought it might help."

"Your intuition served you well. It is stouter than I had anticipated and we have wasted valuable time trying to get it open. We could not break it down without giving ourselves away but I was getting desperate. I knew Cowper arrived at the front lodge some time ago, and I was about to resort to kicking it in when I heard the bolt slide back." He smiled into her eyes, his expression full of admiration for her quick thinking. "Nice outfit," he whispered, a wicked lilt to his tone. "It could give a man ideas."

"I shall use the pan on your head if you do not behave," she said severely, unable to keep the smile out of her voice.

"Is there anyone else abroad?"

"No, they are all abed."

"Good, then let us to it."

"Are you all right, Mr. Bradley?" she asked as Alex's servant came up on her other side. "You appear to have a rather nasty bump on your head."

"Not nearly so bad as the master would have given me if we hadn't found you safe and well, ma'am," he said with a cheerful grin.

"Fortunately he has a very thick head and is none the worse for his experience," said Alex. "Come, all of you."

Taking Estelle's hand he allowed her to lead them into the hall. At a motion from Alex, Matthew turned the key silently in the lock of his father's study and pocketed it. If things got out of hand neither man would now be able to escape through that door. They all paused to listen to the voices coming from the room, relieved to hear the two men exchanging civilities and the sound of glasses being filled.

"We are just in time, I think. It does not sound as though they have started discussing the reason for Cowper's visit yet."

Alex followed Estelle into the next room and cautiously opening the adjoining door a few inches.

She stripped off the maid's uniform to reveal her travelling gown beneath it. Impatiently pulling the cap from her head caused pins to fly in all directions and her hair to tumble round her shoulders.

Alex stared at her with a slow, appreciative smile spreading across his lips that made her blush deeply. "What are you doing?"

"I have no intention of confronting my father dressed as a maid." She tried hard to compose her features into an expression of disapproval as he continued to stare at her tangled hair but was aware that her reproachful attitude lacked true conviction.

"Spoilsport!"

He relieved her of the apron which she was holding behind her back. His hand briefly made contact with her body, causing her to wince.

"What is the matter? Are you hurt?" He whispered the words for fear of being overheard by the men in the adjoining room.

Ashamed and humiliated, she could not meet his eye and stared intently at the floor.

"You are." His flirtatious expression gave way to one of fulminating anger. "He did this to you? Estelle, look at me. Tell me who harmed you."

Estelle still could not meet his gaze and merely nodded once. Alex paced out his agitation in front of the empty fireplace, clenching his fists and swearing beneath his breath. She had never seen him lose his temper before and wondered why the knowledge that her father had chastised her should cause him such anguish. After all, he knew what sort of man he was.

Her father's mocking voice reverberated inside her head, reminding her that Lord Crawley would never make an alliance with a creature of such lowly social standing as her. She had known that, of course. But knowing it and hearing it put into words by a third party was altogether another matter.

She chanced a glance at Alex's noble profile. His brow was creased in an expression of concentrated fury, his eyes were as black as obsidian, and he was grinding his teeth as he struggled to control his temper. Her heart swelled with love for this complex yet compelling gentleman who had been part of her life for just a few days but whom she could no longer imagine living without.

Perhaps her father had been right about Alex's intentions. If his anger now was anything to go by, he did have feelings for her and meant to make her his mistress. If her father was right about that, then he was right about something else too. She had changed beyond recognition from the person she used to be just a few short months ago. If Alex wished her to live beneath his protection, far from being shocked by the suggestion, she would agree without hesitation. Having a part of him—for as long as it took him to get bored with her—would be far better than being excluded from his life altogether.

"By all that's holy, Estelle," Alex exploded, "he will pay for his iniquitous deeds before this night is out!"

"Shush!" Estelle, astonished by the outburst, recalled him to the business in hand. "They have settled with their drinks and I think I heard my father ask Cowper what had promoted a visit at such a late hour."

They crowded round the slightly open door and listened.

"Have you been playing it straight with me, sir?" they heard Cowper ask.

"What the devil are you talking about, man?"

"So, Mrs. Travis and her sister are missing, are they?"

"Yes they were, but—"

"And you were doing everything in your power to find them?"

"You know damn well that I was. I am in no mood for games, Cowper. You did not come here this late just to talk about my daughters, so out with it, man. What is it that could not wait until a more social hour?"

"All right then, I'll say it plain. You have been playing me for a fool, Winthrop. I should have thought you would have known better than to try it, aware as you are of what I'm capable of when roused."

"I have had the very devil of a day and I don't need you coming here with wild eyes flashing accusations, talking in riddles."

"You have known all along where your daughters were and deliberately pretended they had absconded so that neither of them could marry me. I would then assume you had done everything in your power to persuade them and feel duty bound to hand over the papers you want so much to possess. And I right?"

"Not only are you wrong but you are completely out of your mind."

"Am I? Then why were your daughters seen together in Ramsgate this very morning entering a solicitor's office?" Cowper paused. "Nothing to say for yourself, Winthrop? You don't know anything about it, is that what you would have me believe? Well, it won't serve and—"

"Poppycock! They—"

"No, don't interrupt me, for I know it all and it is useless your denying it. You promised to split your fortune between the two girls if they did as you asked. That is why they attended an out-of-the-way solicitor today, where they were unlikely to be recognized, to sign the papers and seal the agreement."

"Do you not know me better than that?"

"You are very convincing, Winthrop, I'll give you that. Were it not for the fact that I saw them there myself I might almost be persuaded to believe you."

"You saw them there and so did Johnson. He brought them home and they are upstairs now. That is what I was trying to explain to you when you first brought their names into this ridiculous conversation and started on your groundless rant."

"Huh, do not think to play me for such a clunch. I have your measure. If the girls are upstairs it is only because you ordered them to come home as soon as their business in Ramsgate was complete."

"Indeed it is not. You know nothing about it."

"Then send for Mrs. Travis. I will hear it from her own lips that she intends to marry me."

"I cannot do that," said Winthrop with transparent reluctance.

"Because she is not here. Huh, I thought as much. You are still trying to gull me."

"She is here but she is not yet ready to think about marriage."

"And I cannot afford to wait. As you know, if we do not register our find at the Patents Office very soon then someone else will beat us to it."

"Look, Cowper, I have given you my word that you can have Estelle and I will not go back on it. But if you know anything about women you will also appreciate that they get silly romantic notions in their heads about matrimony and cannot be rushed into it. She will come round in time. You will just have to take my word for it. Besides, she is still in mourning and cannot marry you for another nine months, and if we wait that long Aspdin will definitely steal a march on us. Come man, get your head out of the clouds and remember that which is really important. This discovery will set us up for life."

"I am aware that I must wait for her but if I hear Mrs. Travis agree to the engagement with her own lips then I will accept her word for it."

"I have already told you, she is not ready to commit herself yet." The listeners heard Winthrop sigh, as though holding on to his patience by the merest thread. "If I were to give you my assurance in writing that the union will take place, will that satisfy you?"

"No, Mrs. Travis is of age and you can no longer speak for her."

"Calm down, Cowper, and tell me how far ahead Aspdin is with his patent application."

"He is almost ready to submit it but is a perfectionist and has a few refinements that he wishes to make before he does so."

"Damn the refinements! For God's sake man, we must beat him to it. Surely you can appreciate that? Cement of the type Aspdin has invented is inspirational. Burning ground limestone and clay together is a stroke of genius. It has created a much stronger finished product than crushed limestone on its own. Think of the demand there will be in Leeds alone, what with the redevelopment of the waterfront. I will be able to undercut the other bidders and produce better buildings as well, which will promote further business. And the requirement for more and cheaper housing will spread throughout the country, you just mark my words. And we can be at the forefront of it all, raking in the money. Come on, Cowper, don't let your lust for my daughter govern your brain."

"I know you are desperate to refill your coffers and set yourself up as a real connoisseur of the arts." Cowper's voice dripped with scorn. "But I will not be gulled, do you hear me? If your daughters were not at that solicitor's office at your specific request, then what were they doing there, uh?"

"I haven't a clue since I have never set foot in the place myself."

"Really? Then how did the clerk who tipped me the wink know about Travis being helped on his way to the next world?"

Estelle gasped audibly. She had not wanted to believe that her father and Cowper had actually gone that far. Alex squeezed her hand and quieted her by placing a finger gently against her lips.

"For the love of God, lower your voice, Cowper," said Winthrop, sounding shocked. "He cannot have known. He must have made it up in order to trick money out of you. I assume you did pay him?"

"That does not account for him having invented such a story. I do not believe in such coincidences, so how could he have known?'

"How do you expect me to answer that?" Winthrop's voice resonated with anger—and underlying fear. "Only you, I and Sir James know of the scheme. When I purchased Sir James's vowels from the moneylender I was exceedingly cautious and the purchase cannot be traced back to me. And did you not approach Sir James anonymously? Did he ever learn your identity?"

"No, of course not. That was part of the deal. He did not care, as long as he got his vowels back."

"Well, then. Sir James has good reason to keep his part quiet, so no one could know. They are simply guessing. Someone is trying to scare you into doing something stupid, like confronting me with these Banbury tales. They are trying to drive a wedge between us for some reason that currently escapes me. And you have fallen for the ploy with tedious predictability."

"I might accept that," said Cowper, sounding slightly placated, "but for the fact that the ladies *were* at that office this morning."

"And now they are here and will not escape me again."

"But that does not put us any further forward if Mrs. Travis will not entertain my suit."

"God's teeth, man, give her time!"

"No, I have risked too much for her sake and will have my answer now. I arranged to have her husband killed because you persuaded me—"

"Travis is no great loss. He was always at me for money and then gambled it away. And his son was no better. He hankered after Estelle too, you know."

"The devil he did!" They could hear Cowper pacing out his agitation. "I must know what the ladies were doing at that office this morning. I will not rest easy until that has been explained. Given what's at stake, I should have thought you would feel the same way."

"Lord Crawley is behind this. I would wager everything I own on that fact."

Estelle felt Alex tense at the mention of his name.

"Explain yourself," snapped Cowper.

"Estelle was staying with that interfering friend of hers, Mrs. Cleethorpe, and met Viscount Crawley there. I believe, although she will not confirm or deny it, that he was taken with Estelle and offered her a *carte-blanche*."

"And you have not made her tell you if this is true? What sort of father are you? Did the bounder touch her?"

"That sort reckon they can do as they please with widowed women, but I doubt Estelle would have fallen for such an obvious ploy. Perhaps that is why they were at the solicitor's establishment. To form a binding agreement before she submitted to his advances."

"The blaggard!' cried Cowper. "If he was here now I would plant him a facer for his impertinence."

"Then here is your opportunity, Cowper."

Alex, his expression set in stone, moved the curtain aside and stepped through the adjoining door.

Chapter Twenty

Estelle followed Alex into the room and enjoyed the sight of her father's face turning white with shock. Cowper looked equally astonished but was the first to recover.

"Has...has this person made inappropriate advances towards you Mrs. Travis?"

"Unfortunately not." Estelle shook her head, smiling in a secretive manner that implied precisely the opposite.

"Estelle, return to your room," said Winthrop in a belated attempt to take command of the situation.

"I think not."

"And you, sir." Winthrop turned his attention towards Alex. "What is the meaning of this intrusion?"

"Oh, is that not obvious, Winthrop? Well then, permit me to explain. We understood that Cowper was in possession of something you wanted badly enough to offer him the selection of either of your daughters in return. However, we could not begin to think what it might be and so we contrived this little gathering in order to get to the bottom of the matter."

"God damn your impudence, sir."

"Cement, hum," said Alex, ignoring the interruption. "I congratulate you on your foresight, Winthrop. This new combination of ground limestone and clay you spoke of will indeed revolutionize the industry, you are right about that. I can quite see why you were willing to sacrifice so much in order to be the first to the Patent Office with the idea."

"You have been eavesdropping and yet call yourself a gentleman. Shame on you, sir."

"It is not me who is likely to suffer shame, Winthrop. Stealing another man's ideas for monetary gain is enough to have you transported. But plotting to murder another man because he stood in the way of your ambitions? Tut, tut." Alex shook a finger beneath Winthrop's nose. "Whichever way you look at it, there's no escaping the fact that you are overdue an appointment with the hangman."

"I shall deny it, of course, and you can prove none of it."

"Oh, but I think we can."

At a motion from Alex, Bradley and his colleague moved to subdue Cowper, but he adroitly evaded them and moved towards the door which Matthew had earlier locked. Finding his exit barred, Cowper turned with a growl of rage to face Bradley, only to discover that it was Alex who now stood between him and the connecting door.

Estelle watched the developing situation with a combination of fascination and dread, surprised that Cowper could absorb Alex's chilling expression with every outward appearance of calm.

"Let me pass or it will be the worse for you."

"Indeed, I should be most interested to learn how."

"Then you will get your wish." Cowper drew a shiv from his pocket and waved the weapon beneath Alex's chin.

Alex laughed in his face. "With that toy? I hardly think so."

"I shall enjoy extracting revenge for the heartache you have caused Mrs. Travis."

"I was unaware that I had broken her heart. Are you fading away for want of my regard, Estelle?"

"Quite the reverse." Estelle smiled at Alex. Fade away? Far from it. She had never felt so alive as when he had awoken her senses.

Cowper's face darkened with obvious anger as he looked in her direction. He let out a frustrated roar. "You bastard! You would be wise to step aside and not antagonize me further. I think it only fair to warn you that I learned to fight in the rookeries and don't abide by your gentlemanly rules of conduct."

"Somehow that does not surprise me."

"Do not imagine the fact that you are unarmed is likely to bother my conscience."

"Thank you for the warning." Alex bowed with mock solemnity. "Although it was scarce necessary. I did not suppose that you intended to fight fair, not if you entertain serious hopes of besting me."

"You think yourself better than everyone. But your arrogance will be your downfall."

"Undoubtedly, but not today, I think."

They circled one another stealthily. Watching them, Estelle felt as though her heart had leapt into her mouth, aware that should Cowper win through underhand tactics she would be at his complete mercy. They were fighting over her, she realized with a jolt: Cowper because he wanted to own her, Alex because he wished to protect her. Cowper was armed with a dagger but Alex had nothing more than his wits to call upon. She was encouraged by the fact that he did not seem deterred by the unevenness of the contest. In fact he looked supremely confident.

Bradley and his colleague looked equally unconcerned, standing with arms folded as though they planned to enjoy the unfolding drama. Their faith in their master's pugilistic abilities helped to calm her frazzled nerves. Would even Cowper dare to fatally injure a viscount or did he merely intend to get past him and through the door? Knowing how determined he was to possess her, she very much feared it might prove to be the former.

And he appeared to be gaining the upper hand. He forced Alex into a corner of the room and lashed out with his shiv when Estelle least expected it. It tore the fabric on the sleeve of Alex's coat and Estelle could not prevent a small gasp escaping her lips when a thin line of blood seeped through the cloth. Alex fell to one knee, clutching his injured arm and Estelle feared that the fight must be over before it had even begun. Cowper clearly shared that view, his lips stretching across yellowing teeth in a parody of a smile as he observed Alex's distress.

"This is likely to be easier than I imagined," he said, his tone laden with satisfaction.

"So it would appear." Alex, his attitude defeated, remained on the floor, completely at his attacker's mercy.

"No!" cried Estelle as Cowper raised the dagger and angled it towards Alex's heart. "Don't harm him. Let him live and I will marry you."

Cowper turned towards her, smiling in satisfaction. "So be it, my dear. Consider it my wedding present to you."

Alex uncoiled his body from its crouched position, still clutching his arm. Estelle wanted to rush to him, to attend to his wound. But even more imperatively, she wanted to make him understand that she had done what she just did, promised herself to this odious man, for his sake. She would never be able to live with herself if he sacrificed his life on her account. But her feet appeared rooted to the spot and she could not move. Cowper, apparently convinced that Alex posed no further threat, stared at her with a hunger that turned her stomach.

Cowper's momentary distraction was all Alex had been waiting for. With one swift tug that belied his injured status he pulled the rug from beneath Cowper's feet. With a startled oath, Cowper tumbled to the floor, the shiv clattering on the wooden boards and coming to rest a safe distance away. Bradley swiftly claimed it whilst Alex, with an air of considerable satisfaction, buried his fist in the middle of the startled Cowper's features.

"Did you really imagine you were the only one who was prepared to fight ugly?" he enquired mildly as Cowper swore profusely and dabbed ineffectively at his bloody nose.

Alex reached inside Cowper's coat and extracted a sheaf of papers. He moved to stand beside Estelle and offered her a smile of reassurance, brushing away her attempts to look at his wounded arm.

"It is nothing more than a scratch. A convenient means to make Cowper think he had the upper hand. There was no need for you to offer yourself as sacrificial bait," he added in an undertone, "although I appreciated the gesture. Ah, here are all the details of the cement that you were so anxious to get your hands on, Winthrop," he said in a more normal voice. "Right here in Cowper's coat all along. And in his own handwriting, too, I shouldn't wonder. Well, if he used his position of trust in Leeds to steal the particulars, then he could hardly ask anyone else to write them down for him, could he now? Nor could he take the original papers or they would have been missed in an instant. So this scrawl must be his."

Cowper was still sprawled on the floor with Bradley's boot resting heavily on his chest. He regarded Alex with an expression of unmitigated loathing. Alex, impervious to his dislike, ignored him.

Estelle gazed at him, her emotions in turmoil. She had just witnessed the man she loved with a passion that scared her risk his life for her sake. She was overwhelmed by his willingness to take such a risk. Only slowly did she become conscious of Cowper's gaze resting upon her in an attitude of such acute longing as to make her shiver. She turned away in contempt.

Her father appeared oblivious to the crowd of people in his study. He did not display the slightest anxiety about Cowper's defeat, barely glancing in his direction. He clearly considered him to be expendable and rested his chin on steepled fingers, staring into the distance. "You have entered my house without my permission, Crawley."

"I invited him in," said Estelle.

"You are a woman and so your word carries little weight." He waved her assertion aside. "Nothing you have heard here can be used against me," he said to Alex, his voice gaining in confidence. "I would not recommend that you make a fool of yourself by repeating what you think you know. I will simply deny it, as will Cowper."

"They are here with my permission, Father." Matthew entered the room looking frail but resolute. "I believe I am still your heir, not banished from these premises and therefore in a position to invite whomsoever I please to join me here."

"Matthew." Her father appeared to deflate at the sight of his son, obviously aware that the game was up.

"And so, you see, Winthrop," explained Alex, "your position really is completely hopeless."

"What do you want of me?"

"I am glad you are prepared to be reasonable. It means we will be able to conclude our business more quickly and save the ladies from any more unpleasantness. But I think your son should be the one to outline his terms on behalf of himself and his sisters. After living beneath your tyranny for so long, it seems only just."

"Father." Matthew cleared his throat and spoke in a level voice that did not once waiver beneath his father's blistering gaze. "You and Mother will leave this house within the next two days and go abroad. Forever. Porter here is an officer of the law and has a record of everything that was said in this room about Travis's death. He will lodge those papers in his employer's office, and if you step foot on English soil ever again, charges will be brought against you."

"You cannot mean that." The hands supporting her father's chin were now visibly trembling, whether with rage or in frustration Estelle could not be entirely sure. Nor did she much care. "I am your father, when all's said and done."

"A father who was prepared to disown me."

"I was not serious about that."

"Were you not?" Matthew quirked a brow. "That is not how it felt to me. You, Cowper, will also leave the country or risk meeting a similar fate."

"Matthew, you forgot to explain that your father and Cowper will sign confessions before they leave, which Porter will also lodge in his place of employment," said Alex.

"Never!" cried both men together.

"Good," said Alex in a languorous tone. "That is precisely the reaction I was hoping for. I personally would prefer to see you taken in charge immediately, you see, but for the sake of your children and their reputations I was persuaded to offer you a way out first." He strolled across the room, confident and authoritative, the planes of his handsome face relaxed yet resolute. Estelle followed his every elegant move with her eyes, completely and absolutely in love with a man who could never be hers.

The two miscreants looked briefly at one another with calculating expressions, both appearing ready to shift the blame to the other in a last desperate attempt to save themselves. But Alex stood firm, deaf to their entreaties and the clumsy attempts on her father's part to bribe him.

"Very well," said her father, with a deathly look in his eye. "Since you leave me no alternative, let us be done with this."

The confessions were written, signed and witnessed and the business was complete.

"Oh, just one thing more, Winthrop," said Alex.

"What now?"

"Only this."

Alex drew back his fist and planted it in the centre of her father's face with considerable force. Her father looked at Alex in surprise and slowly crumpled to the floor, blood pouring from his mouth.

"That was in revenge for your abuse of Estelle," Alex said, capturing her hand and leading her from the room.

Chapter Twenty-one

Somehow, late as it was, room was found for the entire party at the inn in Farnham and Estelle was at last able to reflect upon the extraordinary events of the day. In all the confusion following her father's capitulation, they had restored a drowsy Marianne to the anxious Mr. Porter and roused her mother from a drunken stupor to inform her that she would be travelling abroad. Her mother had been totally perplexed by the whole business, unable to understand the necessity for this sudden journey. She did not once express pleasure at the unexpected appearance of her daughter but that did not prevent Estelle from experiencing a pang at regret at the thought of never seeing her again.

They also made plans to acquaint the servants of Matthew's return as head of the household. There was so much to organize and Estelle had not managed a single private word with Alex. At Marianne's request she intended to return with her to Ramsgate on the morrow and remain with her until she was wed to Mr. Porter. Then she would consider Matthew's request to return to Farleigh Chase and help him with his new responsibilities.

But the idea did not sit comfortably with her. The place held too many unpleasant memories for her ever to be comfortable there. Images of her father would always haunt her. Every minute she would expect him to appear and issue some unsavoury command that required her instant obedience. She would not mind if she never set foot in the place again and would, perhaps, seek a position as a governess after all. But she understood that in her current emotionally turbulent state, now was not the time to make decisions about her future.

She and Marianne were sharing a room in the inn and they had talked for some time about the extraordinary events of the day. Her sister was keen to hear every detail of their father's downfall, furious to have slept through it all. Still drowsy, she had closed her eyes again half an hour previously, but Estelle was too energized to even consider sleep. For the first time in her adult life, the spectre of her father did not loom large, and she was finally free to behave as she saw fit. And the heady feeling of liberty streaking through her veins was all due to one man's determination to fight on her behalf.

She must see that man one last time to thank him and wish him adieu. They would part in the morning, and she would never get another opportunity to see him alone. Checking to ensure that Marianne was soundly asleep, she pulled the robe taken from her room in Farleigh Chase tight about her body and slipped from the chamber before her courage failed her. She knew Alex's room was the second on the left on the other side of the corridor. Boldly she entered it without knocking, lest he thought to observe the proprieties and send her away when he saw it was her seeking him out.

He was seated at the window in shirt-sleeves, staring out into the dark night, apparently deep in thought. He started when he heard the door open and looked up, seeming to resent the intrusion. But when he observed her standing on the threshold, his face broke into a slow, intimate smile that set her pulse racing.

"Estelle, I hoped you would come." He held out his arms and she ran into them without hesitation. He crushed her body against his and claimed her lips with an avidity that stole what little breath she had remaining. His tongue ruthlessly plundered her mouth as though seeking release at the end of a day that had been fraught with danger for them both. He deepened the kiss and she did not scruple to follow his lead, boldly drawing the tip of his tongue deeper into her mouth and lacing her fingers through the tangled mass of hair that hung below his collar. Desire streaked through her body in dizzying waves as his hands lazily explored the contours of her back, stroking her bruised rear with a delicate touch and drawing her ever closer, allowing her to feel the full extent of his own desire.

"I came to thank you for freeing me from that tyrant," she said, when he finally released her and gave her an opportunity to speak.

"The pleasure was all mine." Alex re-seated himself and drew her onto his knee.

"I did not wish to thank you in front of the others, you see, when I take my leave of you in the morning."

"And why would you be taking your leave of me?"

"Well, Marianne has asked me to stay with her in Ramsgate until she is married."

"I see."

"Indeed, and then Matthew wishes me to return to the Chase but I am not so sure I should like to do that."

"I should think not." He sucked gently on the lobe of one of her ears and she squirmed on his lap as he sent pleasure spiralling through her.

"And so perhaps I shall seek a position as a governess after all."

"That is hardly necessary."

"Why? Oh, that was pleasant. Do it again."

He obediently reapplied his lips to the pulse beating at the base of her neck. "You appear have overlooked one small consideration."

"What might that be?"

"Have you forgotten that you have undertaken to be my mother's companion—"

"Yes, but that was only because—"

"And that she is expecting me to return you to Crawley Hall at once." He slid the robe from one of her shoulders and possessed himself of her breast.

"Oh, but I cannot. You must ask her to beg my pardon. I deceived her, and I would hate to see the disappointment in her eye when she learns the truth."

"Well," he said, dealing with the inconvenience of the robe which still clung stubbornly to her other shoulder, "I think we can resolve that. I have a suggestion to make."

"The answer is yes."

He nibbled at her bare shoulder. "But you do not know what I was about to suggest."

"Oh, but I think I do. My father was right. You wish to have me living beneath your protection and I would be more than willing to enter into an arrangement of that nature."

He ignored her strangled protest as he abandoned his nibbling and stood so abruptly that she slid from his lap. "Is that what you think of me? I had not appreciated that you consider me to be as lacking in moral fibre as all that."

"No, of course I do not," she said, bewildered by his anger. "You just risked your life on my behalf and so it is obvious that you must have some feelings for me. But consider. You are an aristocrat, expected to marry well, whereas I am the daughter of a disgraced builder who murdered my husband. We desire one another, which is most inconvenient, but there is nothing to be done about that other than to adopt the solution I have suggested. Are you not pleased with me for saving you the trouble of asking?"

"You would prostitute yourself for me?"

"It hardly seems creditable, I do agree. But then I was even prepared to marry Cowper to save you, remember, which told me something important about my feelings for you. And now, I find the prospect of parting from you too painful to endure and if you really are in need of a mistress—"

"I did not say that."

"You see, Alex, you have awakened something in me and I find that I cannot bear the thought of not seeing you any more, of not feeling you—"

"God's teeth, Estelle, will you let me explain myself! That was not what I meant at all."

"Oh." She dropped her head to hide both her blush and her disappointment. "You do not desire me then?"

"I desire you so much that I cannot think about anything else for more than five minutes at a time."

"Then my solution would best serve."

"Indeed it would not and that was not what I was about to suggest."

"Then what?"

"I was going to suggest that you return to Crawley Hall and that we tell my mother the truth about you."

"That I am about to become your mistress? I think she might be rather shocked if she were to learn that, Alex."

"Will you oblige me by putting mistresses out of your mind for just one moment?"

"Well, I suppose if you can forget about them then I ought to be able to manage it," she said dubiously.

As he sat down again, he pulled her back onto his knee and his hands reclaimed her breasts. "I suggest we explain your reasons for coming to Crawley Hall in the first place and give her an edited account of how we have bested your father. Naturally, we would leave out all reference to murdered husbands."

"Yes, I can quite see that it would be better not to mention anything about that. But do you not think she will be cross with me? I like her very much and should not like to disappoint her."

Alex chuckled. "My mother is not as easily shocked as you seem to imagine and would love the romantic story of your sister's flight to Porter. And she would, of course, insist upon your resuming your position as her companion. Not that you were officially her companion. But if she considers you to be homeless because you cannot bear the thought of returning to the odious Chase, I daresay she will not be able to help taking you under her wing."

"And save you the expense of setting me up as your mistress." Estelle tilted her head to one side, allowing Alex's marauding hands easier access to her body. "Yes, that would be a wise economy, I suppose."

"Estelle, my dear, you are in danger of trying my patience beyond endurance. I have no intention of taking you as a mistress. I want you for my wife."

Estelle's mouth fell open. "But that is impossible!"

"I know that it is, for the present. I am not so ill-mannered as Cowper in that I would propose to a lady who is still in mourning."

"Oh, I see." A tremulous smile tugged at lips. She bit them, afraid that she might be about to disgrace herself by crying.

"But since gaining a liking for doing as you please, you appear to have developed a penchant for frequenting concealed passages, drugging maids, crowning butlers with frying pans and masquerading as governesses. I do not think that such qualities ought to be encouraged in a future viscountess. I should keep you where I can see you until such time as I can decently propose to you."

"Hum." She traced the line of his lips with her finger. He responded by sucking that finger into his mouth and smiling into her eyes, passion and amusement competing for domination in his expression. "It is a tantalizing prospect, I must confess."

"And when I am in a position to propose, what do you imagine your response will be?"

"It is hard to say and, anyway, I think it excessively cruel of you to excite my anticipation since I cannot see the situation ever arising. Your mother will be grievously disappointed that you have chosen so poorly. She puts great stock by such matters you know." She wagged the finger he had just released beneath his nose.

"My mother says all the things she thinks people wish to hear and then does precisely as she pleases." His lips brushed the sensitive spot beneath her left ear. "It can be terribly trying. You are very much like her in that respect, you know."

"Yes, I daresay that I am. Would you not find that rather frustrating, having two such contrary females under your care, I mean?"

"I certainly feel frustrated at this precise moment. But we were discussing my mother. She is a romantic at heart and since she already adores you, I do not anticipate any difficulties when I take her into my confidence and tell her that I plan to propose to you as soon as I decently can. That will save her the trouble of finding suitable young ladies to parade for my attention, of course."

"Do you really think it will be that simple?"

"Indeed, I do. In fact I believe she noticed my partiality for you even before I became aware of it myself. If she did not approve she would have been sure to let me know."

"Oh." Estelle appeared to have lost the ability to say anything that made the slightest bit of sense. She blamed his hands, of course. How could anyone be expected to think coherently when he was doing such wonderful things with them? But she was not about to say so in case he felt honour bound to bring them under control. "Then why did she go to the trouble of discussing your potential brides with me?"

"I would imagine it was her convoluted manner of judging if you returned my regard."

"She was assessing my suitability for the role, you mean?"

"I daresay she was. But regardless of my mother's feelings about our union, the plain fact of the matter is that I love you to distraction and cannot conceive of a life without you in it. You are everything I have ever wanted in a woman, Estelle. You are brave, principled, intelligent and witty and, when I ask you that question, I think it only fair to warn you that I shall not take no for an answer."

"Well," she said, smiling openly as happiness invaded ever corner of her body. She slipped her arms round his neck, lifting her face to receive his kiss. "Since you put it like that..."

About the Author

Wendy Soliman grew up on the Isle of Wight in the south of England. She now lives in Andorra, a small principality nestled in the Pyrenees mountains between France and Spain, with her husband Andre and a rescued dog of indeterminate pedigree.

To learn more about Wendy Soliman, please visit www.wendysoliman.com or

http://historicalromanceuk.blogspot.com/.

You may send an email message to Wendy at write2wendys@yahoo.com

One promise, two pendants…love that was destined to be.

Gypsy Legacy: The Marquis
© *2007 Denise Patrick*
Book One in the Gypsy Legacy series.

Lady Christina Kenton's life is turned upside down when her gypsy great-grandmother gives her a pendant, along with a deathbed request—Tina must promise to marry only the man wearing its mate. But Tina cannot bring herself to make the promise, for her late stepfather has already pledged her hand to his long-absent heir.

Jay Collings, now the Marquis of Thanet, returns to England after an eighteen-year absence to honor a promise to a gypsy who once aided him, only to discover he must break his vow in order to secure his inheritance. The last thing he wants is a wife chosen by the father he despised.

Tina's gentle strength touches Jay in ways no other woman has. And, unknown to them both, she holds the key to Jay's promise and his inheritance. But just as their fragile relationship begins to take root, the legacy of her gypsy blood brings danger to their doorstep.

Jay and Tina's destinies may be entwined—but will they live long enough to fulfill them?

Available now in ebook and print from Samhain Publishing.

A passion they never expected...
a mystery that could cost them everything.

Yorkshire

© *2008 Lynne Connolly*

Richard and Rose, Book 1

Rose Golightly is a country girl who thinks her life will continue on its comfortable course, but a series of events changes that for good. On a visit to the ancestral estate of Hareton Abbey, Richard Kerre, Lord Strang, enters her life. A leader of society, a man known for extravagance in dress and life, Richard is her fate. And she is his.

Richard is to marry a rich, frigid woman in a few weeks, and has deliberately closed his heart to love. Then a coach accident throws his wounded body into Rose's arms.

With one kiss, Richard and Rose discover in each other the passion they thought they'd never find.

But the accident that brought them together was an act of sabotage. Somewhere, in the rotting hulk of a once beautiful stately home, a murderer is hiding.

Richard and Rose set out to solve the mystery, and find the layers of scandal go deeper than simply determining who is guilty. And that doing the right thing could separate them—forever.

This book has been revised from a previously published edition.

Warning: This series is addictive. Passion and murder are a potent mix.

Available now in ebook and print from Samhain Publishing.

hot stuff

Discover Samhain!

THE HOTTEST NEW PUBLISHER ON THE PLANET

Romance, fantasy, mystery, thriller, mainstream and more—Samhain has more selection, hotter authors, and everything's available in both ebook and print.

Pick your favorite, sit back, and enjoy the ride! Hot stuff indeed.

Samhain Publishing Ltd

WWW.SAMHAINPUBLISHING.COM

GREAT
CHEAP
FUN

Discover eBooks!
THE FASTEST WAY TO GET THE HOTTEST NAMES

Get your favorite authors on your favorite reader, long before they're
out in print! Ebooks from Samhain go wherever you go, and work with
whatever you carry—Palm, PDF, Mobi, and more.

Lightning Source UK Ltd.
Milton Keynes UK
14 May 2010